WHAT SHE LEFT

MARTINA MONROE BOOK 1

H.K. CHRISTIE

KEEKSTAR
MEDIA

Copyright © 2021 by H.K. Christie

Cover design by Odile Stamanne

First edition: July 2021

ISBN: 978-1-953268-02-0

1

BEFORE

I gazed down at her and wondered how something so magnificent could have come from something so horrible.

When I learned I was pregnant, I didn't know what I would do. Terrified and confused, I had busied myself with activities until he noticed my rounded belly. He'd seemed as surprised as I was by the predicament. To my astonishment, he hadn't ordered me to terminate; instead, he'd kept me hidden away until she was born. I wasn't sure how I would react to her birth. Would I accept her, or would I despise her because she reminded me of him? *Him.* A horrible man. A despicable tyrant. A phony and a fraud.

The moment I pressed her against my chest and heard her cry, for the first time in my life, I understood what love was. Since then, she made my miserable days tolerable and became my reason for living.

I lightly skimmed her scalp with my fingertips, careful not to wake her. My angel, my Amelia. I lowered my lips to plant a soft kiss on the top of her head, inhaled her scent, and then pivoted to head back to my bedroom.

My pulse quickened at the sight of him. I hadn't realized

he'd been standing in the doorway. I stepped closer and whispered, "What are you doing in here? I don't want you waking her."

"Come with me, now."

"What? Why?"

"I'll tell you on the way. Hurry up."

I didn't know what all of this was about, but I knew better than to fight him when he had that look in his eyes and a revolver in his hand. "I have to get Amelia."

"Leave her."

I shook my head. "No, I'm not leaving her."

He raised his arm and pressed the revolver to my abdomen. "You will leave Amelia, or I'll kill her while you watch."

My body trembled. Was he going to kill me? What would happen to Amelia? I glanced around the room, trying to find an escape, but there was none. He was blocking the door. "I won't leave her. You'll have to kill me," I said, hoping he was bluffing.

He hesitated. "Fine. Take her, but be quiet about it. I don't want to hear her cries."

I swung around and scooped up Amelia as carefully as I could. She wiggled and cooed as I picked her up and held her firmly to my chest. I glanced back over at him. "Fine, let's go."

"Now. Hurry. Do as I say, and be quiet." He waved the gun and said, "Go."

I led the way out of the nursery and down the stairs before I hesitated. What if I called out? Would someone save me? I could feel the muzzle of the gun pressed into my lower back. No one was coming to save me.

I continued down the steps, reached the front door and stopped. He spat, "Open it. We're going for a drive."

I silently opened the door and exited our home as he held the gun on me. "Put Amelia in her car seat and then get in the front."

I obeyed and entered the passenger side of the vehicle.

He pulled out of the driveway with one hand on the steering wheel and the other holding the revolver that was pointed right at me. I recognized the weapon with its nickel-plated barrel and wood grip and knew he could shoot as well as I could. "I don't understand what's going on. Why are you doing this?"

"Be quiet. This is best for everyone."

"Please, can you just tell me what is happening?"

"Say another word and I'll shoot you right here."

I swallowed my thoughts and my words. At least I had Amelia with me.

We drove for ten minutes before he pulled the car over to the side of the road and put it in park. He reached over, using his free hand to open the glove box, and pulled out a leather pouch. He handed it to me. "There's five thousand dollars in here. The train station is less than a mile down the road. Now go, never return, and erase us from your memory. We don't know you, and you don't know us."

He was sending me away. I didn't understand but knew better than to ask any more questions. I cracked open the door and stopped. "I don't have her ear drops."

"She'll have her drops. Now go."

"But, I'm taking her with me."

"No, you're not. Now go, before this ends badly for both of you."

He couldn't mean it. Without budging, I stared him in the eyes with as much determination as I could muster. "Not a chance. I'm not leaving her."

His eyes went dark and then he swung his arm around to the back seat, the revolver now pointed at Amelia, who slept soundly in her carrier. "I'll shoot her right now if you don't get out of the damn car."

My heart beat pounded in my ears, but I was frozen by the thought of leaving Amelia.

He growled, "I'll count to three. One. Two..."

I pushed open the car door and stepped out. Before I could fully exit and close the door behind me, he shoved me to the pavement and sped off.

I scrambled to my feet and broke into a sprint, trying to catch up to the car. As the taillights disappeared into the darkness of night, I fell to my knees and screamed.

MARTINA

CLICK CLICK CLICK.

That ought to do it, Mr. Jones. I lowered my camera and placed it into the leather case sitting on the passenger seat before I rolled up the car window. *Another one bites the dust.* I shook my head as I considered Mr. Jones's situation. He was going to have a tough time explaining why he could play basketball but still needed to be on disability from his job in the warehouse. He was one of thousands of people who thought they could get away with defrauding their employer. It probably never occurred to them that their workplace's insurance company would hire a private investigator to follow them around to see if there were any cracks in their claim. Newsflash, they did. They always did. Well, I didn't know that for sure, but considering the number of folks I had been following around lately to uncover evidence of insurance fraud, I assumed so.

Yes, that was my job now—following around people who had open workers' compensation claims. I didn't go into the private investigations and security business to hunt down people trying to cheat their companies out of insurance money. I almost felt sorry for those people I followed around—at least the ones who were legitimately injured. I didn't shed any tears for the others. It was hard to feel sorry for someone when they were stupid enough to play a game of basketball on a public court while claiming they were too injured to return to work. Mr. Jones wasn't even the worst of them.

Over the last six months, I'd seen tons of people who thought they were fooling everyone. One subject, out on workers' comp from a roofing company, had been caught doing a roofing job for cash. That was bold. And stupid. When I handed over the report to his employer, the man's face turned beet red, and I thought I had seen steam come out of his ears. The employer insisted he'd not only fire him immediately but also pursue criminal charges. I didn't blame him. If I had an employee and they pulled that with me, I'd probably do the same. Our past always seemed to have a way of coming back to bite us. That was a little tidbit I knew firsthand.

I'd messed up, and now this soul-sucking work was my penance. My days now consisted of tracking fraudsters or cheaters. I wasn't sure whom I detested more. Even I recognized I had begun to turn cynical. I needed a heavy dose of the goodness I believed was inherent in all of us. It was why I'd chosen this line of work. I wanted to help and protect, not catch petty criminals and capture evidence for divorce court.

My AA sponsor, Rocco, often reminded me I needed to look for the small positive things—the light—and not dwell on the dark. Like the fact that I was healthy and sober for nine months. I was alive, and so was my little girl, Zoey.

To be honest, if it wasn't for Zoey or Rocco, I'm not sure I would've made it through the last few years. Jared's death, and later, nearly losing my life because of a drunk-driving accident— my fault—had been the lowest I'd ever stooped, and that was saying a lot. Despite my dissatisfaction with my line of work, it was boring enough that I was home by six each night. Zoey reveled in having me home each night for family dinner for a change. It was during these meals that my world brightened, as she recounted every detail of her day and her plans for the future. I envied her youth and excitement for all things including snakes, bugs, and glitter. Oh, to be seven years old again and not have a care in the world. My nightly conversations with Zoey were a pleasant distraction from the hole in my heart and the empty chair where Jared used to sit. He would've loved these moments with our daughter.

I shook myself out of the thoughts and started the car. I'd delayed heading back to the office as long as I could. Believe it or not, I dreaded desk work even more than following my subjects around. The office was where I'd sit for hours filling out reports, cropping photos, and sifting through my inbox. I had gone from bad-ass protector to nothing more than a glorified paper-pusher.

As I drove, I tried to stay positive. I was grateful that Stavros had taken me back after what I'd done. I hadn't earned the right to complain or ask for more meaningful work, not yet anyhow. I had to play it cautiously with Stavros. He'd been clear about his concerns about putting me back on higher-level cases. As he explained it, he didn't want to put me in unnecessary danger, leaving Zoey an orphan, or drive my stress levels to a point that might push me back toward the bottle. What he didn't understand was the demoralizing nature of my work had me craving the drink more than ever. I needed to call Rocco.

———————

THE SOLES OF MY SHOES SQUEAKED ON THE TILE AS I walked through the lobby of Drakos Security & Investigations. I headed toward Mrs. Pearson, giving her my best friendly nod. "How are you, Mrs. Pearson?"

She gave me a bright smile outlined with magenta lipstick. "Martina, dear, I'm fine. Thank you for asking. Long day?"

Did I look that defeated? I guess sitting in a stuffy car all day will do that to a person. I needed to hit the gym STAT. Besides Zoey, the other thing that got me through the last nine months was a strict fitness regime and healthy eating. My sponsor, Rocco, was right. Healthy body, healthy mind. I had to stay strong. "Not too bad today."

"Nice to hear. You have a good evening, my dear."

"You too."

I headed back into the cubicle area and past the first three stations before I halted. The six-foot-three-inch burly man leaning over my desk drove a wave of panic through me. Stavros didn't normally drop by my desk unannounced. I actually didn't see him much outside of our weekly debriefs. It hadn't always been that way. In the past, he had been more of an uncle to me than a boss, but after the accident he'd been nearly all business. I'd disappointed him, and from what I could tell, that was worse than a betrayal. I vowed to never let it happen again—I couldn't let it happen again. I owed him my life. I sucked in some air and held my head high. I could face anything, or at the very least, I could fake it until I made it. "Stavros, this is a surprise."

Stavros studied me from head to toe, assessing my current state. Was I drinking again? Was I stressed? Was I too thin from working out too hard? Was I mentally stable? They were all good questions. Fingers crossed one day he'd be able to trust me again. I supposed that was up to me now.

"You're looking well," he said.

"I'm feeling good. What can I do for you, Stavros?" Our relationship hadn't been the same since the accident. He now kept me at arm's length which hurt more than he could ever understand.

He stood, hands on hips, as if he was about to command me

to head out into the field. Some training never went away. Stavros was a decorated ex-special forces commander and all-around tough guy, and I braced myself since I had a hunch he was about to tell me what was what. And I was going to listen. "I was just leaving a note. We received a call today from a potential new client. They requested you specifically. Do you have time to discuss it?"

My body relaxed. "Yes, of course."

"All right. Let's talk in conference room one." He didn't wait for a reply; instead, he headed toward the first conference room on the right.

I followed dutifully behind him, keeping up with his pace. A closed-door conversation with Stavros wasn't typical for a new insurance case or cheating lover. Was it an actual case? Was he going to let me run it? I couldn't get my hopes up. Whatever it was, I'd accept it and be grateful.

I entered the conference room and shut the door behind me. He stood with his hands on the table, as if contemplating how to address the situation. Was I the situation? He pushed off and took a seat. I sat down across the table from him and met his gaze. "Stavros?"

He leaned back. "Here's the deal. The client asked for you specifically. She was referred to us by a previous client of yours, of the firm's, where you were the lead. I'm sure you remember the Rose Green case. Apparently, this woman is a coworker of Rose's. Rose talked you up pretty good."

I nearly jumped out of my chair, but before I could enthusiastically accept whatever it was, he raised his hand to stop me. I settled back down and listened. "The case involves identifying a child in a photo. This photo was found after Ms. Gilmore's mother's death. All we know so far is that when she asked her father about the child in the picture, he was so upset he stormed out of the room and refused to discuss it. This piqued Ms.

Gilmore's interest, and she shared the story with her coworker, Rose. Rose said she should contact you, because you could probably identify the baby in the picture. You know and I know, damn well, that secrets typically get buried for a reason. It could be a can of worms or completely benign. You won't know until you start digging around. The mission is to identify the child. Does that sound like something you would be up for?"

My heart was racing. *One thousand percent, yes.* I would show him I could do this. I could be trusted. I wouldn't let him down. "Absolutely. I am ready."

He squinted. "Have you been keeping up with your meetings?"

He still didn't trust me. I tipped up my chin. "Every day, and Rocco is on speed dial."

His eyes bore into my soul as if he was assessing whether I could be trusted. "I'm not completely sure that you're ready for this."

I hadn't had a sip of alcohol in nine months. I had done everything right. I could do this. Not that I hadn't wanted a drink or that I didn't call Rocco several times a week. I don't know what I'd do without Rocco. Or my spunky seven-year-old, who kept me honest every single day. We called my addiction an illness because it was. I'd been sick, but was getting better every day. I was okay. *I'd be okay.* I knew that I'd have to fight every day for the rest of my life to stay this way. I stared Stavros directly in the eyes. "I'm ready, Stavros."

His body relaxed. "All right. Ms. Gilmore has an appointment tomorrow morning at nine. You'll be the lead investigator."

My insides jumped up and down. A real case. It was the reason I had become a private investigator. It was the reason why I got up every day to do this job. I needed to know I was doing something more than just taking care of myself and my daughter. I wanted to be a part of something bigger—bigger than me. I was practically vibrating in my seat.

Stavros pushed off the chair and stood. "Don't think I won't be watching closely. I'm talking about daily check-ins and weekly summary reports."

I grinned. "I look forward to it."

"Good." He started to exit the room when I stopped him.

I stood up and called out to him. "Stavros."

He turned around. "Yes."

I stared into his deep-brown eyes. "Thank you."

He nodded. "Have a good night, Martina."

I eked out a, "you too," before he exited the conference room. In that moment I felt I was getting my life back after I'd nearly lost it all. I was just given my second chance, and I wasn't going to screw it up.

3

MARTINA

My pink, sparkly girl fidgeted in front of the door, waiting rather impatiently for me to take her to school. I couldn't understand how I had given birth to a daughter who loved all things pastel and glittery. She was small, like a sprite, with bright-blue eyes from Jared and dark-brown hair from me, with a fierce focus and determination I had never seen in a child. It was one of the few ways I knew she was mine.

Today was no exception. Her current outfit included bubblegum-pink jeans with a white sweatshirt adorned with a heart made of fuchsia sequins. With Valentine's Day coming up, she'd insisted on wearing hearts every day until the holiday.

Her pink backpack was slung over her arm, and her tiny fist rested on her hip. "Mom, I can't be late today. You know today is the day the class is going to discuss our plans for Valentine's Day. By the way, we still need to buy Valentines. Everybody in class has to have them and we give them out at the party. Kaylie's older sister told her all about it. And I, for one, can't wait."

I'd completely forgotten that I needed to buy Valentine's cards. If I hurried, I could pick up a pack before heading into the office. I felt like I was always coming up short in the mother department. I supposed it was the curse of a working, single mother.

I studied Zoey and her obvious enthusiasm for the class Valentine's Day party. What I wouldn't give to be excited about a Valentine's Day party. Even before my heart had been ripped out by the loss of Jared, I wasn't into celebrating Valentine's Day. It was a sappy, made-up holiday designed to sell candy and jewelry. *Lame.* Although, I remembered one Valentine's Day where Jared had surprised me with flowers and candy while dressed in the tuxedo he wore to our wedding. He had hit all the clichés. My belly ached from laughing so much at each goofy gesture.

I sucked in my emotions and headed toward Zoey. "I'm ready."

"Thank goodness," she said with a coy smile.

The girl hated to be late—same as me. I supposed she was like Jared and me, after all. She was a mini soldier ready to take on the world in battle, one Valentine's Day party at a time. I reached for the doorknob when Zoey said, "You aren't going out there without a coat, are you?"

Did I mention that my almost-eight-year-old acted more like an eighteen-year-old? Too often, she was trying to take care of me when it should be the other way around. "I was just about to grab it." I hurried to the closet and pulled out my black down jacket, lifting it up for her to see. "Got it." Boy, my head wasn't on straight. Maybe it was the strange butterflies in my stomach. I was nervous and excited about my first real case and client in nine months. The thought of an actual case made me feel alive. Working fraud and cheater cases these past six months had left me feeling partially dead inside. "Would you like to do the honors, my dear?"

"Of course." Zoey turned the knob and opened the door. She stood to the side and said, "Madam, after you."

I smiled at her. "Why thank you, kind girl." I stepped outside, turned around, and locked the door before heading toward the car. The butterflies fluttered. I thought, *I can feel it in my bones that today—everything would change.*

I RUSHED THROUGH THE FRIGID AIR TOWARD THE FRONT OF the office building. Stopping to purchase the Valentine's cards had taken longer than I'd expected, and I only had three minutes to make it to my appointment on time. I entered through the automatic doors and raced toward the stairwell. There was no time for the elevator. I swung open the door and ran up three flights of stairs before reaching the floor of Drakos Security & Investigations. I slipped off my jacket and entered the office, hoping the sweat under my pits wasn't noticeable. I approached Mrs. Pearson. "Good morning."

Mrs. Pearson tipped her head down. "Good morning, dear. I put your first appointment, Ms. Kennedy Gilmore, in conference room two. She has coffee and a bottle of water."

Wait? Kennedy Gilmore? I knew that name.

"You're the best," I said before subtly rushing to the conference room. I knocked on the open door and eyed the woman sitting and sipping coffee. I was about to introduce myself when it hit me. I stood stunned for a moment before gathering my composure. "Kennedy?"

Kennedy's bright-green eyes met mine. She cocked her head. "Martina Koltz?" She paused. "From Stone Island?"

I nodded. *I didn't see that coming.* "It's Monroe now, but yes. What a surprise. It's been years. How are you?" A flood of emotion shot through me. I hadn't been prepared for this, not even a little. I took off my coat and draped it and my bag on the back of the chair before sitting across from her.

Kennedy gave a friendly smile before speaking. She had matured into a stylish woman with red hair and freckles and reminded me of the girl next door meets supermodel, not the bookish girl I went to school with.

"Before these past few months, great. Actually, I live in San Francisco and work in communications now. Wow, this is such a coincidence. How about you? Married now? Kids?"

I hated this part. "I have a daughter. She's almost eight. My husband passed almost two years ago."

Kennedy's face fell. "I'm so sorry."

Where is your head, Martina? She had just lost her mother. "Thank you, and my deepest condolences on the passing of your mother."

"Thank you."

A deep silence filled the room. I was usually better at this. The small talk before getting into the serious stuff. Kennedy's presence threw me off my game. I needed to turn this around. "So, you know Rose?" Better to stick with the present. I hadn't wanted to get into the past. Not when I was unprepared.

"Yes, we're coworkers and friends. We have lunch together almost every day. She has glowing reviews of you and your work."

"That's always nice to hear. How is Rose?" Rose was a fighter. She'd had an abusive ex-husband and a stalker, both of whom decided she belonged to them despite her feelings on the matter. Thankfully, the ex was in jail and the stalker was dead. Good riddance to both of them. I hadn't spoken to Rose since her case ended. I had wondered about her from time to time and considered reaching out to her but never had. I thought maybe she'd think it was weird if I, the private investigator she hired to figure out who was stalking her, wanted to have coffee after the case was finished.

Kennedy nodded. "Oh, she's great. She was promoted recently, and she started up a self-defense class for everyone at the office. She is fierce up and down. I just adore her."

"That's great to hear. Please tell her I said hello."

Rose had been nearly killed—twice. Now she was thriving. I made a mental note to get in touch with her, at the very least to thank her for referring Kennedy. It was because of Rose that I was getting out of my dreadful probation.

"Will do."

Time to get down to business. "I was briefed a little on your case, but why don't you tell me about what brought you here today."

Kennedy bent over and reached into her purse and pulled out an item. She then slid an old photograph across the conference room table. I looked down at the young woman and infant in the picture and flipped it over. In cursive letters was the name Amelia, with a heart drawn next to it with a date. I glanced back up at Kennedy and in her emerald eyes she held a mix of sadness and excitement and frustration. "Tell me about the picture."

Kennedy looked down. "As you've heard, my mother passed away a few days ago. Pancreatic cancer, it was fast and sudden and terrible. She was my..."

I slipped the box of tissues across the table to Kennedy. She plucked one from the box as she apologized and dabbed at her eyelids. "We were very close, closer than most mothers and daughters. We were best friends. I thought we didn't have any secrets, but I had started going through her things, as suggested by the funeral home, and I found the picture. I'd never seen it before, and I didn't think Mom had any living family. When I asked my father about it, he became angry and told me to never ask about it again, but something in my gut is telling me I need to know who she is."

I think if I had been in Kennedy's shoes, I would have wanted to know who the baby was too. I hadn't been friends with Kennedy while growing up. She was more of an acquaintance because she lived next door to my best friend. We never hung out. I remembered her as a quiet girl who followed the rules, and well, Donna and I, not so much.

She continued. "The picture is dated two years before I was born, so I don't think I've ever met her. I have little family left, and if the baby is a relative, I'd like to find her. Do you think you can find her?"

"I hope so. What can you tell me about your mother and her family?" I didn't want to alarm Kennedy, but the baby bore a striking resemblance to both Kennedy and her mother. All three of them had a widow's peak and a similarly pointed chin. My bet was that the baby was a relative. A close relative.

"I can tell you everything I know—it's not as much as you'd expect. She was always guarded about her childhood, but she said she grew up on the East Coast, in the state of Pennsylvania, before her parents and brother were killed in a house fire. She said she didn't have any aunts or uncles still around, but she had a distant cousin who took her in for a little while after she finished high school. After a few months, she moved out to California where she met my father. They were married, moved into a house on Stone Island, and shortly after, they had me. They lived there ever since. She was a stay-at-home mother and volunteer. She was the best mother."

My gut clenched. I wondered if Zoey would say that about me after I was gone. "She sounds amazing."

"Do you think that's enough information to identify the baby?"

"You haven't found anything else in her things that might give you more clues?"

"I don't think so, but to be honest, I'm not sure what I'd be looking for. Maybe you could come out to the house and look through her things. Is that something you do?"

I was going to have to. It would be the first time I would visit Stone Island in thirteen years. "Of course." I would do everything in my power to make sure I found this baby, even if it meant returning to my hometown, something I hadn't ever planned to do.

"So, you can find her?"

"I'll do my best."

Kennedy frowned ever so slightly.

I placed my hands on the table and leaned forward. "I promise you, I will do everything in my power to find baby Amelia's identity."

Kennedy's frown faded. "Thank you, Martina. Rose said you wouldn't let me down."

I sure hoped not.

4

ALONSO

He arched his back and stared up toward the heavens. "I could get used to this California weather," he mumbled to himself before straightening his posture and gazing out at the blue-gray waters of the San Francisco Bay. *Perhaps I'll need to extend my trip longer,* he thought. His break on the beach was interrupted by the buzz of his cell phone in his inner jacket pocket. He dug inside the blazer and studied the screen. *Figures.* "What's up, boss?"

"What have you learned?"

He'd only been in town for forty-eight hours. What was the rush? Charlotte was dead. If he took another day to poke around, it wasn't likely to make much of a difference.

"I've only had a chance to swing by her house."

"Did you get eyes on the husband or her daughter?"

"Affirmative. The daughter was over at the house when I checked it out. She's now a spitting image of Charlotte with her red hair and peaches-and-cream complexion. Her widower looks pretty distraught and from what I can tell, he just mopes around the house." He wasn't sure what the boss expected him to find. The obituary in the newspaper said as much as he'd found. Regardless, he would dig around and make sure there was nothing out of whack or anything that could lead to trouble for the boss.

"Have you had a chance to take a look at the inside of the house to see if there's anything I need to be worried about?"

"Not yet."

"What are you waiting for?"

He knew the boss was impatient, but this was a bit much, even for him. If he was expecting something, it would be nice to know what it was because it would make his job easier. As it was, he'd made the trek out to California every few months to keep an eye on Charlotte. Now that she was deceased, he didn't think it was necessary, but at the same time, he wasn't about to turn down a free trip to the state known for sun and fun.

"I was waiting until the house was empty. I didn't think you'd want me making friends or anything. However, I tailed the daughter when she left the island." He was distracted by a couple of fellow tourists running into the surf with their pants rolled up and their shoes gripped in their hands. *Good for them. Life was for moments like these.* He realized he was in a desperate need of a vacation. Maybe after he was done looking into Charlotte's estate, he'd hang back in the Golden State for a week or two.

"And?"

His thoughts returned to the call at hand. "It may or may not be related to Charlotte, but I saw the girl visit a private investigations firm."

Charlotte had been a good girl, and he couldn't imagine what the boss thought he would find. It didn't matter. He was simply glad not to be on the frigid East Coast. It was February, and he was wearing a T-shirt and khakis, standing on the beach. Nobody else was wearing a similar outfit, likely because these Californians didn't know what it meant to be cold. *Shoot, it was*

60°F. In his book, that was beach weather, yet he'd seen more than a dozen folks wearing down jackets. *Wimps.* After he was done updating the boss, he was heading over to the ice cream shop to get a cone. Mint chocolate chip was calling his name.

The boss spoke. "Which firm? You ever heard of them?"

"It's called Drakos Security & Investigations. I did a quick search and called a few buddies out here. They're the best in the Bay Area, probably best in the state and some say arguably one of the best in the country. The firm was founded by an ex-special forces guy who hired many of the same. Word on the street is, if someone needs protecting or someone needs to be found, Drakos and his team will deliver."

"It would be tricky to find out if Drakos and team knows anything, but you can, right?"

He took the phone away from his ear and stared at it. He shook his head. Get inside of Drakos Security & Investigations? That would be a damn suicide mission. Lord only knew what kind of tech they had inside. It wouldn't surprise him if they had poison darts shoot from the ceiling as he broke in. *No thanks.*

Those ex-military types rarely left things up to chance. He had a better chance of surviving, or at least remaining a free man, by limiting his search to the Gilmore house and avoiding the investigations firm all together. "I'll start at the house and see what I can find. If she left any mementos behind, I'll find them."

"All right, I want a full report. Also, I want a full report on the husband and daughter."

"You got it, boss."

He shoved the cell phone back into his pocket and slipped his sunglasses on. He'd check out the Gilmore house tomorrow; at that moment that mint chocolate chip was calling his name.

5

MARTINA

I HELD MY BREATH AS I DROVE ONTO STONE ISLAND. Glancing across the two-lane road, I felt as if I had been transported back in time. Suddenly, I was eighteen with a chip on my shoulder and saving all my pennies for a one-way ticket out of there.

In my youth, I had vowed to leave that life behind me and never return. I had thought it would be too painful to return. I supposed it hadn't occurred to me that one day my work would bring me back. It was only ninety minutes outside of San Francisco, but you'd think you were in a different world.

I continued driving, quickly recognizing the town market and the small café where I had gone on my first date with a boy who attended my high school. I didn't need directions. I remembered exactly where Kennedy Gilmore lived. Even if my memories were foggy, the island only had a few major roads. It would be trickier to get lost than to find the house.

I continued down Main Street as a pang of guilt shot through my chest and sat there. My mother still lived in that same trailer in the middle of the island. My brothers were probably somewhere on the island as well. Over the years, communication with my mom had dwindled to Christmas cards and a phone call on Mother's Day and her birthday. The conversations were brief and mostly about her cats. It surprised me she was able to keep those kittens fed and alive. She'd barely cared for her human children back in the day. I supposed I should have had more empathy, considering I knew firsthand that alcoholism was a disease. But you can't help someone who doesn't want it or doesn't think they need it.

As I drove past houses on stilts and roads that seemed to lead to nowhere, I turned along a bend in the road and continued toward the water. I saw the sign and my heart raced. It had been painted and looked new, but it was the same as it ever was, The Boathouse Bar and Grill. It was the place my best friend and our dates went to before our senior prom.

We decided we were grown-ups, all of us destined to leave the island and move on to more exciting places. We were dressed up and had the time of our lives, eating shrimp cocktail and drinking Shirley Temples, secretly spiked with vodka that Donna's boyfriend had swiped from his parents' liquor cabinet. I wished that was where the memories of The Boathouse Bar and Grill ended, but it wasn't. My thoughts drifted to that last night. More Shirley Temples spiked with vodka.

Distracted by my thoughts, I slammed on my breaks, nearly blowing through a stop sign. I shook my head and tried to forget the past as I continued down to Marina Road, then made a right on Conrad Court. My breath seized as I approached Donna's old house, which sat next to Kennedy's parents' home. I didn't know if Donna's family still owned it or if they'd sold it. I hadn't reached out to them in years. It was too painful. Like me, they didn't think Donna had run away.

I rolled past and pulled into the dirt driveway in front of the Gilmore's residence. I parked the car and turned off the engine. I saw another car, presumably Kennedy's, and stepped out of my vehicle and headed toward the stairs. I climbed up the two flights to the front door and knocked, glancing around as I waited for the door to open. From where I stood, I could see the bay and boats docked in front of the neighboring houses. An eeriness washed over me. It was surreal. I'd spent so much of my teen years out on the back porch with Donna or walking the levee down to the marina store to buy soda and candy. This was where I'd spent most of my time. It had been my escape from the trailer park.

The door swished open and Kennedy flashed a nervous smile. "Martina, you made it." She threw her hands up. "Of course, you made it. You grew up here. But you found it okay?"

"Yep, I remembered the way."

"Great. Come on in."

I stepped inside. As I imagined, there were floor-to-ceiling windows on the front of the house with views of the choppy blue water and green hills in the distance. I stepped into the living room.

Kennedy chewed her lower lip.

"What is it?" I asked.

"Seeing you yesterday, made me think of Donna. Did you ever hear from her again? We weren't good friends in our later years, but we were friends as kids, and I know they thought she ran away, but..."

"I don't think she ran away. And no." My gut clenched. "I never heard from her again."

"If it's worth anything I don't think so either."

I cocked my head. "Do you have any specific reason to believe that she didn't leave on her own?"

"Well, like I told the police, that night I saw someone out on the levee with her. I couldn't make out their face. They were wearing a hoodie and sunglasses at night. It seemed off."

What? Back then, the police wouldn't tell me anything, and

I hadn't the inclination to do my own investigation. I was eighteen years old and when they wouldn't help me find her—insisting she was a runaway—I was the one to do the running and joined the army. This new information was interesting and could help find out what happened to her. I'd file this information away, because I needed to find baby Amelia first.

"It's been my experience that the police aren't always the best at getting the job done. Hence, my line of work. Speaking of..." I was curious to know if Kennedy knew anything else that could help find Donna, but first things first.

Kennedy took the hint. "Right. So where do we start? Should I give you a tour of the house and show you where all Mom's things are?"

"Sounds like a great plan. Show me the way."

She led me on the tour of the house and its four bedrooms. One was obviously her childhood room that hadn't been redecorated. The walls were a dark shade of purple. A twin-size bed was situated in the corner with a lavender-colored comforter embroidered with flowers. A matching white dresser and vanity lined the walls, along with concert posters and a bulletin board with photos pinned to it.

The last bedroom she led me into was bigger than the others and was configured in an L-shape, wrapping back around to the front of the house. Sliding glass doors and a window displayed bay views. Kennedy stopped and said, "This is Mom and Dad's room. Although, Dad hasn't been able to sleep in here since she died. I can't say I blame him. This is the room where I was boxing things up and came across the photo. I was too freaked out by Dad's reaction to continue looking through the boxes. Mom never told me where in Pennsylvania she was from. She usually waved it off by saying I'd never heard of the small town. Which, by the way, we only have a few hours. My dad is at the doctor's office in Grapton

Hill. I didn't tell him I'd hired a PI since asking about the photo had upset him so much. I prefer he didn't know for the time being."

"Understood." The room was tidy, aside from the stacks of boxes. I walked over to the dresser, surveying the framed photographs of various sizes and shapes. There were plenty of what I presumed was a young Kennedy and family photos of the three Gilmores. I picked up a small photo of a young man in a dark suit. "Is this your dad?"

"Yep."

"How did you say he and your mother met?"

"Mom was working at a diner that Dad would visit frequently. They both said it was love at first sight."

"That sounds wonderful." I continued studying the photographs. The faces wore smiles most of the time. "Is it okay if I look in the drawers?"

"Yes, of course. Can I get you anything? Water, tea, or coffee?"

"Coffee would be great, thank you."

Kennedy gave a quick nod and headed out of the room. I slid open the first drawer, hoping to not be too terrified by any of the contents. People had a tendency to hide secret or valuable items in underwear drawers. I carefully surveyed the first drawer's contents. Nothing out of the ordinary. There was nothing unusual in the next two drawers either. One contained tanks, T-shirts, and long-sleeve shirts, and the other, trousers and athletic wear. I knelt down to go through the bottom drawers and continued to search the rest of the drawers, which appeared to be mostly Mr. Gilmore's things.

Empty-handed, I headed over to the closet and rifled through the hanging items, some in plastic from the dry cleaner and even a dress with tags still attached that would never be worn by Mrs. Gilmore. I squatted down to look for any clues at the bottom of the closet. I tapped the spotless floor, hoping for a secret hiding spot. No dice.

I stood up and placed my hands on my hips and glanced at the top shelf that held shoe boxes and a collection of handbags. There was nothing that appeared to be a keepsake box or anything that may provide a clue. I pulled down each item, then studied the inside of each purse and box. What I found was that Charlotte Gilmore was tidy—a woman who didn't leave old receipts or lip gloss in her purse when she wasn't using it, like I did.

Who was Charlotte Gilmore? All I could tell was that she was a well put together woman, a pillar of the community, and according to Kennedy, an exceptional mother. She probably never left Kennedy at home with the nanny all day long and sometimes all night, working a dangerous job. Or forget to buy Valentine's Day cards. *Shoot*, she probably made hand-crafted cards each holiday. I wondered if I'd ever measure up to such a good mother.

Kennedy entered and then handed me a cup of steaming coffee. "Thank you." I took a sip. It was smooth and rich.

"Sorry it took so long; I had to brew a fresh pot. Find anything?"

"I didn't see anything in the drawers or in the closet. I haven't started searching in the boxes. Where did they come from?"

"I brought them up from storage, downstairs. I brought up all the ones labeled as hers. There may be a few more down there, near the laundry."

"All right, let's start looking through these boxes."

A while later I closed up the lid on the last box in the room. There was nothing that could tie Charlotte to her past before she'd met Theodore Gilmore. The photograph was literally the only thing that appeared to have existed before Charlotte had married her husband. No childhood mementos or photographs of her family, which was odd considering Kennedy had said they died in a fire. Perhaps all the family photos went up in flames as well? It was as if Charlotte Gilmore didn't exist before her time in California. The only evidence that she did was the picture of her and Amelia.

"Is it okay with you if we head downstairs now?"

"Sure, I'll lead the way."

We descended the wooden steps until we reached a door halfway down the stairs. We entered, passing laundry machines on the left and a bedroom with bunk beds. A full bathroom was situated on the right. In the center of the space was a living area with a TV, sofa, and video game consoles. A fun place for kids or kids-at-heart to play. "Did you hang out down here a lot when you were younger?" I asked.

"Oh, yeah, all the time. This was like my sanctuary, where me and my friends would hang out. I begged my mom to let me live down here, but she refused, saying that there wasn't any heating or air conditioning."

"Sounds nice." I continued to one of the storage closets and opened it. I found a set of plastic bins, one on each of the shelves. I searched through each one. The last one was full of what looked like handmade quilts. "Did your mom make these?"

Kennedy stepped closer and ran her fingers across the top quilt. "Yes, she was quite crafty." She began to tear up.

I placed my hand on her shoulder to comfort her. "Are you all right?"

"Yes, I'll be fine. I forgot these were here. I have so many memories of Mom with all the fabric laid out on the table, cutting out squares and working away at the sewing machine. She spent hours and hours creating quilts for friends and family."

"Your mother sounds like she was an amazing woman, mother, and wife."

"That she was. There are people coming from all over the Bay Area to attend her memorial on Saturday. She touched so many lives. She was a volunteer at the hospital and at the school. She had a lot of friends."

"That's so nice."

"You know, maybe you should come to the memorial. Who knows, maybe someone will know something. I can tell Dad you're just a friend of mine or that you're from one of the places she volunteered at. He could never keep track of all of them anyhow. What do you think? Can you make it?"

Not a bad idea. Who knew, maybe if somebody from her past read about her death in the newspaper, they would attend the service to pay their respects. Those people may have some useful information. Saturday? Did Zoey have a Brownie meeting? "What time is memorial?"

"It's at one o'clock."

I'll have to call Claire to see if she can drop Zoey off at the meeting. "I'll be there."

I clicked the lid on the bin of quilts and pushed it back on the shelf. It got caught on something halfway back, and the sound of a pebble dropping caught my attention. I glanced down at the ground. Nothing appeared to have dropped. I pulled out the bin and heard the rattle once more. I set it on the ground and removed the quilts. At the bottom of the box was a ring. I picked it up and studied the engravings. It was a class ring. Why would it be in a storage bin full of quilts? I called out to Kennedy. "Hey, have you seen this before?" I knew it wasn't hers since we'd graduated from the same high school.

Kennedy scurried back over, and I handed the ring to her. It contained a mother-of-pearl rectangle stone with a C inlaid in gold. She studied it before looking up at me. "No. I don't know what the C could stand for, but the year 1966 is about right for when my mom would have graduated from high school. It could have been Mom's."

"Mind if I take it with me? Maybe I can find out what school it's from."

Kennedy's eyes brightened. "A clue! Maybe it will be the key to finding out who baby Amelia is."

"It's very possible." I prayed it would because we had little else.

"Great. Thank you, Martina."

After saying our goodbyes, I jumped back into my car and hit the road. For a moment, I had forgotten where I was. I couldn't wait to get off this damn island.

6

MARTINA

I drove past the Boathouse Bar and Grill and my heart clenched. I needed to have a clear head. I needed to focus on finding Amelia and learning more about Charlotte's past. I continued driving and thought, *only a few more minutes and I'll be out of here.* A thumping sound and wobble of the wheel threw me out of my thoughts. "You've gotta be kidding me," I mumbled. I pulled the car over to the side of the road next to the small lot across from the town market.

I stepped out of the car, slamming the door behind me, and headed to the rear right of the vehicle and knelt down. Sure enough, I had a flat tire. I didn't see any obvious issues like a nail or a gash, just a flat.

I stood up and went around to the trunk and pulled out the jack, set it in on the ground, and then retrieved the spare. Thank goodness I'd opted for the full-size tire and not the little dinky one. I leaned the spare against the back of the car and went to work on replacing the damaged tire. I was on the last turn of the tire iron, securing the bolt, when I heard footsteps on the gravel. I finished the turn and stood up.

"Martina Koltz, is that you?"

"Dave?"

He grinned, showing off his dimples, like he'd always done back in high school. He was a year older and Donna's brother. All the girls had crushes on him, even me, for a time. I would bet money he was married with kids—a picket fence—the whole nine yards. He approached for a hug, and we embraced. He shook his head, keeping that killer smile on full display. "My gosh, you look exactly the same."

"You too. You look great. How are things?"

"Great. I'm still on the island." He lifted his hand, showing off a silver-toned wedding band. "Been married five years, and my wife and I just had our second baby. It's been an exciting time," he said with a chuckle. "What are you doing back here, visiting your mom?"

A stab of guilt shot through me. "No, I'm working. After the Army, I became a private investigator. I'm here working a case."

"No kidding." He glanced at my ring finger. "You're married? Have any kids?"

I glanced down at the gold and diamond band on my finger. It had never occurred to me to take it off. "My daughter, Zoey, is almost eight. My husband passed almost two years ago now."

He put his hand to his chest. "I'm so sorry."

"Thank you." Neither of us were talking about the elephant in the room, or rather, on the island. I didn't need to ask him if he'd heard from Donna. She had been missing for thirteen years. I knew the likelihood of her still being alive was slim to none. Hoping she was alive was a pipe dream. The awkward silence remained. "How is your family?" I asked.

"They're surviving. Nothing has quite been the same since Donna disappeared and now with this detective reopening the case it's brought it all up again."

Of course they weren't the same. I had worked enough missing persons cases to know how such an event could affect the family. Not knowing if their daughter or sister was alive or dead. If they were being held captive or if she had simply run away and was now happily sipping margaritas on the beach. Not knowing was worse than knowing. *Wait, what did he just say?* "I hadn't heard that they were reopening the case."

"Yep, a detective came by my parents' house last week. I'm surprised he hasn't contacted you yet."

So was I. As far as I knew, I was the last person to see her before she disappeared. Strike that. If what Kennedy said was correct, I was the second to last person. "Do you know the name of the detective?"

"Not off the top of my head. He's with the sheriff's department, I know that. My parents told me about it. They're pretty shook up but happy there is someone still looking for her. They've never given up hope that she's alive."

In that moment I think my body was comprised of eighty percent guilt and the rest was bones, tissues, blood, and water. The guilt for not visiting my family. The guilt over Donna's disappearance. I needed to get off this island.

"I hope they find her. It was good seeing you, but I really gotta get back to the city."

"Good to see you too. Take care, Martina."

"You too." I placed my tools in the trunk, shut it, and hurried back into my driver's seat. I sucked in my breath and made my break for it.

As I drove over the bridge, my nerves were rattled, and my mind drifted into a fog. I hadn't thought too much about what it would be like to return to Stone Island. I just knew that I shouldn't. Now I knew what it was like and I wished I hadn't. It was as if I were eighteen again and my world was crumbling out of my control. It was clear what I needed to do. I took one hand off the steering wheel, grabbed a stick of gum from my bag and popped it into my mouth. Chewing furiously, I clicked the button on the steering wheel and made my command, "Call Rocco, mobile."

7

MARTINA

I sat in my seat and swirled my coffee, waiting for Rocco to arrive. Like the coffee, my mind and my thoughts were spiraling. It wasn't a good place to be. As much as I had protested to Rocco that we didn't need to meet in person, I was thankful he had insisted. At that moment, I really needed his wisdom and reason. The jingle of the bell at the coffee shop door garnered my attention. I glanced to the left and saw the imposing figure. Donned in a black leather jacket with tattoos on his neck and salt and pepper hair pulled back into a ponytail, Rocco entered wearing a sheepish grin. I lifted my hand and waved. He strutted over. "How you holding up, Martina?"

"I'm glad you're here," I said weakly.

"Will you be okay if I grab a coffee?"

I nodded. "Of course. I'm so sorry, I should've gotten you something. I just wasn't thinking straight."

He came over and placed his hand on my shoulder. "Martina, it's okay. We'll get you through this. I don't want to hear you apologize. I'll be back in two shakes. I just need some caffeine, cool?"

"Cool." I picked up my coffee cup with shaking fingers and

took a sip. I placed it back down and realized I probably should have ordered an herbal tea rather than the coffee, but for some reason caffeine was calling my name. I fidgeted as I waited the short amount of time it took for Rocco to pay for his coffee and bring it back over to the table.

He sat down, placing his helmet on the empty chair next to him. To most, he was a big bad biker-dude, and in some ways he was, but not in a negative way. He was, in fact, an ex-Hells Angel and ex-felon, but he was also my AA sponsor. My savior. My rock. He was the only person who could talk me down off the ledge, or away from the bottle. It had been nine months since my accident, and I had admitted that I had a problem with alcohol. Rocco was tough on me, but that was exactly what I needed. He sat down and took a long sip of his coffee before leaning back. "So, you want to tell me what's going on?"

"I had to return to Stone Island for a case I'm working. I knew it would trigger me, being back there, but it's my first actual case since before the accident, and I don't want to screw it up. I haven't been to the island since the summer before I went into the Army. Between my family and what happened to Donna, I didn't want to face it. Cowardly, I know, but here I am, triggered. I never really dealt with Donna's disappearance. I was so young, my approach was to run, and that's what I've been doing—until now. Between Kennedy and running into Donna's brother—it's all coming back in full force." I bowed my head and inhaled, trying to stop the tears from falling. I needed to suck it up. I dabbed my eyes and looked back up at Rocco. "You know I still have family on the island. My mother and my brothers. My father ran off when I was in middle school. I don't talk to them except for the Christmas cards I send to my mother. It wasn't a terrible childhood, but it wasn't great either. So many kids have had it worse off than me, I know that now. At the time, I was hell-bent on getting out of that trailer park and making something of myself. My best friend and I had plans for after graduation. We were going to see the world, do all the things and see all the places." I chuckled at my naivety. "I actually did it, but my best friend, Donna, didn't. Well, I assume she didn't. She disappeared. The police called her a runaway, but even back then, I knew better. She wouldn't have left without telling me." I paused, trying to compose myself.

Rocco reached out across the table and placed his hand on mine. "I see why you're upset."

I pulled my hand back and shook my head. "No, you don't. It's my fault Donna was taken. We had gone out to the Boathouse Bar and Grill. It was one of our favorite places to go out and feel like grown-ups. We'd order Shirley Temples and spike them with vodka. That night we'd been drinking and eating nachos, having a great time being young and carefree, thinking that nothing could ever happen to us. A couple of older boys we'd never seen before joined us toward the end of the night. In hindsight, I'd had far too much to drink and planned to leave with one of them. I was so stupid back then. Donna wasn't so into the other guy and declined his offer to go somewhere more quiet. Being a drunk teen, I half-heartedly said I'd stay behind and walk home with Donna. Donna insisted I go have fun, and she'd walk home. We hugged, and I went off with the boy. I never saw her again. I should've never left her there alone."

I stared deep into Rocco's dark eyes.

He tilted his head. "It's not your fault she went missing, Martina. I know you, of all people, know that."

"If that's true, then why do I feel so guilty? It's my fault that she's probably lying dead somewhere. You and I both know the probabilities. Thirteen years and not a word or reported sighting of her. I know she didn't run away."

"The island brought all that buried guilt up to the surface," he said.

"That's not all. I had a flat tire before I could get off the island. When I was on the side of the road fixing my tire, Donna's brother spotted me. We chatted. Looking into his eyes —the same eyes that Donna had—nearly crushed me on the spot. Not only that, he told me that there's a detective reopening the case. Not that they did much investigating the first time around. Knowing what I know now, the police basically didn't do any sort of real investigating. They were quick to label her a wild runaway. Sure, they had asked a few locals if they had seen her that night, but that was about the extent of it. I know someone did something to her. They had to. She wouldn't have left on her own."

"How do you feel about them opening up the case and trying to find out what happened to her?"

"I guess, I'm afraid. Afraid that they'll find her and that she's not alive. I've made so many mistakes. Rocco, mistakes that can't be undone. Donna, Julie DeSoto, my car accident... the list goes on and on."

"Martina, you can't beat yourself up. It was not your fault. You were only eighteen years old. I know I'm preaching to the choir here. What would you say to you, if you were sitting in my chair? I'd think you'd say, it isn't your fault someone took your friend. It's the monster's fault, not yours. You know, it sounds like what you're experiencing is survivor's guilt. That'll eat you up pretty good. I'm sorry you're feeling this way. I got my demons too, Martina. You know that. You either have to learn to let it go or do something about it so you can get some closure. I'll tell you where you won't find closure and that's at the bottom of a bottle. Are we clear?"

I nodded.

"Say the words."

"Booze is not the answer. It will only make me feel worse in the end." I raked my fingers through my pixie cut. Why was life so hard?

"Okay, now that we've gotten that out of the way, any ideas of how to move forward? You have to know by now, that God kept you here for a reason. I think one of those reasons is that beautiful little girl of yours and another is because of all the people you help and will help in the future."

I sank into myself. How could I possibly get past Donna's disappearance? In my mind, the wound was still wide open. "That's it, Rocco. If it's open, I need to close it."

"I'm not sure I'm following."

"Don't you see. I'm an investigator now. The case is still open—I can find out what happened to her."

Rocco shook his head. "Is that a good idea? Do you have the capacity? You have a lot on your plate. You have your first real case, Zoey, and yourself to take care of. That's a lot. Maybe you can reach out to the detective working the case and lend a hand, but going it alone may be too much."

He was right. I couldn't take on another full investigation on top of the Gilmore case and take care of Zoey and myself. I could find out who was working the case. They'd want my statement anyhow. I stared at the ground, thinking of what I could do to help the case, where I could start, and where I would find the energy. Rocco's voice knocked me out of my thoughts. "Martina, how are you feeling now?"

I glanced up. "I feel better, more calm. I like your idea. I need to take action. Control what is within my control and all that. I'll take care of my mind, my body, my daughter, and my job."

"That's the idea, Martina."

"Thank you, Rocco. I don't know what I'd do without you."

"Just paying it forward, Martina. I know one day when

you're ready, you'll make a great sponsor—mark my words. Now that you're feeling good and have a general plan, do you know what your next steps are going to be?"

"I do." Not only was I going to find Amelia and figure out why Charlotte Gilmore's past was as buried as a pirate's treasure, but I was also going to find out what happened to Donna.

8

MARTINA

I RAN MY FINGERS THROUGH MY HAIR AS I CONTEMPLATED the results of the background check I had performed on Charlotte Gilmore, maiden name Charlotte Jamison. It made little sense. It was as if she didn't have a past before she had become Charlotte Gilmore. That was impossible; everyone had a past.

She told her daughter she was from Pennsylvania, but there was no record of a Charlotte Jamison in Pennsylvania, matching her age and date of birth. I tried multiple spellings of the last name Jamison to see if I had recorded it wrong.

According to Kennedy, Charlotte had moved to California in the late 1960s. Record keeping in the sixties wasn't great and certainly not electronic. Was it possible she just happened to not leave a trail from her trek across the United States, where she ended up settling down with a husband and daughter for more than thirty years?

Something in my gut was telling me there was more to it than that. I had a hunch it wasn't just a matter of lost records. I heard the printer spit out the last page of the list of high schools in Pennsylvania, starting with a C. There were far more than I had expected. I pushed myself off the seat and walked over to the printer, grabbed the pages, and headed back to my cubicle. Firmly planted in my seat, I flipped through the pages and thought about my next steps.

What if Charlotte hadn't been from Pennsylvania, and everything she'd told Kennedy had been a lie? She could have been from anywhere. The best, and only, lead I had was the class ring. It was old and worn, but the *C* across the mother-of-pearl stone in the center was distinct.

More disturbing was the story that Charlotte's family had died in a house fire, but so far we hadn't found any news stories matching such an event. I had one of our interns go to a library and sift through microfiche after microfiche of news articles from the 1960s, looking for house fires in Pennsylvania. They hadn't completed their search yet, but so far there was nothing. Had Charlotte made up her entire past and lied to her daughter all these years? And who was baby Amelia? What if we found Amelia and she wasn't even alive anymore?

The sound of footsteps grew louder as he approached my desk. It was that time of day. Daily debrief. Check. I glanced up at Stavros, who stood casually at the opening of my cubicle. "Hey, Stavros."

"How's it going with the Gilmore case? You find out which school the ring is from?"

"No, nothing definitive. So far I can't find a history for Charlotte Jamison, and there's a long list of schools starting with the letter *C* in Pennsylvania—and the rest of the United States. I'll need to reinterview Kennedy and see if maybe there's something about Charlotte's past I'm missing. Maybe she got the last name wrong or the wrong state. Or maybe she could let me speak with her father. Maybe he knows something that he just didn't want to share with his daughter."

Stavros nodded. "That is strange that you can't find

anything on her. Maybe she was running from something or someone?"

"That's what I think, but until we have proof, I don't want to tell Kennedy that. This case may uncover a lot more than the identity of the baby in the photo."

"Looks like it. Do you need anything from me?"

"No, I've already got the interns looking into news articles from nineteen sixty to nineteen seventy for house fires in Pennsylvania where entire families had perished. They're halfway through. So far nothing. Next, I'll start requesting yearbooks once I narrow down the list of potential high schools."

"Another part of Charlotte's history that can't be verified," he commented.

I had a feeling I knew what Stavros was going to say. I wanted to beat him to the punch and let him know I wasn't off my game. "You know, the absence of evidence is evidence in itself."

Stavros cracked a smile. "Very true. Keep up the good work, Martina. Let me know if I can be of any help."

"Will do. Thanks."

I was frustrated that I hadn't learned more about Charlotte, but I could feel Stavros trusting me again, and I was feeling like my old self. Well, except sober. My phone buzzed. I looked down. I grinned and picked up the phone. "Hi, Claire."

"Hi, Martina, I just want to remind you that we have the interviews with the first two candidates in about an hour. I just wanted to check to see if you'll still be able to make it?"

I didn't know what I was going to do without Claire. She was the best nanny anyone could ever ask for, and she was graduating from nursing school in three months. She was so good that she had even set up interviews for her replacement. Since Jared died, there was no way I could've done my current job if I didn't have someone like Claire as a full-time nanny. Because she was a student and worked for us full-time, she often agreed to last-minute requests for pick-ups or drop-offs, overnights with Zoey, or for making dinner. She was a godsend. I truly believed that Claire was my angel. It sounded a little hokey, but it was true. "Yes, I'm just about to head out now. Did you need me to pick up anything for dinner?" I hoped the answer was no. I didn't think I'd make the interview on time if I had to stop at the store or at the local pizza joint.

"Nope, I have lasagna in the oven."

"Thank you, Claire. I really appreciate everything you've done for me and Zoey. You truly are a gift."

"I appreciate that, Martina. We'll see you soon. Oh, actually..." I heard rustling and muffled voices through the line.

"Zoey, would like to say hello. Here she is."

"Hi, Mommy."

"Hi, sweetheart. How was school?"

"It was so great. Oh my gosh, we just found out today that we're going to get a new pet for the classroom. Do you want to guess what it is?"

Based on how excited Zoey was, it was probably some sort of reptile or equally slimy creature. She was fascinated by nature, especially the parts that gave me the creepy-crawlies. "A rat?"

"Hey, how did you know?"

Only my daughter would be excited about a rat. "Just a guess."

"You must've used your investigator skills. Were you using my modus operandi?" She emphasized the *I* sound.

"I think you're learning my secrets," I teased.

"One day I want to be a super-investigator just like you, Mommy. That is, if I don't become a veterinarian or an astronaut."

Of course. "I need to wrap things up here, but I'll see you when I get home, okay?"

"Okay, Mommy, I love you."

"I love you too, sweetheart, bye."

Just twenty-four hours ago, I was having a complete meltdown after being on Stone Island and being faced with my past. Now that I had dove headfirst into my investigation, I was practically floating. That reminded me. I still needed to call the CoCo County Sheriff's Department to find out who was reopening Donna's case. It wasn't uncommon to use civilian contractors to help with cases, so if I offered my services pro bono, you'd think they would be cooperative or even grateful. Since my conversation with Rocco, I was empowered and taking action. It was my happy place.

Next on the list, dinner and interviews for a new nanny. After that, I would figure out who Charlotte Gilmore really was, so that I could identify baby Amelia as I had promised Kennedy, and then I was going to find out what happened to Donna, whether the sheriff's department wanted me to or not. I was back.

9

MARTINA

I stepped into the hall of the church where Charlotte Gilmore's memorial luncheon was being held. The hall had banquet tables along the walls with finger foods, pasta with red and white sauces, and a green salad. A table with beverages and cookies sat on the other side of the room. The rest of the area was set up with round tables draped with lavender table cloths and bouquets of white, pink, and lavender roses in the center. I stepped closer to the table and admired the tiny silver frames with old photos of Charlotte, with whom I presumed were friends and family. It wouldn't be a bad idea to sit down with Kennedy and peruse family photo albums for additional clues into her past.

I surveyed the hall. Kennedy hadn't exaggerated when she'd said her mother had left many people behind who cared about her and would miss her. Cancer was devastating. Not only had it obliterated Charlotte but parts of her family and friends as well. I watched as most mourners were clumped in groups, nobody ready to sit or touch the food yet. Most were dressed in dark clothing or in their Sunday best. It appeared to be a well-to-do group.

I searched the crowd for Kennedy. She was easily spotted with her strawberry-blond hair tied back and wearing a black sheath dress. Her father, standing next to her, looked like he would crumble at any moment.

My heart ached for Theodore Gilmore. I understood what he was going through. The sudden loss of a spouse was devastating. Without them by your side, you aren't sure where you fit in the world anymore. He had probably assumed he and Charlotte had many years ahead. Charlotte wasn't that old, and neither was he. I would have guessed if they were healthy and took care of themselves, they could have twenty more years together. I could almost feel his pain from across the room. I had two years to find my new normal and still struggled. I empathized with Theodore, who'd had less than two weeks to try to comprehend what his life would be like without Charlotte.

I continued toward the crowd around Kennedy, not to talk to her, which I would do later, but to check out the other guests who wanted to be by her side.

The night before, Kennedy and I had created a game plan for me at the memorial. For starters, I needed to blend in and act as if I was just another mourner while trying to obtain more information about Charlotte's past. I hadn't told Kennedy about the strange fact that there were absolutely no records of Charlotte Jamison in Pennsylvania that fit her mother's description and date of birth.

What I had told her was that so far we hadn't had any luck, but I didn't elaborate. I explained to her it would be helpful to talk to people who knew her, especially people who knew her shortly after she had arrived in California or, with any luck, people who knew her before then. It was starting to look like everything Charlotte had told her daughter about her past was a total fabrication. I'd be surprised if she was even from Pennsylvania. I felt a light touch on my shoulder, and I glanced over at an older woman who wore her silver-gray hair up in a bun like a librarian. *Wait. Is she the librarian from my high school?* "Hello," I said.

"Hello, dear, you look so familiar. How did you know Charlotte?"

Here goes. "I went to the high school where she was a volunteer. I was friends with her daughter, Kennedy."

A wide smile showed off a little red lipstick on her front teeth. "I thought that was you! Martina?"

I was nearly stunned. How could she have possibly remembered me? Not that we'd gone to a large school, but it had been so many years. "Yes. My goodness, you have a great memory. I thought you looked familiar. You were the librarian, right?"

"Oh, yes, you can call me Edna now. It would have meant so much to Charlotte that you came. How have you been, dear?"

"I've been all right."

"That's great. Do you have any kids or a husband?"

I hated this part about running into old friends and family and... librarians. "I have a daughter, she's almost eight. My husband passed a couple years ago, but I'm doing well now. Thank you."

"Oh, dear, I'm so sorry. Oh, I think I see Randy. Well, dear, you take care. I'm sorry for your loss."

I mustered a tight-lipped grin as she wandered off to meet up with Randy. It hadn't occurred to me that anybody would know me or recognize me. I continued on through the crowd, trying to listen to people's conversations as they shared stories about Charlotte. They all seemed to have memories from the past thirty years, but none from as far back as her childhood or teen years.

My stomach rumbled. I'd forgotten to eat in the rush to get out of the house. Claire had arrived to watch Zoey ten minutes earlier than I needed her to, but I still wasn't quite ready on time. I had forgotten that I had promised Zoey pancakes for breakfast this morning and, of course, I didn't have all the ingredients, so I had to negotiate with Zoey until she finally agreed to have cold cereal in exchange for a pizza and movie night.

We took promises seriously in our house. I really should start writing some of these promises and commitments down. At work I was organized, neat, and put together. I would never forget a detail like the ingredients for pancakes if it had to do with work. I really needed to get my parenting life together. Maybe an all-in-one planner might do the trick, considering my professional and personal lives tended to intersect.

After a few more awkward, 'How did you know Charlotte?' encounters and sharing a few stories I had created that would align with interactions of a high school student and an office volunteer, I scanned the crowd to get eyes on Kennedy. I spotted her shaking hands with a fit older man with a receding hairline and thick dark eyebrows. The curiosity in Kennedy's eyes made it appear as if it was the first time they'd ever met. She eyed me, and my gut stirred. I shuffled over to the table of cheeses and crackers directly behind the man. I grabbed a small paper plate and stacked crackers with cheddar cheese and what looked like Monterey Jack. I took a bite and my mouth watered. It was heavenly. I nibbled on my cheese and crackers as I listened in on the conversation.

"Yes, Charlotte was a delightful girl," I heard the man say. "All the boys had crushes on her in school."

My body stiffened. This was somebody from Charlotte's past. No wonder Kennedy gave me that look. I slowed my chewing to hear the conversation better.

"Did she have a lot of boyfriends in high school? Were you a boyfriend of hers?" Kennedy asked. "Mom never liked to talk about her childhood. I would really appreciate anything you can tell me."

Nicely done, Kennedy.

"Oh no, I was a family friend. We never dated. I never had the pleasure. She didn't have too many boyfriends, but she was a looker. She had a lot of admirers. She was quiet, studious, did well in school, and was a superb tennis player."

"Have you been in contact with my mother all these years?"

The man hesitated for a moment. "No, we lost touch over the years, but I saw the announcement of her passing in the newspaper and wanted to pay my respects."

"I'd appreciate anything else you can tell me about my mother. What was it like growing up in Pennsylvania? Did she like the cold weather? Did she ski?"

Well played, Kennedy. It would be nice to confirm that she was actually from Pennsylvania.

He chuckled. "It's funny. She didn't like the cold much. In our senior year, she told me she wished she could move to California one day. She liked the warmer months, and she swore one day she'd live near the water—it looks like she got what she always wanted. I'm glad to see that she followed her dream. I'm just sad that I hadn't reconnected with her earlier—before her passing."

"You were a family friend? She told me her brother and parents had all died in a fire."

The man cleared his throat. "Yeah, that was tragic. It really was. The family were good people."

"How long had you known the family?"

"Her brother and I were good friends in high school. He and Charlotte were only a few years apart. I was close with her brother until the accident."

Something was telling me that this guy was putting on a performance and if you asked my opinion, it wasn't a very good one.

"Do you still live in Pennsylvania?"

"Yes, but I moved out of the area where we grew up. I now live in..."

Before the man could finish his thought, Theodore stormed over. "How did you know Charlotte?"

Kennedy placed her hand on her father's shoulder. "Dad, this is Alonso Davidson—he went to school with Mom. He came out when he heard the news. Alonso, this is my dad, Theo."

Theodore's face turned beet red. "I don't remember ever hearing about you. Who are you really?"

My heart raced. Why would Theodore think somebody would impersonate a friend of Charlotte's? He had to know more about Charlotte's past than he had told his daughter.

"Sir, I swear it's true. It's so nice to meet you and to meet Kennedy. I hadn't kept in touch over the years, but we were friends in school. That's all. I didn't mean to upset you."

Theodore's hand shook as he pointed at Alonso. "You. I don't like you. You need to leave."

"Yes, sir. I don't want to intrude. Kennedy, it was nice meeting you, and to both of you, my deepest sympathy," Alonso said before he hurried out of the hall.

I turned around and looked at Kennedy, who eyed me as well. She was clearly suspicious of the entire encounter and her father's reaction to Alonso.

I rushed out after Alonso and watched as he got into a blue sedan. He drove off before I could record the license plate number. Frustrated, I watched him drive out of the church parking lot before heading back into the hall.

Kennedy gently grabbed my arm as I reentered the room and pulled me to the side. "Did you talk to Alonso?"

She'd clearly seen me go after him. I wasn't terribly inconspicuous. "No, but we have his name. I'll try to get his contact information."

Kennedy nodded nervously. "What do you think of my dad's reaction? Strange, right? He must know more than he's telling me. Do you think I should confront him?"

I'd love to say I didn't want to get involved in family matters, but seeing how I was already in it, I figured I'd give her my best advice. "Yes, but not today. He just buried his wife. Give it a day or two before confronting him."

"You're right. I don't know what I was thinking. Thank you, Martina."

"No problem. I'm going to head out and see what I can find out about Alonso. Maybe he can give us some details about your mother's hometown."

"Okay, but..." Kennedy hesitated. "Would you be willing to come over when I ask my dad about my mom's past?"

Oh, boy. "Are you sure I should be there?"

"I was thinking about it, and I don't like sneaking around behind my dad's back. Can you come over on Monday, and I'll introduce you, and we can ask some questions and let him know what we're looking for?"

I was in deep. "Of course."

She wrapped her arms around me and squeezed. "Thank you."

I admitted I was curious why Theodore had gotten so upset by Alonso. What else did Theodore know? He clearly hadn't told his daughter everything he knew about her mother. There were definitely secrets, and I had the feeling they were about to be revealed.

10

ALONSO

He finished his Caesar salad and threw the container in the waste bin inside the budget hotel room. He reflected on the day. The memorial had been nice. It was obvious Charlotte had lived a good life and had been loved. It was what he had suspected, based on what he'd seen over the years.

Charlotte and he hadn't been terribly close in their younger years, but he knew she had been a good girl and that she had been kind toward him. It was true he'd attended school with her and her brother, but most of their interaction was when he was running errands or performing odd jobs for the family. He hadn't exactly been in the inner circle, not until his job had been elevated to "special advisor." Now, he was the boss's right-hand man. It was a position he'd enjoyed over the years. Whatever the boss needed, he'd do it. He actually preferred the more clandestine work. You know, the type of things that if they needed to be done quickly and/or quietly, he was the guy. Being on an assignment was kind of fun. The job paid well, and he liked the prestige associated with it. Lately, though, he wondered if he was getting a bit old for the work. Retirement was looking pretty good these days.

Inspired by Charlotte's full life, he wondered if he'd missed out on having a family. A person with whom he could come home to or celebrate the holidays. Her daughter, Kennedy, seemed like a smart, sweet gal. He hoped he hadn't given her too much information. She had seemed so desperate to know more about her mother, and he truly wanted to give it to her, but his loyalty was to the family not just to Charlotte. The information he provided was fairly nondescript and accurate. He hoped it gave Kennedy some comfort. However, he also hoped it was all she knew. If she knew anything more, he would know soon enough.

He pulled out his phone and called the boss. "Hey, boss, I just got back from the memorial. It had a real nice turnout. Charlotte had a good life."

"Good to hear. Did everything else go smoothly?"

"Mostly okay. The house is all set."

"What do you mean? Do we have anything to worry about?"

"Maybe, maybe not. The husband was pretty upset by my presence at the memorial. I don't think he actually knows who I am, but he seemed to know enough to be upset by the fact I was someone from her past. He practically threw me out of the church."

There was silence from the boss.

"That is strange. I wonder how much he knows. It could be problematic if he knows too much."

"The Gilmores may not know anything important."

"True, maybe he just thought you were some creep."

Thanks. "Well, I got my eyes, and my ears to the ground, so we'll know soon enough if there's anything to be worried about."

"That's what I like to hear. Give me an update tomorrow, okay?"

He glanced out the window. "You got it."

"Thanks. Talk soon."

He hung up and placed the phone back down on the desk. He hoped all went well, but if, or more likely when, Kennedy started asking her dad about why he had reacted the way he did when he saw him, they would know if there was anything to worry about. The Gilmore place was good and bugged, so if they had any conversations about Charlotte's past, he'd have a front-row seat.

Maybe he could stretch this assignment out to a week or so. He'd like to check out the area more. It seemed like a nice place to spend his golden years. He was thorough. He could simply tell the boss he needed to make sure there weren't any stones left unturned.

He logged into his laptop and opened the software program connected to the listening devices he'd planted inside the Gilmore house. It would likely be at least an hour or two before they were home. It looked like he'd have a couple of hours to kill. Perhaps a stroll along the water would be nice, and so would some mint chocolate chip ice cream. *Yes, please.*

11

MARTINA

I gave my best, most non-threatening smile to Theodore Gilmore as he apprehensively shook my hand. He didn't smile back. He eyed his daughter and then me. "What exactly is it you're looking for?"

He wasn't even pretending to be friendly. Maybe he was grumpy or sad or not feeling well. His skin was pale and his eyes were lined with bags. He could have easily been all three. "Maybe we should sit down at the dining table and discuss this," I suggested.

He mumbled something under his breath before shuffling over to the dining table with his fragility on full display. If I had to guess, I'd say he wasn't well, physically, and not just from the despair over his wife's passing. I eyed Kennedy. She shrugged and followed behind her father.

Theodore situated himself at the head of the table. My guess was that was where he always sat. Kennedy pulled out the chair next to him and sat by his side. I took a seat across from Kennedy and next to Theodore. I glanced over at Kennedy. "Do you want me to explain what we're looking for or do you?"

Her hands were shaking, and her eyes were fixed on her father.

I took the cue. "Why don't I explain?"

She looked at me and nodded. I wasn't sure if she was afraid of her father, or she was just nervous to tell him that she had gone behind his back and continued to investigate the baby in the photo.

I turned to position myself so I was directly facing Theodore Gilmore. "Mr. Gilmore, your daughter hired me to determine the identity of a baby that is in a photo with your late wife. Do you know which photo I'm talking about?"

"Yes," he said without emotion.

"In order for me to find out the identity of that baby, I have to look into Charlotte's life. Her life before she met you and before she arrived in California. In that pursuit, I will be able to also provide Kennedy more information about Charlotte's family and where she's from."

I stared at Theodore Gilmore, who sat quietly with his head bowed and his wrinkled hands raised to his forehead.

He clearly didn't like the fact I was investigating his wife's past, but I also suspected he held some, if not all, of the answers to his daughter's questions. I prodded him. "Kennedy has told me that your wife's maiden name is Jamison, her date of birth, and that she was from Pennsylvania. We also found a class ring from 1966 that we think was Charlotte's. Charlotte apparently told your daughter that her parents and brother died in a fire many years ago, which was the event that prompted her to move out to California and stay with a relative after she graduated from high school. I was told that relative has since passed." I gauged his reaction.

He remained hunched over.

I continued. "To be honest with you, Mr. Gilmore, that's not a lot to go by. So far, we have had no luck in confirming any of that information. Is there anything you could share with us about your wife's past that would help us to learn more about her family and the identity of the child in the photo?" I glanced over at Kennedy. She frowned at her father's demeanor. I tried to keep my tone even and matter-of-fact, hoping that this information would convince him to say something, maybe something we didn't already know and that could help the investigation. We sat in silence as both Kennedy and I watched Mr. Gilmore.

He lowered his hands and raised his head before staring into Kennedy's eyes. "I'm so sorry, honey. I hadn't realized how much this meant to you. I should've told you before, but she never wanted you to know. But now that she's gone and my family is dwindling as well, I think maybe you have a right to know." He eyed me apologetically. "I can tell you what she told me." He cleared his throat. "Honey, would you please fetch me a glass of water?"

"Of course." Kennedy hurried over to the kitchen. She glanced over her shoulder. "Can I get you anything, Martina?"

"I'm fine."

She nodded before pulling a glass from the cupboard and filling it from the tap. She set it down in front of Theodore and quickly retook her seat.

Theodore took a gulp and placed the glass back down. "I'll tell you everything she told me when we met. My mind is a bit fuzzy since it was quite a while ago. She didn't like to talk about her past, and we didn't discuss it after we were married. She told me she was from Doylestown, Pennsylvania and that she had a brother and parents who died. She..." He stopped and took another sip of water. His Adam's apple bobbed as he swallowed it, his hands shaking as he placed the glass back down. "She also told me she had been married. They'd been young—married right after high school. Soon after, she'd gotten pregnant, and they had a daughter—Amelia. She died shortly after being born." He stayed focused on Kennedy, who's face had gone long and pale.

Her eyes welled. "Amelia was my sister?"

Theodore nodded.

"What happened? How did she die?"

"Something genetic. I don't recall exactly what it was," he explained.

Case closed? Married before? Perhaps Jamison was her married name, not her maiden name, but even so it would have shown up in the records searches.

Kennedy shook her head back and forth, bewildered. "I can't believe she was married before. What happened to her husband?"

Theodore stiffened. "She told me he was a bad man. They divorced."

"Was it the man at her memorial, Alonso?"

"I don't know what his name was. She said she never wanted to talk about him ever again and that her life started on that day at City Hall, when she and I were married," he said with a sad smile.

"I don't understand why she wouldn't tell me," Kennedy pleaded.

He put his hands up in defeat. "I don't know, but it wasn't my secret to tell. I always had the feeling there was more to it, but every time I'd push for more, she pushed me away and I didn't want to be shut out."

"Was Jamison her family name or her married name?" Kennedy asked.

Theodore cocked his head and shrugged. "I don't know. I guess I always assumed Jamison was her family name, but maybe it wasn't."

"Why were you so upset when I introduced you to Alonso at the memorial?"

"I don't know. I just didn't like the vibe from him. If Charlotte never wanted to talk about her past, she certainly wouldn't be happy to see someone from her past pop up out of the blue. I didn't trust that guy. I have a feeling she wouldn't have either."

As I had suspected, Theodore Gilmore had known a lot more about his wife than he had let on.

Kennedy deflated in her chair. I couldn't blame her. It was a lot to take in. "What else do you know about her past?"

"I'm afraid that's everything I know."

Kennedy pushed her chair back and stepped toward her father and wrapped her arms around him. It was my cue to leave. This was a family moment and my case had been solved. I slid out of my chair and quietly took my bag from the back of the chair and headed toward the door. Kennedy glanced up at me. I muttered, "I'm going to let you two have some space."

She released her father and walked toward me, cheeks still wet. "Thank you for everything." She glanced back at her dad and then back at me. "I want to know where Amelia and the family are buried. I want to go there and pay my respects. Can you help me find them?"

Case *not* closed. "I will." I waved at Theodore. "It was nice meeting you, Mr. Gilmore."

He gave a head nod without a word.

"Kennedy, we'll be in touch. Take care."

She embraced me and whispered, "Thank you." I let myself out of the house and stood on the porch facing the Bernards' house. My heart was heavy as I thought of the other family on this street who grieved for a loved one that had been gone too soon. I would find Kennedy's family and I would find Donna. Both families deserved closure.

12

DETECTIVE HIRSCH

I SHUT OFF THE SHOWER, HOPING TO HAVE GOTTEN THE scent of death off me. I could go the rest of my career without going to another burned-out meth lab and die a happy man. Most people have never smelled the scent of charred flesh, but for those of us who have, you never forget it. It was not something that you can get out of your hair or your clothes with a little spritz of cologne or one cycle in the washing machine. I grabbed the towel from the rack and dried myself off before wrapping the towel around my waist and heading back to the locker room.

This job was damn depressing. Not that my former position at the San Francisco Police Department was any less depressing, but at least it had some variety. A sprinkle of good amongst the daily tragedy. Out there on the Delta, it seemed as if it was one drug deal gone wrong after another. The saddest part was how young the dealers were. I should have done more research before transferring to the CoCo County Sheriff's Department. I had been warned. It was where careers went to die, but I had been intrigued by the cold-case aspect. Not to mention the fact I didn't have a choice after the last showdown with my lieutenant. It was the Sheriff's Department, or I was out of a job.

I thought it might have been a blessing in disguise. I'd get to own and run my own investigations, all without the brass hovering over me. With cold cases, I thought I might be able to make a difference. To find the lost and forgotten. I still had that opportunity, but it was mixed with run-of-the-mill mayhem.

I dressed in a pair of jeans and polo shirt and then threw on a black zip-up sweater before heading back out to the station. I walked in and gave a friendly smile to the receptionist, who I assumed had been with the Sheriff's department since the beginning of time. "Hi, Detective Hirsch. You have a message."

"What's the message?" If I were a preteen, I'd write in my diary how excited I was to get my first message at my new job. It was the first in nearly a month.

"It's from someone who wants to talk to you about the Donna Bernard cold case. She was insistent. She said if she doesn't hear from you, she'll call every day until you call her back."

"What else did she say?"

"Not much, just that she wanted to talk to the detective who was working the Donna Bernard case."

I grabbed the slip of paper Glenda had placed on the desk. "Did you give her my name?"

"Nope. I just took the message."

I lifted my hands into a prayer position. "Thank you." I'd barely cracked the file and didn't need some nut job coming after me.

I reached my desk and plopped down in my chair. I needed caffeine—STAT. Before propping myself up to grab a coffee, I glanced at the note from Glenda. I shut my eyes and shook my head. *You've got to be kidding.* Why was Martina Monroe calling about the Donna Bernard case? I'd nearly forgotten about her and that complete debacle. Or, at least, I'd tried to erase the memory. Martina was the private investigator who had been all over me after the DeSoto case. When I'd told her the husband was free and wasn't being implicated in the murder, I thought she was going to throw a punch. She didn't believe the department's theory that Julie DeSoto's death was the result a robbery gone wrong. She insisted the husband had her killed and that I was an idiot for closing the case. Not that it had been my choice.

My body suddenly froze, and dread filled me. *No.* I straightened my posture and grabbed the Bernard binder and flipped it open. I scrolled through the pages of witness statements and stopped at the one from a Martina Koltz. Was Koltz, Martina Monroe's maiden name? Was I that unlucky, that my first cold case at my new job at the Sheriff's Department was connected to Martina Monroe?

So much for thinking I'd be able to run my own investigation. If that woman was involved, I had no doubt she'd be a thorn in my side the entire way. I one hundred percent believed she would be following up incessantly until we solved the case. I shut the binder and turned on my computer to check my email, hoping for a distraction. I was halfway through a department message when I heard footsteps approaching my desk. I glanced up. "What's up?"

"Hey, Hirsch. We have a dead body on Stone Island."

"Homicide?"

Brown, the head crime scene technician, wore a Warriors jersey and denim with a pair of sneakers. He was tall and a big fan of basketball. He said, "The only information we have is that there's a dead body. First responders are already on the scene. Could be natural or an accident, or it could be homicide. You're the lucky bastard who gets to help us figure it out."

And here I thought this day couldn't get any worse. "All right. I'm ready to go."

"You want a ride with the CSI team?" Brown asked.

"If you don't mind. I've had a hell of a day already."

Brown chuckled and smacked me on the shoulder. "Buck up, it's only Tuesday."

THE CSI TEAM AND I ARRIVED AT THE HOUSE ON STONE Island. In the long driveway, there were a couple of black and white patrol cars mixed with a few others. We stepped out of the van, and I surveyed the house and its surroundings. *Damn. This just got weirder.* The dead body was next-door to the Bernards? It was like the universe was playing with me.

While the crew unloaded their equipment, I jogged up the stairs where there was a patrolman standing outside the door. In these parts, everybody knew everyone. The officer was a fit young guy. He smiled. "Hey, Hirsch, go right inside. The body is in the bedroom. The daughter is inside talking to Lancaster."

"Thanks." I opened the door and stepped inside. A woman with auburn hair and freckles had tears streaming down her cheeks and a shocked look in her eyes. She was being consoled by Officer Lancaster. Lancaster raised her brows and pointed to a box on the ground and then waved toward the back of the house. In the box were booties and gloves. The case was likely a natural death, but until manner of death was determined, we'd treat it like a crime scene. I slipped a pair of booties over my shoes and continued down the hall until I reached the room being guarded by Officer Pickett, a pot-bellied, middle-aged bald man. "Hey, Hirsch."

"Hi, Pickett. What can you tell me?"

"Theodore Gilmore. Sixty years of age. Known heart condition. The daughter, the one in the kitchen with Lancaster, came by and found him like this. She checked for signs of life—there were none—she called 9-1-1. Paramedics checked for a pulse and confirmed he was dead."

"How long ago?"

"About an hour."

"Anything been disturbed?"

Pickett gripped his belt. "Paramedics were careful when they came in. The head paramedic said he was pretty sure he was dead, so he tiptoed over to check the pulse. He was already cold when they arrived."

"Did the daughter have any reason to believe it could be anything other than natural?"

"Nothing definitive. She just said something about it being weird timing or something to that effect. She's pretty torn up."

"That's helpful. Thanks." I sucked in my breath and stepped past Pickett. I never enjoyed looking at a dead body, and I had the feeling this wouldn't be any different. There he was. Mr. Gilmore, fully clothed in denim trousers and a gray sweatshirt, lying on his stomach, arms straight by his sides, and his head turned toward the wall. I would assume that if he'd had a heart attack, he would've clutched his arm or chest and fell. If he'd had a stroke, he also would have fallen. The way Mr. Gilmore was positioned suggested something other than a fall. The word posed came to mind.

I slipped on a pair of purple nitrile gloves and knelt down next to the deceased's face. I didn't see any visible bruises either, which means he likely didn't fall. I glanced over at Pickett. "Hey, does the daughter live here?"

"No, she lives in San Francisco. She came by this afternoon to check on him. His wife's memorial was just a few days ago."

Damn. Mr. Gilmore was having a far worse day than I was. Double Damn. The poor daughter. No wonder she was in shock. I looked back at Mr. Gilmore, who stared at me with vacant eyes. We were going to need the medical examiner to determine cause of death before ruling manner of death, but my gut was screaming homicide. A knock on the door caught my attention. "Hey, Brown. It looks a little suspicious to me. Photograph everything, get prints on the doors and windows, collect any fibers that don't seem to fit, and anything that looks out of place—bag it and tag it. I'll call the ME."

Brown gave me a thumbs up, and I exited the room to search the rest of the house. I didn't find any signs of forced entry or a struggle. I headed back toward the front of the house and inspected the windows. Both unlocked, but both with the screens intact as well. It didn't mean an intruder couldn't replace them after they snuck out. I removed the gloves, shoved them in my pocket, and approached the kitchen. I nodded at Lancaster. She raised a finger for me to wait. I stood until she motioned me over to her and the daughter.

Lancaster spoke in a soothing voice. "Kennedy, this is Detective Hirsch. He has a few questions for you. Are you up for it?"

She nodded as she brushed away the tears from her cheeks with the back of her hand. Her eyes remained listless.

No ring on her fingers. "Ms. Gilmore, I presume?"

She nodded.

"I'm sorry for your loss, Ms. Gilmore."

"Thank you."

"Have we called someone to be with you?"

Lancaster said, "Yes, she has a friend on the way."

"Great. Like Officer Lancaster said, I'm Detective Hirsch and I'll be the one trying to figure out what happened to your father."

"You don't think it was his heart?"

"I'm not sure. The medical examiner will be the one to tell

us what caused his passing. Once we know that, we can determine his manner of death."

"Like, if it wasn't natural?"

"Right. Can you tell me exactly how you found him?"

"I used my key to get in, like I usually do. I called out for him to let him know I was here. When I didn't hear back, I looked for him and found him lying there. I rushed in to check if he was breathing, but I saw his eyes and touched his neck. He was...cold. Then I dialed 9-1-1. I waited in the kitchen for them to arrive."

"Did you touch anything in the room? Or move him in any way?"

"No."

"Can you think of any reason anyone would want to hurt your father?"

She shook her head. "No. Not really."

"The other officer mentioned you said there was something weird about it. Can you explain?"

She let out a breath. "Well, my mother passed less than two weeks ago. The memorial was over the weekend. He had just told me some things about my mother's past that were upsetting. That was yesterday and then... Now he's gone."

"Upsetting how?"

I listened and scribbled notes on my 3x5 notepad as she described how she'd hired a private investigator to look into her mother's past. She told me about a family secret and about a man from her mother's past that had shown up at the memorial. I had to admit it was a little weird. "Did the PI find out anything else that was strange?"

"Just that initially she couldn't find anything about my mother's past. She couldn't confirm the story about her brother and parents or find any records at all."

Her mother had been running from someone. The ex-husband? If that were true, why a made-up story about a family fire? "And what was the name of the PI?"

Ms. Gilmore shifted her focus toward the door. She rushed over to a woman and wrapped her arms around her. A few moments later, they stepped apart. *You've got to be kidding me.* I was convinced my life had become one sick joke. I swallowed my remaining pride and approached the two women. *Maybe she's forgotten who I am?* I extended my hand. "I'm Detective Hirsch, lead detective in the death of Mr. Gilmore."

She eyed me up and down. "How does it look? Robbery gone wrong?"

She remembers. I lowered my arm. "Ms. Monroe, good to see you. The ME should arrive shortly. She'll determine cause of death and then we can work on manner of death."

Ignoring me, she turned to Ms. Gilmore. "Don't worry, Kennedy, if he can't figure it out, I will."

Kennedy's mouth dropped open. "Do you know each other?"

"Our paths have crossed. It's okay, I'll handle it."

I bit my lower lip to contain myself. "Ms. Gilmore, the CoCo County Sheriff's department will do everything in our power to find out what happened to your father." I pivoted toward Martina. "Ms. Monroe, I presume you are the PI who is investigating the late Mrs. Gilmore's past."

"That's correct."

"Is there anything relevant that could help us determine a motive or a suspect in the event the death is determined to be suspicious?"

Martina remained stoic. "Maybe."

Pride gone, I asked, "Perhaps you and I can work together and compare notes?"

"I need to be with Kennedy right now. Maybe we can talk later?"

"Of course. That would be great." I fished a pair of business cards from my inner jacket pocket and handed one to each of the women.

"Ms. Gilmore, again, I'm sorry for your loss. If you have any questions, please call me—day or night. And Ms. Monroe, call me when you're ready to talk. I actually I got a message from you about the Bernard case. I'd like to discuss both with you."

Martina narrowed her light amber eyes, as if assessing me. "I'll call you."

"I'd appreciate it."

I exited the house and made my way up to the levee to look around. There were small houseboats, fishing boats, and empty docks. Houses lined the waterfront. It was time to knock on doors and find out if anyone had heard or seen anything unusual. The niggling in my gut was telling me this was bigger than it appeared at first glance. Between the disappearance of the girl next door, the investigation into the wife's mysterious past, and Martina Monroe connecting all of them, it was too much coincidence for my taste. I supposed I could forget about sleeping for a while.

13

MARTINA

I LED KENNEDY OUT OF THE KITCHEN AND ONTO THE LEVEE outside. The wind picked up, and the icy breeze shot a chill down the back of my jacket. It was still better than being in the home with Theodore Gilmore's dead body. Kennedy stood with her back to the dark gray water. I studied her grief-stricken face. "Kennedy, I'm so sorry."

"Thank you for coming, Martina. I asked you to come because something is telling me this wasn't an accident or because of his heart problems. Yesterday, he was fine. You saw him, he was okay, right?"

He didn't look great to me, but I didn't want to say that to her. I hadn't seen the body and didn't want to speculate until the medical examiner came back with the cause of death. "Was there anything out of place in the house to make you think some-body broke in and hurt your father?"

"No, what's weird is how he was lying on the floor. When I found him, at first I thought he was just sleeping on the floor, which was odd, but he looked peaceful. He wasn't banged up like he might be if he'd fallen down. It was as if he'd laid down, put his arms by his side and went to sleep, until I saw his eyes. They were open and blank. It's hard to describe."

What an awful thing to find your parent like that. "That sounds suspicious. Do you know if he had received any strange phone calls or messages? Or have you received anything that would make you think somebody would want to hurt your father?"

"No. Nothing. Everyone loved Dad. What if it's connected to my mom?"

"I can't imagine what it could be, but I'll keep in contact with the detective and make sure that we know what's going on with the case at all times. If your father's death is connected to your mom's past, we'll find out."

"I sensed a little tension between you and the detective—not friends?"

Darn it, Martina. Very unprofessional. The sight of him just triggers me. "I've only worked with him once before, but it wasn't a good outcome. In my line of work, we also provide security. I had a case where we were helping a woman leave her abusive husband safely. The morning we were supposed to pick her up, he was supposed to be out of town, but when we arrived, we found her murdered in her bedroom. I suspected the husband must have hired someone to do his dirty work, but the detective—Hirsch—of the SFPD said it was a burglary gone wrong and that she'd simply been at the wrong place at the wrong time. It was ludicrous. There was nothing stolen from the house. Long story short, Hirsch and I got into a bit of a tiff, but that was a while ago. I apologize for being so unprofessional, I won't let it happen again."

"It's okay. I suspect you're human too. Do you worry he won't be able to find out what happened to my dad?"

"Maybe, but like I said, I'll be on him every step of the way.

Don't worry, I'll make sure it all goes smoothly, and he does an adequate job."

I glanced next door at the Bernards' house. I still hadn't stopped by to say hello and wondered if I should wait until I met with Detective Hirsch so we could interview them together. Suddenly, I realized my to-do list was growing by the moment. Top of the list was to uncover Charlotte's real past, real last name, and who killed Theodore Gilmore and then to find out what happened to Donna. I lifted my wrist and glanced at my Timex. *Darn it.* I was going to miss another one of Zoey's Brownie meetings. She was going to be one mad little sprite. I'd have to make it up to her somehow. I eyed Kennedy. "Do you have someone you can stay with tonight?"

"I figured I would just go home to my apartment. I have a cat that I need to take care of."

"Are you okay to drive?"

Kennedy shrugged, defeated.

I was already going to miss Zoey's Girl Scout meeting. If Claire could drop her off and stay with her afterwards, I could give Kennedy a ride. "Let me make a quick call. I might be able to drop you off."

Kennedy protested. "You don't have to do that, Martina."

I put my hand on her shoulder. "You shouldn't be driving all that way right now. Give me a sec."

I stepped away and pulled my phone from my jacket pocket. "Hi, Martina. What's up?"

"Hi, Claire. Is there any way you could take Zoey to her Brownie meeting? I'm out on Stone Island, and I don't think I'll be able to make it back in time."

"Sure, of course."

"And could you potentially watch her after the meeting as well? My client has had a rough night and shouldn't drive. She needs a ride home all the way out to San Francisco."

There was a pause. Not a great sign. I hated springing things like this on Claire, especially since I think she may be frustrated that I hadn't picked a new nanny yet. The two I interviewed didn't seem to have the same dedication that Claire did. She finally responded. "It's not a problem. I'll take care of it. Also, Martina, I received a couple new applications today. Tomorrow we can discuss setting up interviews."

"Thank you, Claire." I hung up and returned to Kennedy. "All set. I can give you a ride home. You shouldn't be here right now. Any questions the detective may have, he can call you. Hirsch has your information, right?"

"Yes. I'll go in the house and grab my things."

"All right, I'll wait for you here." I wrapped my arms around myself as the breeze picked up. I heard the crunch of boots on gravel and turned to see the detective heading my way.

I needed to make nice, and quick, if I was going to get access to information on Theodore Gilmore's case and since he was handling Donna's case, it was doubly important. "Detective."

"The two of you are close?"

"We've been working this case, and I've been by her side most of the time. It's been a hard week and a half, and now with her dad's death, it's been rough. I'm going to drive her home. She's holding up here, in front of everyone, but she's pretty shook. I don't want her on the road when she's alone with her thoughts."

"That's good of you."

"I'll call you tomorrow. There are a couple things I want to look into that may be related." The sound of a creaking door stole my attention toward the Bernard house. I watched as Mrs. Bernard let out a black-and-white cat before returning inside the house. My heart sank.

"Okay, I'm ready to go. Detective, is there anything else you need from me?" Kennedy asked.

I turned to Kennedy and Detective Hirsch. He said, "No, we have all we need right now. I'll be in touch."

"My car is the gray sedan. I'll be right down," I said.

Kennedy nodded and descended the steps. I glanced over at Hirsch. "Kennedy grew up next-door to Donna Bernard—her whole life. She needs to be part of the investigation into Donna's disappearance, but I want you to give her some space."

"You and Donna were friends?"

"Best friends."

"We'll find out what happened to her and what happened to Theodore Gilmore. I want us to work together on this. If that's okay with you."

I nodded. "Thank you, Detective."

Great. Now I had a line into the sheriff's department and what was going on there. Maybe Hirsch wasn't as bad as I thought. I recalled him saying that it wasn't his choice to close the DeSoto murder. Maybe he wasn't a total idiot.

I jogged down the steps and wondered why Hirsch was with the CoCo County Sheriff and wasn't with the SFPD anymore. I'd ask him the next day. At that moment, I had to take care of Kennedy.

When I was given her case, I had been excited at the prospect of having my old life back. To be working on an active investigation that was something other than cheating spouses or insurance fraud perpetrators, but I was reminded of the reality. The chaos. The adrenaline spikes and what I knew would be a severe lack of sleep. And a lot of making things up to Zoey.

14

DETECTIVE HIRSCH

I TURNED AWAY FROM THE BERNARD RESIDENCE, HEAD hung low. They were the last of the neighbors for me to question about last night. I wasn't a coward but felt awkward since I hadn't given them any updates on their daughter's case yet. The truth was, I'd barely scratched the surface of Donna's disappearance.

However, seeing as their next-door neighbor was possibly murdered last night, it was important to find out if they'd heard anything or if they had any security cameras installed on their home. I hadn't seen any, but I would double-check.

I walked back to levee and spotted the medical examiner arriving. I quickened my steps to meet her at the front door of the Gilmore residence. I'd only met her a few times, but I was sure she remembered me. I was "the new guy." I called out, "Dr. Scribner."

I caught up to her, and she smiled. She was a woman of maybe fifty with shoulder length silver hair she had pulled back in a ponytail. "Detective Hirsch, what do we have here? Did you look at the body yet?"

"I did. I'd like to hear your thoughts on time of death as soon as possible, if you can. I have my suspicions."

"All right then, let's get to it."

I followed her into the house. We both stopped at the same box filled with the booties. I slipped a pair on whereas she pulled out coveralls from her case and slipped into them before putting a pair of booties on. Gowned up, we headed back to the bedroom where Theodore Gilmore's body lay.

Dr. Scribner stepped into the room and studied the body. She scanned it, examining every angle, before kneeling down in front of his face. With gloved hands, she pressed down on the side of his face with her fingers, and then did the same to his neck. She glanced up at me. "Can you help me lift his body up?"

I nodded before hurrying over.

"I just want to lift him up a few inches if we can. On my count of three. One-two-three."

I lifted with all of my strength. Dr. Scribner lifted his shirt and the exposed skin was a ghoulish dark purple. Lividity had set in, which meant he had been dead at least eight to twelve hours.

"We can set him down now."

I slowly lowered him back down.

From her bag, she pulled out what looked like a meat thermometer and plunged into his back. The sound was wet and disturbing. A few moments later, she leaned in and read the temperature. Without looking up at me, she said, "Based on body temp, I'm guessing he died"—she paused and lifted her arm and looked at the digital watch on her wrist—"between midnight and two AM."

I stood up. I don't think it was a coincidence that the neighbor's dog barked at midnight and then again at 1:00 AM. If Theodore Gilmore was murdered, it was likely that somebody broke in around midnight and left around 1:00 AM. Why had they been there for a whole hour? "When do you think you'll be able to do the autopsy?"

She let out a sigh as she examined behind Mr. Gilmore's ear. "Not sure. We're pretty backed up."

"Any way to make an exception and get him to the top of the queue?"

She peered up at me over her glasses.

I pleaded, "He has a daughter. She's the one who found him. His wife, her mother, died a week and half ago. She's lost both parents in less than two weeks. If there's any way we can give her a little closure sooner rather than later, I would appreciate it."

She returned her focus to Theodore. "I'll see what I can do. I don't think this was an accident."

"Why not?"

"Position of the body and the suspicious tiny mark behind his ear. Between you and me and Mr. Gilmore, my guess is somebody injected him with something and then forced him into this position. Don't quote me on any of it. I could be wrong. He could have been sleepy and decided the floor looked comfy and fell asleep and then died of natural causes." She stood up and snapped off her gloves. "I'll see what I can do to get your autopsy sooner rather than later."

"Thanks, Doc."

I left the death-filled room and reentered the front of the house and walked over to Brown. "You guys about finished up here?"

"Just about. You?"

"I need to do a quick follow-up with a neighbor, and then I'll be done. I should be back in five minutes."

"We should be able to wrap up shortly after."

"Great." Now that we had a potential cause and time of

death, I headed back to the neighbor's house two doors down, whose dog had barked in the early hours of the morning. I approached, and the dog went off. The owner wasn't kidding. If there was any activity within ten feet, the dog heard it. I knocked on the door and stepped back. The man opened the door and said, "Detective, you're back."

"Yes, Mr. Piratto, can I ask you to confirm a few things?"

He nodded. "Sure, let me grab my jacket." He disappeared behind the door, returning a few seconds later, wearing a down jacket that went down to his knees. He zipped it up and closed the door behind him. "What is it, Detective?"

"Can you confirm what time you heard the dog barking?"

"First one was right at midnight. I have a clock on my nightstand."

"And the second bark, was at what time?"

"One, one-oh-five, maybe."

So, whoever may have broken into the Gilmore's house and killed Mr. Gilmore had been there for an hour. What would the killer be doing for an hour? The house wasn't ransacked, and there were no signs of forced entry. Was he questioning Theodore? Was he searching for something? "Do you know if any of your surrounding neighbors have security cameras on the outside of their houses?"

"Actually, you know, I think the guy three doors down installed a camera on his dock. This last summer someone had stolen his boat and took it for a ride. He was furious. I'm pretty sure he put cameras up the same day. In the end, it had been a couple of stupid kids, but he still didn't want anybody taking his boat, understandably."

"Thank you, Mr. Piratto. You've been really helpful."

"Anything to help. Take care."

We had ears on a potential suspect, but we needed eyes on him too. I pounded down the gravel until I reached the house three doors down. I glanced down at the dock. It was dark and I couldn't see much. I turned around and knocked on the front door. From the other side of the door, someone said, "Who is it?"

"Detective Hirsch with the CoCo County Sheriff's Department."

The lock disengaged, and the door opened. A man in a thick bathrobe with a receding hairline stood there. "What can I help you with, Detective?"

"I'm not sure if you've heard, but your neighbor, Mr. Gilmore, was found dead this afternoon."

"No. That old guy whose wife died?"

Not a great way to talk about someone who had just died. Not a friendly neighbor, I was guessing, or at the very least, not a sensitive soul. "Yes, there is a possibility that it may be a homicide. Did you hear or see anything out of the ordinary last night?"

"No."

"Your neighbor says you might have cameras on your dock."

"I do, but I'm not sure if it captured anything on the levee. I positioned them mostly for the dock, but I can look and see if there's anything on them."

Maybe he's not so bad after all. "I would appreciate it."

"Any specific times?"

"Between eleven forty-five and maybe two in the morning."

He said, "Let me check," and went back into the house without a word.

I surveyed the area. It was dark and visibility was low. Only a few front porch lights had turned on.

A few minutes later, the man reemerged, clutching a silver flashlight. "I have no footage from last night. I think someone may have disabled my cameras." He stepped out of the house and said, "I'm going to look," before he stormed down to the dock. He reached the gate and muttered, "Son of a bitch." He turned around. "Someone cut the wires."

There was definitely somebody out there last night that didn't want to be seen or heard. Somebody who knew what they were doing and had scoped out the place ahead of time. What were the odds that Theodore Gilmore had a heart attack or died of natural causes on the same night the dog barked at midnight, right around his time of death, and the nearest surveillance cameras were tampered with? Not likely. If Theodore Gilmore was killed, why was he killed? Who had motive?

15

ALONSO

He stepped onto the jetway and peered out the window. Under his breath, he mumbled, "Goodbye, California. I'll miss you until next time." He turned back toward the line of passengers in front of him, waiting to board the plane. He would definitely miss sunny California and would certainly trade the frigid Pennsylvania winters for it, but unfortunately, he had to cut this trip short.

The boss was not pleased when he had explained what he had found out. The boss didn't elaborate why he wasn't happy. He had simply told him they needed to quiet down the source in order to stop the flow of information about the family. He found it strange that Charlotte had told her husband she was married before him, but as far as he knew, she hadn't been. Why had Charlotte told her husband that she had been married before and had a baby? He would've known if that were true, unless she'd been married and fallen pregnant after she had left Pennsylvania all those years ago.

As the line advanced, he moved ahead with his duffel bag over his shoulder.

He was tight with the boss, but usually the information

flowed in one direction, and it was never appreciated when he asked too many questions. His phone buzzed, and he knew who it was.

He glanced at the screen. *Yep.* "Hey, boss."

"Are you on the plane yet?"

"I'm boarding right now."

"Good. We'll discuss our next move when you arrive home. This matter isn't finished. We need to contain this, and fast, but I don't want to talk over the phone. When you land, I'll have a driver waiting to pick you up from the airport."

"Thanks, boss."

From behind, he heard a high-pitched voice say, "Sir."

He looked up ahead and saw that he'd failed to move the obligatory three steps to fill the gap between the passengers in front of him while he was on the phone. He twisted around and said, "Sorry, ma'am," before he stuffed the phone into his pocket and stepped forward.

The boss was talking about containment, which meant Kennedy and the private investigator may need to be dealt with. He didn't like the idea of silencing them the way he had to silence Theodore. He decided against jumping to conclusions. He wasn't sure what the boss was asking him to do. Maybe the boss was being overly dramatic. He had to have faith. If the boss wanted him to take care of Kennedy and Martina, he must have a good reason, right?

16

MARTINA

I PULLED INTO THE PARKING LOT OF THE CoCo COUNTY Sheriff's Department. I shoved down my personal feelings about Detective Hirsch and his inability to solve Julie DeSoto's murder because I needed to be professional, rational, and in control. I parked the car and turned it off before climbing out and slamming the door behind me harder than I had intended to. I needed to breathe and center myself and thank God I was alive and healthy. I couldn't let my anger get the better of me. I could do this.

I buttoned my coat and headed toward the front doors of the station. In my conversation with Rocco last night, he reminded me I was actually fortunate that Hirsch was willing to even talk to me about an open investigation. Rocco was a great sounding board for all things and often the voice of reason. Sometimes I wondered if I leaned on him too much. Maybe I should get a therapist and not burden Rocco with all my problems. He was a sponsor and wasn't expected to be my confidant or my crutch. Before my accident, I would've gone to Stavros to discuss the idea of working with Hirsch, but I couldn't have him questioning my abilities to do the job. I was sober, healthy, and fit, and I was going to stay that way. Healthy body, healthy mind.

I approached the receptionist, who had to be at least eighty years old. She wore cat eye glasses and her dark hair in a short bob. The woman gave me a friendly smile. "Hello, how may I help you today?" she asked with a cheerful tone.

"I'm here to see Detective Hirsch. My name is Martina Monroe."

"Oh, are you here about the cold case?"

"No, not really. It's about another case, actually."

"Oh, two cases. You guys are going to be buddies. He is a looker, you know," she said before chuckling. "I'll get him for you." She picked up the phone and pressed a few buttons. "Hello, Detective Hirsch, Ms. Monroe is here to see you." She nodded and said, "Okay, will do."

She hung up the receiver and said, "He'll be right out. So, did you know Donna Bernard?"

"I did. Do you remember the case?" I asked.

"I do. She was such a pretty girl. I didn't know her personally. I just saw the photos. Do you believe the story that she ran away?"

It warmed my insides to hear that Donna was remembered. I shook my head. "No, I was her best friend, and I don't think that she ran away—not for one second."

"Good. A woman with convictions, I like that. I hope you find her."

"Me too."

"Best of luck, Ms. Monroe," she said before refocusing on her computer screen.

At the sound of footsteps approaching, I glanced across the office and spotted Detective Hirsch. I told myself, *friendly Martina, friendly*. I gave a weak smile. "Detective, good to see you."

We shook hands. "You too. Why don't you follow me back to the conference room and we can talk?"

"Sounds great. After you." I watched as the receptionist's eyes followed us as we started down the hall. If she thought I was there to make a romantic connection with Detective Hirsch, she was way off base. Maybe she had read too many romance novels or watched too many telenovelas. Not that Detective Hirsch was bad-looking. He was attractive in a Ken Doll kind of way.

Hirsch led me into a medium-sized conference room with a table and seating for eight. "Can I get you anything to drink? Coffee, water, or soda?"

"I'd love a cup of coffee. Thank you."

"I'll be right back. Go ahead and make yourself comfortable."

I slipped off my coat and draped it on the back of my chair before pulling my laptop from my messenger bag and setting it on the table. I sat myself down and centered the computer directly in front of me. I supposed if he would give me information on the cases, I could do the same. Quid pro quo and whatnot. Usually, two minds were better than one. I hoped that was how it worked out with Hirsch.

With his information and the sheriff's department behind him, we should be in pretty good shape. Plus, we'd need Hirsch to arrest whoever we found to be responsible and make sure they were locked up good and tight.

Detective Hirsch reentered with two paper coffee cups in his hands. He handed me a cup and placed a handful of sugar, cream, napkins, and stir sticks on the table. "I didn't know how you took it, so I brought a little of everything."

"Thank you, I take it black."

"I'm impressed. You're tougher than me." He took the seat across from me, removed the plastic lid from his coffee, and dumped in two creamers and a packet of sugar. He stirred with a wooden stir stick and then rested it on a paper napkin. He took a sip and set it back down.

Who would be the first to speak? Where would I even start? Probably with the active potential homicide investigation and then we'd get to Donna's case.

We sat silently across from one another for a little longer than was comfortable for most folks. I assumed we were both familiar with interrogation techniques. I doubted he would break first. I eyed him and then reminded myself I was supposed to be playing nice. His focus was impressive. Maybe he wasn't a doofus after all. "For starters, Detective Hirsch, I wanted to thank you for meeting with me. I appreciate it. Both cases are pretty important to me, and I know you don't have to share information with me, so please know it's appreciated."

Hirsch gave a lopsided grin. "You're very welcome, Ms. Monroe."

"Please call me Martina," I said in a friendly tone.

"Thank you, Martina. After we spoke on the phone, I talked to my supervisors. They're fine with you helping with the cases so we don't have any issues there. However, I need one thing from you and that is the promise that we'll share information with one another and neither one of us goes to the press or outside this investigation with information unless there's agreement between the two of us. In a sense, we work like a team. Obviously, you have your part. You'll work your current investigation, share information you may have about Donna, and I'll share with you what we have on both cases as well. You have quite the reputation for being a top-notch private investigator, so I know you can do the job. I trust you'll do your part, and I'll do mine. We share what we find. How does that sound?"

He was a straight shooter. Good. "Sounds like a solid plan. Maybe you can start with what you have on the Theodore

Gilmore case, and I'll tell you what I have found about his wife's family."

Hirsch explained what he'd learned from the medical examiner and from interviewing the neighbors. I nodded and said, "Interesting. The day the camera was tampered with was the day of Charlotte's memorial."

He said, "A day that the perp would know nobody would be home."

"Exactly."

Hirsch continued. "We haven't determined it to be a homicide yet. The autopsy is scheduled for tomorrow. I practically begged the ME to get it in sooner rather than later to give Kennedy a bit of peace. I can't imagine what she's going through —losing two parents in a week and a half. It's horrible."

"It is. I appreciate it and I'm sure Kennedy will too. What is your take—do you think it's homicide? Kennedy told me she said his body looked peaceful but oddly displayed."

Hirsch nodded. "She's right. My take—he looked posed. His body was face down, his arms down by his sides. His head was on its side, staring at the wall. Unless he purposefully laid down on the ground in that position and fell asleep and then happened to die in his sleep, which is possible, then it's murder. Plus, the ME pointed out a puncture mark behind his ear. He could've been injected with a chemical that killed him."

I leaned back in my seat, thinking about what Hirsch had just explained to me. It was starting to sound like a professional hit, assuming that Theodore was murdered and his death wasn't from natural causes. Had Theodore been murdered because of Charlotte's past or something completely unrelated? Donna's case, the disappearance of his next-door neighbor, was also just reopened—another coincidence? Did Theodore know something about Donna's disappearance? I mumbled, "Interesting" to myself before meeting Hirsch's baby-blue eyes.

"Let's assume homicide. Does it seem like a professional hit to you?"

"Forensics hasn't come up with any prints or obvious signs of a break-in. When you add it all up, if it was a hit, it was a pretty good one."

I still can't imagine why someone would have killed Theodore. I had just met with the man the day before. He wasn't in good health, that I could tell. If that was the case, why take out a sick, old man? What would be the purpose? Somebody was hiding something and doing everything they could to protect it. But what?

"Penny for your thoughts?"

I glanced back over at Hirsch. "I was just trying to figure out motive. I haven't seen his medical records, but from what Kennedy has told me, he didn't have a very good heart. I saw him the day before he was killed, and he didn't look well. Why take out a sick man? What is somebody hiding or trying to protect that only Theodore knew?"

"I'm not one who believes in coincidences. The fact that you're investigating his wife's past, and he supposedly spilled the beans the night before he was killed is too coincidental for my taste. Maybe what he told her wasn't everything he knew?"

"You also just reopened up the Donna Bernard case. Maybe he knew something about that? They lived next door at the time of her disappearance."

"Did you know the Gilmores back then?"

"Not well. Kennedy and I were in the same graduating class, but we didn't run in the same crowd. The only connection I really had to her was that Donna lived next door, and I was at Donna's house most of the time. We'd wave, and she was friendly, but we never hung out. We may have had a few classes together. I wasn't always the best student or best kid back then. Kennedy was an honor-roll kid."

"From reading the files, I'm assuming Donna wasn't on the honor roll either?"

"No—not so much. Neither one of us was fond of rules back then. We drank and smoked and spent too much time daydreaming and vying for the attention of older boys. I was from the trailer park, but the Bernards were different. They were a good family, a little strict. I think her parents thought I was a bad influence. I hope I wasn't." I shook my head and tittered. "Now that I'm a parent myself, I can understand their concerns. As hypocritical as it sounds, my daughter is only seven, but I don't think I'd like it if she started hanging out with someone from the wrong side of the tracks."

"I'm sure you weren't so bad. Did you ever have any interaction with Mr. Gilmore when you were a teenager?"

"No, not that I can remember."

"Do you remember if Donna interacted with him at all?"

"I wouldn't think so. I mean, in our later teen years, we were practically inseparable." I lowered my head and remembered the last time I'd seen her, not knowing that it was the last time I'd see her. I hadn't been an excellent friend. I'm not proud of that. But I turned my life around from my wild teen years. The Army helped with that. The Army opened up a lot of opportunity for me. It's how I met my husband, who gave me my beautiful daughter, and the opportunity to become a private investigator. Now there I was, investigating Donna's disappearance all these years later and the mysterious death of her next-door neighbor. I picked up the cup of coffee, sipped it, and set it back down. "Not bad for police station coffee."

"Sheriff's department coffee is better than police department coffee," he said with a twinkle in his eye.

"If you don't mind me asking, how long have you been here at the sheriff's department? When did you leave the SFPD?"

I watched as he fidgeted. It wasn't something he wanted to

talk about. I bared my soul about my wild teenage years, so he should be able to give me this, right?

"It's not a glamorous story. I joined the sheriff's department a little less than a month ago. I was looking for a change of scenery and a chance to make a difference. This job would allow me to spend half my time on cold cases, and that intrigued me. But to be honest, it was a bit forced as well. My LT and I didn't always see eye to eye. Actually, I'm not sure we ever did."

Interesting. I wanted to ask about the DeSoto case, but we already had a lot on our plate. I'd have to save those questions for later—once we solved the two open cases we had. "Are you liking it here?"

"It's different. A lot of meth labs."

He hated it. "Yikes."

"Yeah. So, what's your take? Did you find anything in Mrs. Gilmore's past that could have made someone want to silence Mr. Gilmore?"

I flipped open the lid of my laptop and powered it on. I then explained the history of the investigation starting from the mystery baby in the photo to the night before Theodore's murder.

Hirsch tapped his fingers on the table. "With the lack of any evidence to support what she had told her daughter or husband, do you think Charlotte was running from something or someone?"

"That's what I suspect."

"The ex-husband?"

"I don't know. Even with the hometown identified, I can't corroborate the story that Charlotte's family died in a house fire or that anybody's family died in a fire during the timeframe Kennedy gave me. If she was running from her ex-husband, why say your family died in a fire?"

"You think it's her family that she's running from?"

"Maybe. Another odd thing that happened—a man, supposedly from Charlotte's past, showed up at her memorial. Claimed he was a childhood friend. He said his name was Alonso Davidson. So, I ran a background check on Alonso Davidson."

"Let me guess, no records for an Alonso Davidson in Pennsylvania?"

"You got it. I think the key to unlocking Charlotte's past is finding out her family's actual name. Maybe she was running from them. I just don't know why. I think the only way to find her maiden name is by searching high school yearbooks."

I watched as Detective Hirsch took all this information in. "How quickly do you expect to get the books?"

"That's the thing. I've made some calls to the schools in the area, but none of them will send me a copy. They suggested I try eBay. Right now, I'm trying to get clearance through my office to fly out to Doylestown, Pennsylvania and look firsthand. It's a long trip, but I have a feeling there's a lot more to this."

"If Theodore's death is related to Charlotte's past, it could be dangerous for you to go out there and start poking around."

I straightened myself in my chair. "I can take care of myself. I'm adept at hand-to-hand combat."

His eyes scanned me, as if assessing my abilities. "Ex-Army?"

"Yes, sir." I said with a smile.

He chuckled. "Do you know when you'll be able to make the trip?"

"I'm hoping this week." Assuming I can get Stavros to approve it and convince Claire to stay with Zoey. Maybe I should just cave and hire a live-in nanny, like Claire's been suggesting lately. I didn't like the idea of sharing my house, but considering how often I'm out at night and have last-minute situations, it may be the right thing to do. I wasn't loaded, but I had money from Jared's life insurance and his pension from the

Army. I'd have to consider it but not then. "So, what are your next steps?" I asked Hirsch, hoping to not appear too forward.

"I'll be questioning family and friends, looking at financials and his job history. I don't want to be too laser-focused on Charlotte's past. Plus, it sounds like you have that covered. As of right now, we don't have a solid motive, and I need to find one. Assuming, of course, that he was, in fact, murdered. My gut says he was."

"Mine too."

"We'll know for sure tomorrow. I'm going to need to requestion Kennedy. Do you think she's up for it?"

I nodded. "She's tough. She's got keen skills too. You should have heard her questioning Alonso, or whoever the guy really is, at the memorial. She knew the right questions to ask and how to ask them. She's pretty determined to find out who killed her father. Who knows, maybe it's helping her. I know from experience, it's much easier to be taking action toward something than sitting around doing nothing. I think she can handle it."

"Good to hear."

Hirsch and I continued to discuss the case and how we were going to focus our attention and the plan for our next meeting. He didn't seem terrible, like I'd thought he might be. His ideas were good. His intuition was on track. Maybe his disagreements with his LT had everything to do with closing the DeSoto case. I was woman enough to admit when I was wrong. For the sake of the Theodore and for Donna, I hoped I was wrong and that Hirsch and I would find out what happened to both of them, and fast.

17

DETECTIVE HIRSCH

I took shallow breaths, attempting to minimize the scent of death as I watched the medical examiner explain what had happened to Theodore Gilmore. She peeled back his ear. "Remember how I pointed out the puncture mark behind his ear?"

"I do." I didn't think I'd ever forget. It was hard to get the images of dead bodies out of your mind, no matter how hard you tried.

"Was he injected with a special chemical that stopped his heart?"

She shook her head. "Nope, he or she was not that sophisticated. When I got him on my table, I found some additional markings that I thought were interesting."

She pulled back the sheet, exposing Mr. Gilmore's torso. It was dark purple with a crude Y incision from the autopsy. She pointed to his abdomen. "You see that cluster of punctures right there?"

"I see them."

"They got me curious. I rushed the toxicology screen. It came back with a few strange results. One was the presence of ketamine and sky-high levels of insulin. I went through his chart —he wasn't diabetic."

I stared at the cluster of puncture wounds on his abdomen again. Somebody injected several doses of insulin into his belly. "What was the cause of death?"

"Overdose of insulin."

"Not the ketamine?"

"Given the condition of his heart, it may have eventually killed him. But no, my guess is the killer gave him a quick jab of ketamine to get him on the floor and then gave him seven injections of insulin into his abdomen before rolling him over and posing him."

"So, there's no way he did this to himself?"

"Not a chance. Once he had that ketamine in his system, he wasn't going anywhere or doing anything on his own."

"Did he suffer long?"

"No. I'd say it was peaceful and relatively quick due to the ketamine."

"Well, that's at least something. When will we have the final report?"

"Probably not until next week, but it's definitely homicide."

"Thanks, Doc."

"Good luck, Detective."

I waved as I hurried out of the autopsy suite. It was as we suspected, but it wasn't exactly a sophisticated hit. Ketamine and insulin were commonly-used drugs and easy to get. Something rare would have been easier to trace, or at least would stand out—less of a needle in a haystack.

Maybe our perpetrator was a diabetic and had used his own stash for the kill. Or, maybe the insulin came from a loved one or friend. The ketamine could've been obtained on the street or at a vet's office. It was something to check out. I could call around and find out if there had been any break-ins in the last week or so where ketamine had gone missing. Now that we had the official ruling of homicide, I'd be able to question friends and family and request financial records. That was the good news. The bad news was I was also going to have to tell Kennedy that her father was murdered. Although it sounded like she'd already suspected as such, it wasn't going to be pleasant.

In my car, I decided to share the news. I pulled out my phone. "Hi, this is Martina."

"Hi, Martina, this is Hirsch. I just got out of the autopsy suite. Definitely homicide." I explained the findings from Dr. Scribner.

She said, "As we suspected. Thank you for calling, Detective."

"No problem." It was nice to have someone to discuss the case with. Most people don't realize that a detective's job could be lonely. It was not like on TV where everyone had a partner to investigate alongside you. In some ways, it was nice to be able to bounce ideas off of Martina and, if I was being honest, it was simply nice to have someone to talk to about the case. She was definitely growing on me. She was sharp and had good instincts. She would've made a great cop.

"Oh, before you go, I wanted to tell you I received approval from my boss, and I'll be flying to Pennsylvania on Sunday."

"Great." My phone vibrated. I removed it from my ear to see who was calling. *Damn it.* "Martina, I have to go; I have another call I have to take, but I'll call you back."

I clicked over to the other caller. "Hey, Dan. What's up?"

"I have the final papers for you to review. Can you stop by the office today and pick them up? If not, I can send them overnight for you."

"Ship them. I just caught a case." And I wasn't exactly in a rush to read through my divorce papers. I supposed I should have been glad to be rid of my lying, cheating wife, but like most things in life, it wasn't that simple. Love truly was blind, deaf, and dumb. I blamed myself for not seeing the signs. I had spent too much time hunting murderers and fighting office politics to put together the not-so-elaborate string of lies my soon-to-be ex-wife had concocted. All the "girls' trips" and "girls' nights" and yet I'd never met any of the girls, and none of the girls had spouses for us to go out with for a couples' dinner.

"Okay, I'll have my paralegal send them over."

"Thanks." I hung up the phone and contemplated my failures. My inability to tow the company line and do as I was told. The inability to be there for my wife when she had been lonely and wanting a partner instead of a pissed-off detective who only wanted to hide away or work a case. I wasn't a great husband. It was probably a blessing that we never had a child. We could both start over without having to develop co-parenting skills or have a lifetime of awkward events with our new partners and our shared child. I'd wanted children, but it never seemed to be the right time for me or for her. I was nearing forty, and it was looking like the idea of fatherhood was slipping away along with my youth.

I started up the car and headed back to the station. I had work to do.

I HEADED OVER TO MY SERGEANT'S OFFICE AND KNOCKED on his door.

"Hirsch, how's it going? What did we find out about the Gilmore death?"

"Just back from talking with the ME. Definitely homicide."

He nodded as if it was what he'd also suspected. He cocked his head. "Do you think it's strange that there was a murder next door to the cold case you just opened?"

I nodded. "I do."

"Okay. What do you need?"

"Financials and work history, quick if we can. I'll reinterview the daughter and get a line on family and friends to determine who had a motive to kill this guy. So far, it's not very obvious. Just a lot of strange coincidences."

"All right, I'll make a few calls and try to get the records fast so you can get this case closed. Maybe it'll help our stats. Can you get the forms completed today, before six?"

"Can do. I'll work on them now."

"Great."

"Thanks, Sarge."

I strolled back to my desk. Yes, it would be nice to have a solid closure rate at my new job, but there were definitely more important things than statistics. Like bringing closure to the family, to Kennedy. The one thing I didn't like about this job, well, one of the main things I didn't like about the job was that sometimes people lost sight of the human aspect of it all.

We were supposed to be protecting and serving, not just closing cases for the sake of numbers and reports. I wanted to close the case because I wanted a family member to have closure. I wanted to find Donna Bernard to figure out what happened to her all those years ago and to bring her home to her family. I wasn't in this job for the accolades or awards. I wanted to make a difference. I couldn't help everyone, but to the ones I could, I knew it would mean the world.

I reached my desk and sat down. I supposed it was as good a time as any to give Kennedy a call and let her know we had some news on her father's case and that I needed to do another interview. I slid the folder over and flipped it open. I picked up the desk phone receiver and dialed Ms. Gilmore's number. The phone rang while my belly did flip-flops. I shouldn't be nervous, but these types of calls were never easy. "Hello."

"Hi, Ms. Gilmore, this is Detective Hirsch."

"Hi, Detective Hirsch. Is there any news in my dad's case?"

"There is. The medical examiner performed the autopsy today, and we've deemed your father's death a homicide. I'll need to meet with you to go through some questions I have. Do you have time tomorrow or sometime over the weekend? I could meet you if that's helpful."

Kennedy didn't speak, but I could hear the faint sound of a sniffle. Suspecting her father was murdered was one thing, but I thought hearing the truth was harder. To think that somebody would intentionally take away your loved one. Your one remaining parent. It was devastating. Hopefully, we would get answers for Kennedy, and soon.

18

MARTINA

I STARED AT THE PINK, FRILLY, HEART-SHAPED BOX OF chocolates that sat across from me on the dining table. For the Valentine's Day party in her classroom, Zoey and each of the kids had decorated heart-shaped boxes and filled them with the best chocolates in the Bay Area. She'd been talking about the party for weeks, and I'd done everything in my power to attend, and I did. I'd mingled with the other parents while the third-graders worked on their crafts. After Zoey finished the project, she skipped over to me with the box firmly in both hands. She lifted it up and said, "Mommy, I made this for you because I want you to be my Valentine today and always. So, will you? Will you be my Valentine?"

It took just about all I had in me to not tear up. I responded, "Yes, I accept the role of your Valentine" and bent over and gave her the biggest hug she had ever received in her young life. I swear, when God took Jared, I suppose she knew what she was doing by leaving me with the brightest light that anyone could ever imagine.

I kept the cherished memory in mind as she was driving me

bonkers by running around the house, singing her favorite song at the top of her lungs. I let out a breath and called out to her, "Zoey, can you please keep it down? I'm trying to do some work."

She skittered into the kitchen, where I sat at the table with the case file on Donna Bernard. "What are you working on? Is it something super important?"

"It is important. Did I ever tell you about my friend, Donna?"

Zoey stood stiff as a board, and her eyes widened. "No, please tell me about Donna."

Zoey was a multi-faceted child. One of those facets screamed, *dramatic'*. "Why don't you have a seat and I'll tell you about her."

She pulled out a chair and perched herself on the edge. "I'm listening."

I smiled at her. "Donna was my very best friend when I was growing up. We were inseparable."

"Oh, like me and Kaylie?"

"We were just like you and Kaylie."

"Is she coming over?"

I shook my head. "Nope. When we were teenagers, she disappeared. I never saw or heard from her ever again."

She rested her chin on her tiny fists. "Where did she go?"

"Nobody knows. The police said they think she was a runaway. But that's not what I think."

"Oh my gosh, Mommy! Are you investigating what happened to Donna?"

"I am. I'm working with a detective at the sheriff's department. They reopened her case, and we're going to work together to find out what happened to my best friend. What do you think about that?"

Zoey sat back and put her hands up in the air. "Mommy, I think that is amazing. I hope you find her. I really want to meet her."

"Me too, honey."

"What have you found so far?"

"Well, I just received the file last night from Detective Hirsch. He's the detective I'm working with. This morning, I'm going to read through her case file and start my investigation."

"Oh, that's why you need me to quiet down. Can I help in any way?"

"Well, maybe it would help if I had colored stickies or colored markers that I could use to color-code the case file. Do you think that is something you could help with?"

"Oh boy, do I. I'll go look through my supplies. I'll be right back, okay?"

"Okay."

I smiled as she ran off to find supplies.

Statistically, Donna was likely dead and had been for some time. But wouldn't it be something if she wasn't, and I found her living her best life, and she could meet my daughter? We could reconnect and eat nachos and drink Shirley Temples—not spiked. This was the kind of hope that fueled families and friends of missing people. I didn't have the optimism of Zoey, but I wish I did.

Zoey padded back into the kitchen with colorful papers and markers clutched in her hands. She set them down on the dining table. "I brought you some highlighters. There is pink, blue, green, and yellow, and I also brought you some sticky notes. Some are heart-shaped and some are sparkly. Do you think you'll need anything else?"

"Nope, that's perfect. Thank you so much, Zoey."

"No problem. So, since you're leaving on your trip

tomorrow and Claire is going to stay with me, can Claire and I order pizza for dinner tomorrow night?"

This girl's love for pizza was limitless. "I'll talk to Claire and see what she has planned. But it's okay with me."

"Speaking of Claire and nannies ... Have you decided who you want to hire to replace her after she goes off to become a nurse?"

Don't remind me. "Not yet. How do you feel about Claire becoming a nurse and not being your nanny anymore?"

"Well, I know she's worked really hard, and she's going to be an awesome nurse. I just know it. But I'm sad too. I'll miss her. But she told me I'll get a new nanny who will be really nice, and she said that maybe the new nanny will spend the night when you have to work late on special cases."

"How do you feel about having a nanny who lives with us?"

She cocked her head. "I think it would be okay. Do you think it would be okay?"

"I think so."

"Good. Well, I have my art project to do, and you have your investigation to do, so I'm going to leave you to it."

I shook my head in amazement as I watched Zoey skip down the hall and into her bedroom.

I flipped open the file and read through the initial report. It felt like a series of flashbacks. That night. The next day. Her parents reported her missing as soon as she missed her 1:00 AM curfew. By sunrise, police were at their house and I was calling everyone I knew to find out if they'd seen or heard from her. It wasn't like Donna to disappear and not let anyone know where she was.

I flipped through the witness statements. The first ones were from her parents. I read through them and my heart broke a little more. The sight of my own statement made my body stiffen. It was surreal. I was so young, so angry, and so hell-bent on getting out of that town. Never in a million years would I have thought I'd be back there investigating Donna's disappearance. I read through my statement and felt like I'd taken a gut punch. I had been so naïve and stupid to have left her at the Boathouse Bar and Grill to go off with some guy I had barely known.

I flipped to the next page and read Kennedy Gilmore's statement. My mouth dropped open as I read Kennedy's account of that night. *What the heck?* I read through Theodore and Charlotte's as well. I shook my head in disbelief. Both Kennedy and Theodore saw Donna that night, around ten thirty, with someone out on the levee. According to the statement, it was dark and they couldn't give an accurate description.

Heart racing, I read through the pages but saw nothing about a follow-up to figure out who was with her out on the levee. I checked through the folder twice. Nothing. The detective didn't follow up on the only potential suspect in her disappearance?

I shut the folder, opened up the box of chocolates and popped one into my mouth, chewing and enjoying the dark chocolate and crunchy almonds. I swallowed and then grabbed my phone and called Hirsch. It was Saturday, but I had a feeling he was working. He seemed like the workaholic type—it took one to know one. "Hello."

"Hey, Hirsch, it's Martina. I'm just going through the Donna Bernard file. Did you notice that the Gilmores saw Donna with somebody on the levee that night, but no follow-up by the detective to figure out who was with her?"

"Everything I have on the case is in that file. The original detective retired a few years ago—he didn't have a great reputation. I've read through it and notified the family that we are reopening the case, but that's about it. Do you have any idea who she could have been with?"

"I don't know. Maybe a family member or a boy? She wasn't dating anyone at the time, but maybe she met someone after I left? I'll put together a list of all her old boyfriends I can remember and any guys who hung around her. The person on levee, that the Gilmores spotted, may have done something to Donna. If they did, and they knew the case was reopened, they may have decided to get rid of any witnesses. The two cases could be related." I paused for a breath. "I can't believe I didn't know about this."

"You didn't know that she had been seen on the levee that night with another person?"

"No, all these years, I thought I was the last person to see her alive. We were standing outside the Boathouse Bar and Grill, and I waved goodbye and she waved back as I drove off with some guy. I can't believe this. We also need to reinterview Kennedy."

"I have another formal interview scheduled with her for Monday. I can ask her about it then, since you'll be in Pennsylvania."

"Well, I think we should talk to the Bernards as soon as possible to find out if it was a family member who was with her that night. I have a few other questions too."

"I'll call them and see what we can do. What time is your flight on Sunday?"

"Seven PM out of SFO."

"I'll give the Bernards a call to let them know I'm working with you."

"I'd appreciate it." With my heart still racing, I hung up the phone and started making a list of potential suspects.

MY STOMACH WAS A BALL OF NERVES AS I KNOCKED ON THE

Bernards' front door. As Hirsch and I waited for them to answer, I contemplated all the things I should've done. I should've called when I had gotten in town. I should've called or visited over the years. I should've looked for her before. I shook it off. This was it. We were going to find out what happened to Donna. The door opened and Mr. Bernard gave a friendly hello and welcomed us inside the house. He'd gone completely gray since I had seen him last and was much heavier and his skin had paled. I stepped inside. My mind fluttered as all the memories from my youth came rushing back into my mind. They hadn't redecorated, except for a few new family photos on the walls. I remembered all the times I spent in the living room with Donna, planning our futures, eating popcorn and watching TV, or teasing her brothers.

He motioned to the sofa. "Please have a seat." He sat down in one of two loungers across from it.

Mrs. Bernard entered as we sat. My heart was practically thumping out of my chest as our eyes met. I got up and smiled as a tear escaped. "Sandy, it's good to see you."

Sandy broke down and stepped closer to embrace me in a hug. "Oh, Martina, it's good to see you too." She stepped back. She shook her head and looked me up and down. "My goodness, look at you all grown up and a private investigator. I'm so proud of you," she said, her voice cracking.

I stared into her eyes. "We're going to find her."

Sandy wiped her tears. "Can I get either of you anything to drink?"

Detective Hirsch said, "No, thank you."

"Some water would be great. Thank you," I said, before taking a seat. I glanced over at Mr. Bernard. He had worked a lot when we were young and wasn't home much. Sandy, on the other hand, was Miss Suzy Homemaker. She baked and cooked dinner every night.

Sandy returned with a glass of water and sat across from Hirsch and I.

He nodded. "Mr. and Mrs. Bernard, as I mentioned in my last visit and on the phone, we are reopening Donna's case. As of right now, we haven't made a lot of progress. The only news I have for you is that Martina and I are joining forces to investigate the case together. In case you didn't know, Martina is a private investigator with a very prestigious firm in San Francisco. She's at the top of her field and is known for getting results. I'm feeling pretty fortunate that she's helping us out. And I know Martina is pretty invested in this too." He paused and surveyed the room. He nodded and continued. "I'm going to be straight with you. My current focus is on the homicide investigation next door."

Sandy gasped. "Theo was murdered?"

Hirsch nodded. "Yes, it was determined by the medical examiner. One thing that stands out to me about Mr. Gilmore's murder was that it was just two weeks after we reopened Donna's case. I'm not sure if you remember this, or not, but both Mr. Gilmore and his daughter, Kennedy, witnessed somebody on the levee with Donna that night. The Gilmores said it was dark and couldn't make out who she was with, but she was definitely with somebody. We're trying to determine if there's maybe a connection between his murder and Donna's disappearance. Do you recall if it was one of you who was with her that night on the levee, it would've been around ten thirty in the evening? It doesn't say so in your statements, but we need to confirm this and rule out anyone who was living with you at the time."

"The last time I saw my daughter was when she left with Martina to go to the Boathouse," Mr. Gilmore stated.

Sandy said, "That was the last time I ever saw her too."

"Could it have been one of her brothers?" I asked.

"The boys were at their grandparents' house that weekend."

"Okay, thank you. It's been a long time, and we just wanted to confirm."

"It wasn't one of us who was with her." Sandy reached for the arm of her husband. "I can't believe there was somebody with her that night, right here in our front yard."

"The police never told you that?" I asked.

"No."

Darn shoddy police work. I composed myself and looked ahead at the Bernards. "Another thing that they didn't do after her disappearance was look at her financials or her bank accounts, but that is something that we can do this time. I remember she had a pretty generous allowance that last year. Do you recall how much it was that you gave her each week?"

Mr. Bernard and Sandy exchanged glances. "Donna didn't receive an allowance."

No allowance? I distinctly remembered her telling me she had an allowance. She always had cash when we went out and had been very generous with her money, offering to pay for dinners and gas. She'd told me it was "no biggie" since it was her parents' money.

"And she never had a part-time job that I can remember. Did she do any odd jobs around the neighborhood?"

"No, she didn't work any jobs. You should know that—you two were as thick as thieves back then."

I scratched the back of my head, trying to make sense of what they were saying. Where was her money coming from? How did she have money to go out or buy clothes? That summer, we went out every night. She always had money. She said that her parents had increased her allowance. "So, you're saying she never had an allowance? Did you ever just give her spending money?"

"No. The kids only received allowance if they did all of their chores. Donna wasn't big on chores."

My gut was stirring. Donna had a secret source of income that she had lied to me about. She had lied to me, her best friend. Why? What was it she had felt she couldn't tell me? And who was she on the levee with that night?

19

DETECTIVE HIRSCH

I TYPED UP THE LAST OF THE NOTES ON THEODORE Gilmore's family, friends, and acquaintances. Basically, anybody who crossed paths with him over the years and that his daughter knew about. From my computer, I glanced back over at Kennedy, who sat quietly with her hands in her lap. She hadn't shed any tears during our interview, but her slumped posture and slowed speech gave away the fact that she was grieving deeply.

"Thank you, Ms. Gilmore. I think this will definitely help the case along. There is another case I'd like to ask you about. It was a long time ago, but I'd like to ask you about your witness statement regarding the last time you saw Donna Bernard. If you're up for it?"

"I'm up for it. I'd like to help how ever I can."

She was a tough woman to have gone through so much loss in such a short amount of time yet be able to answer questions and keep a level head. She was remarkable. "Great, it could actually help your father's case."

Her eyes widened. "Do you think Donna's disappearance may be connected to my father's murder?"

I slid the Bernard binder in front of me and flipped it open to the Gilmore statements. "We're checking out all angles right now. In your statement, you and your father both said that you saw Donna out on the levee that last night around ten thirty PM." I pointed to the statement. "It says here you couldn't make out who it was, but that it was somebody who was taller than Donna. Do you remember any more details from that night?"

"That's all it says? I remember it pretty well. We'd been celebrating my mother's birthday. It was a pleasant night out, so we sat on the back deck. My father and I were cleaning up when we spotted Donna and the other person."

"It was dark, right? What alerted you to the fact Donna was there with someone?"

She picked up the bottle of water and took a gulp. "Well, it's pretty quiet out on the Delta at night. Especially that late. I heard the crunch of gravel and voices."

"Do you remember anything specific about the voices? High? Low? Male or female?"

"I recognized Donna and her voice. She was wearing a white top. I'd seen her earlier wearing the same thing. The other voice was deeper, like a male."

I tapped more notes into my computer. "Do you remember anything else about this person? Like height, weight, or coloring?"

"He was a little taller than Donna. He must've had darker skin and darker hair since I couldn't see him very well as opposed to Donna, who had light hair and fair skin. She showed up a bit more in the dark."

"Could the other person have been African-American?"

"No, I don't think so. Maybe Latino or Italian. They had tan or olive skin with dark hair."

How on earth had this not been recorded in her original

statement? "Could you hear what they were saying or if it was an argument or a friendly conversation?"

"No, their voices were muffled, like they were trying to be quiet. They must have spotted us. I couldn't make out what they were saying."

"Did you see them leave?"

"No, we cleaned up the dishes and locked up for the night. They were still out there when I shut the door."

"This is very helpful, Kennedy. Thank you, again."

"I still don't see how this could be connected to my father's murder."

"Well, we just reopened the Donna Bernard case, and your father was one of the last people to see her and whomever she was with. It's possible that person she was with found out we'd reopened the case and were trying to silence him."

Kennedy stiffened. "If that's the case, then I'm a target too."

She had gotten there fast. She was sharp. "If it's true, then yes, you could be in danger."

She fidgeted in her seat. "What am I supposed to do now?"

"Until we can rule out the Bernard connection, I'm going to request a patrol unit be put on your apartment. Or is there someone you can stay with?"

"I have some friends, but I also have a cat, so I prefer to be in my own home."

"Okay, why don't you stay put, and I'll go speak to my sergeant. I'll be right back." I wasn't sure if my supervisor was going to go for this plan or not. It was going to take some luck to use taxpayer dollars to have a patrol watch an apartment building all night and day. We may have to pull in favors from SFPD. I wasn't sure if I was the guy to get those favors. I approached Sarge's door and knocked lightly. He glanced up from his readers. "What's up, Hirsch?"

I explained the situation to him and requested a round-the-clock patrol on her apartment building in San Francisco.

Sarge removed his glasses and set them on the desk. "Do you have any friends in patrol over at SFPD?"

"Maybe—depends on if my old LT has been playing nice or not."

"I'm afraid he may not be. Look, why don't you put in a few calls. If that doesn't lead us anywhere, I'll make a few calls and see what I can do. Let them know that you have my full backing on this."

"Thanks, Sarge." I headed back to my desk and dialed the number to the SFPD. I held my breath as the line rang. "San Francisco Police Department. How may I direct your call?"

I recognized Maria's gravelly voice immediately. "Lieutenant Tippin, please."

"Who's calling?"

"Detective Hirsch."

"Hirsch, how are you? How's the sheriff's department treating you? Hopefully, better than old baldy did."

The riff between my hairless LT and me was no secret at the station. "It's going well. It's a nice change of scenery. How are you?"

"Same old, same old over here, but I'm all right. I'll put you right through."

Lieutenant Tippin was an outstanding leader of the SWAT and special operations teams. Our paths crossed a few times when we were taking down the bad guys. Tippin was known for being good police and for always doing the right thing and not just what the brass demanded. Part of me thought maybe I should've transferred over to his group, but my heart wasn't in it. I was a detective through and through.

"Hirsch, how the heck are you?"

"I'm doing all right, sir. I'm working a case out here on the

Delta with the daughter of a murder victim. It's a bit of a complicated situation." I described the case, including Martina Monroe's role and investigation into Charlotte Gilmore's past.

"You're working with Martina?" He chuckled. "She keeping you on your toes?"

"She is, but I'm also finding she's an asset and excellent ally to have."

"That she is. Give me the address, and I'll make sure we've got twenty-four-hour patrol on your witness's address. Give me an hour to make the assignments and to get the team assembled."

Tippin was solid. "Thank you, sir."

"Any time. Tell Martina hello for me, and tell her not to be a stranger."

"Will do." I hung up the phone and was pleased to have a win for once. I wasn't sure how Martina knew Tippin, but it seemed that anybody who had worked with her in the past had the highest respect for her.

My thoughts lingered back to the DeSoto case and how angry she'd been. I, myself, wasn't entirely convinced the husband wasn't involved, but the certainty Martina expressed made me rethink the case, and I wondered if it warranted taking a second look. After we took care of the Donna Bernard case and found Theodore Gilmore's murderer, maybe I'd ask Martina more about what she had on the DeSoto case. Martina was tough, highly intelligent, and driven. I could only imagine what it would be like to be around her all the time. Professionally, of course.

I snapped back to the present case and jogged back to the conference room, where Kennedy sat, peeling the paper label off her water bottle. I gave her a reassuring smile. "Good news. The SFPD will have twenty-four-hour patrol on your apartment building, starting in about an hour."

Kennedy set down the water bottle. "That's good news. Thank you."

"No problem. Is there anything else I can do for you, Ms. Gilmore?"

"No, I don't think so. You'll let me know if I can be of any help, on Donna's case or my dad's case?"

"I will. It's appreciated."

I walked her out of the station and waved as she was tucked away safely into her car. If we had more manpower, a full surveillance team to follow Kennedy wouldn't be a bad idea. Maybe someone was following her, and maybe that someone was her father's killer.

When Martina returned from Pennsylvania, I'd run it by her. It was one thing to get a team watching her building, but a surveillance team was a whole different ask. I only had so many favors to call in, but maybe Martina had a few more.

I pulled up the email where Martina had provided the names of all of Donna's boyfriends that she could remember and started on the background checks. My fingers and toes were crossed that we'd get one that matched the description Kennedy had given. We needed a break in either case if we were going to close them anytime soon.

20

MARTINA

I jogged up to the high school reception office and opened the door with determination. I'd had a great workout at the hotel gym and a hearty breakfast at the local diner. I was operating at full capacity and it was great. I approached the counter, unzipped my down coat, and unraveled my scarf. There were multiple desks with what looked like a mix of student workers and regular employees. A perky young redhead approached me. "How may I help you?"

"I have an appointment with a Jill Williams. My name is Martina Monroe."

Before the student could request assistance, a woman in her early forties approached. She was dressed in head-to-toe black with cropped dark hair and bright-blue eyes. Except for the piercing eyes, she was practically my twin. "I'm Jill."

I extended my hand. "Martina." We shook and then I handed her my business card. "Thank you for meeting with me."

"No problem. I have the yearbooks in my office, all ready for you."

And she was organized and efficient. I liked her already. "Great."

"Follow me and I'll show you." As we walked, she said, "So, you're looking for a former student?"

"Yes, I'm afraid I don't have a last name. Just a photo, the potential year of graduation, a class ring, and the city she grew up in." We thought. Who knew what was true anymore? It was pretty clear Charlotte had spun a lot of lies when it came to her past.

We stopped down the hall. "Well, I hope you find what you're looking for. I'll leave you to it. Just holler if I can help."

"Thanks, I appreciate it."

I sat down at the desk that had a stack of eight yearbooks on it. I read the spines of each. *Interesting.* Jill had pulled a range of yearbooks from the period of time that Charlotte may have been a freshman to her senior year plus or minus two years. *Thorough.* If Jill were in the Bay Area, I'd ask Stavros to offer her a job.

I pulled the yearbook for 1966 and hoped I'd get lucky. I set it down and flipped open the cover. The pages were yellowing and smelled of mildew. I thumbed through the pages until I reached the senior portraits. Black and white photos of boys in bow ties and neat haircuts were mixed in with girls with short, puffy hairstyles. It was the sixties. I pulled my bag onto my lap and fished out the photo of Charlotte. Who knew if her name was even Charlotte? I would need to compare faces. I took the photo of Charlotte and placed it on the page next to each female photo.

An hour later, I'd had a few near matches, but none were Charlotte. Maybe the year was off? I looked through the earlier and later years. Three hours later, no dice. Charlotte had not graduated from Central East between 1964 and 1968. I checked the time. I had about thirty minutes to grab something to eat before heading over to Central West High School.

I placed Charlotte's photo back into the envelope and in my bag and headed out to the reception area. I gave a sheepish grin to Jill-the-amazing, and said, "No luck, but thank you for all of your help."

Jill frowned. "Bummer. What are you going to do next?"

"I'm headed over to Central West. Is there a spot between here and there for a quick, healthy bite to eat?"

"Sure. You know, about a mile from Central West High is Henley's Bistro. They have great salads and sandwiches." She gave me directions to Henley's in great detail. I didn't have the heart to tell her I had GPS in my rental car.

"Perfect. Thank you."

"Best of luck."

I zipped up and headed out into the freezing Pennsylvania air.

Tucked away in the corner of Henley's Bistro, I practically devoured my turkey and avocado sandwich. I hadn't realized how hungry I was until the server set down the piping-hot bowl of tomato-basil soup and the sandwich in front of me. After swallowing the last bite of the sandwich, I grabbed the spoon and slowly dipped it into the thick orangish-red soup that smelled of tangy tomato and fresh basil. It was just what I needed. I raised the spoon and my phone buzzed. Of course. I set the spoon back down and glanced at the phone before answering. "Hi, Kennedy."

"Hi, Martina, I hate to bother you, I'm a little stir crazy and I was wondering how it's going out there?"

It wasn't surprising Kennedy was unnerved. Between her

father's death, wanting to learn more about her mother, and not knowing if she was in danger, she was probably going nuts thinking through all the different scenarios. The not-knowing part was a killer. I explained in a quiet voice. "I went to the first high school. No luck there, but I'm about to head over to the second one now."

"So, nothing yet?"

"I'm afraid not. I'll let you know as soon as I have something, I promise. How are you holding up?"

Kennedy seemed to hesitate before replying. A sure sign that Kennedy was not doing well. I should probably make a call over to Hirsch to have him check on her. I knew they had surveillance on her apartment, but she probably could use a friend, or maybe even a counselor at this point. I made a mental note to give Hirsch a call as soon as I finished my lunch.

Kennedy finally responded with a shaky voice. "I'm hanging in there. I just got back from the funeral home to make arrangements for my father's memorial."

My heart ached for her. "How did it go?"

"Well, fortunately and unfortunately, I am now very familiar with the process and how it all works. I knew exactly what my father wanted, since during the preparation for my mom's memorial, he made sure to tell me what he would like when his time came. I doubt he realized how soon that would be. It was so like Dad to make things easier for everybody else."

"He seemed like he was a great guy."

Sniffles came through the phone before she responded. "Thanks. I won't keep you. You'll let me know as soon as you hear anything?"

"Absolutely."

I set the phone down and glanced around the restaurant. There was a good number, maybe twenty or thirty, patrons eating and chatting away. This was a popular spot. The decor was modern and tasteful, gray tones mixed with natural wood. I wondered if it was a new business. If it was, it appeared as if word spread fast that it was the spot to go to.

I returned my focus to the soup and spoon. It was warm and tangy, just right for the weather. I wasn't sure I'd ever get accustomed to the frigid Pennsylvania weather. I was a California girl all the way. I finished my soup and took a big gulp of water from my glass before I looked up and lifted my hand to get the attention of someone to retrieve my bill so I could be on my way.

An attractive woman with strawberry-blond hair and freckles approached. She wore a cream blouse and a navy pantsuit. I assumed she must be the manager or owner. She wasn't the same person who had taken my order or brought me my lunch. There was something familiar about her. She gave a wide smile. "How did you enjoy your lunch?"

I nodded. "It was perfect. Exactly what I needed. "

"Great to hear." She sifted through the receipts in her hand. "This must be yours." She handed me the white printout. "Typically, you pay at the counter. But if you'd like, I can take your payment here."

"No, I hadn't realized that. I can go up to the counter."

"Are you new in town?"

"No, I'm actually just visiting from California."

"Really, whereabouts?"

"The Bay Area."

"I've never been, but I've heard it's beautiful. I bet you don't get this hale or snow?"

"No, not usually."

"All right, well, enjoy your time here in Pennsylvania."

"Thank you."

I slipped my parka back on, grabbed my bag and headed over to the counter to pay my bill. After the transaction, I zipped up my coat and strolled through the dining room, dialing on my phone as I walked. He picked up after the first ring. "Hey, Hirsch."

"I was just about to call. You find anything yet?"

"No luck so far. But, hey, I just talked to Kennedy. She doesn't sound like she's doing so great."

"Does she seem spooked?"

"No, more like unnerved. I'll check on her when I get back, but I was wondering if maybe you could swing by to check on her and ease her fears a bit. She seems on edge."

"Will do. I was calling to let you know that I reinterviewed her, and now I think we have a lead on Donna's case."

"What did you find out?" I listened as Hirsch gave me the physical description of the person who'd been seen with Donna that night. I knew who it might be. "Were you able to locate him?"

"Yep. And guess what?"

"He has a record?"

"Yep. He's currently serving time for sexual assault and attempted murder."

My stomach soured, and I stopped in my tracks before I pushed opened the door of the bistro. One of Donna's previous boyfriends was in jail for sexual assault and attempted murder. I shook my head. It shouldn't have surprised me. I always knew Diego was no good. What if he had done the same thing to Donna—except his attempt to kill had been successful. I shoved open the door and the ice-cold air smacked me straight in the face, returning me to the present.

"Are you going to interview him?"

"I have an appointment for tomorrow at the prison. Anything you can tell me about the guy?"

"Well, I remember he was a total creep back then. He wasn't someone who liked to be told no, and he wasn't respectful to

Donna. He was controlling and possessive, but I'm not sure if he ever physically hurt her. But looking back, I wouldn't be surprised if he had. Wait, if he's in jail, he couldn't have killed Theodore, right?"

"True, but if it's not him, we can rule him out and move on. The original detective never even questioned him."

I can't believe they never questioned any of Donna's ex-boyfriends. Although, since I'd seen the file, I knew it was true. A teenage girl had disappeared, and they never thought to question old boyfriends or romantic connections? Anybody who's seen a single episode of *Law & Order* knew that was who you looked at first. If I had to speculate, I'd say that the original detective did exactly nothing to find Donna.

"All right, sounds like you've got it covered. I gotta head over to the second high school."

"Good luck."

"Thanks. I have a feeling I'll need it." I climbed back into my car, not bothering to remove my coat, and drove down the street rather slowly because of the icy road. I wasn't used to these road conditions, and I didn't like it. Thankfully, Jill was not exaggerating, and the school was only about a mile down the street. I parked in the lot and checked my watch. I had two minutes until my appointment. I hoped Central West was as organized as Jill had been at Central East High School.

I jogged to the front door of the school office. I hoped to wrap this case up quickly; I did not like the snow. It wasn't the winter wonderland I'd pictured. The snow was dirty and gray, not white and fluffy, like when Jared and I had rented a cabin in Lake Tahoe—away from any major roads. I pulled on the door and entered the office. The only sound was of tapping keys on a keyboard. A woman was sitting at one of the five desks behind the counter. She peered over her black-framed glasses and stood up. She was a stocky woman with silver and brown hair that rested on her shoulders. She ambled up to the counter. "You must be Martina Monroe."

"That's me."

"I'm JJ. We spoke on the phone. You're right on time—perfect timing since all the kids are in the cafeteria for lunch, making it nice and quiet in here. I pulled the yearbooks from 1965 to 1967. Hopefully that'll help you. If you need more, I can request them from the library and they'll bring them right over." I watched as she walked back to her desk, picked up the stack of three yearbooks and clutched them to her chest before returning to the counter. She set them down in front of me. "I'm sorry we don't have any open offices for you to use, but you're welcome to sit in the waiting area. There's a small table at the end that you can set them on."

"That's fantastic. Thank you so much." I lifted the books and carried them over to the waiting area that consisted of a row of plastic chairs on each side with metal tables at the ends. I set the yearbooks down on the table before taking off my messenger bag and unzipping my jacket and placing it on the chair next to mine. I sat in the bucket seat, grabbed the yearbook from 1966, reached over, and pulled out the envelope with Charlotte's photo from my bag.

I flipped the cover open and studied the pages, one by one. It was nearly identical to the yearbooks at Central East. I reached the section with the senior portraits and started studying each and every photograph, sliding Charlotte's photo next to each one of the female pictures, hoping to find a match to the hairline, eyes, nose, and chin.

I leaned back and thought about my time at the bistro. Now staring at Charlotte's photo again, the woman who brought the check bore a resemblance—and even more so to Kennedy. I contemplated a connection to Charlotte but shook it off. Many people had red hair and freckles, especially in these parts. I returned my attention to the yearbooks. With each comparison I began to lose hope that I would ever find Charlotte's actual name or where she was from.

I wanted to give Kennedy answers about her mother and father, since she was without parents and barely had any family remaining on her father's side. It was sad, especially since she so desperately wanted a connection to a family member. I flipped the next page and pressed Charlotte's photo against the next female graduate. And the next. And the next, and then my pulse quickened. My eyes darted from the yearbook to the photo. The hairline, eyebrows, eyes, cheekbones, nose, and chin. It was a match. I'd found her. I skimmed to the left of the year-book to find the name of the woman whose picture matched Charlotte's. Her last name wasn't Jamison, though. It was Henley. Charlotte Eloise Henley, member of the graduating class of 1966 at Central West High School.

21

DETECTIVE HIRSCH

AFTER THANKING THE GUARD, I ENTERED THE MUSTY ROOM and eyed the man who may have killed Donna Bernard all those years ago. Diego Tarantino. He had dark hair, olive skin, and tattoos on his arms and neck. Mostly skulls and names written in Old English. A real tough guy, the type that ended up right where he was. I grabbed the seat and sat down. "I'm Detective Hirsch." As a sign of respect, I extended my hand to shake his.

He remained seated but extended his hand for a weak shake. I maintained eye contact with him. "Thank you for meeting with me, Diego. I'm hoping you'll be able to help me out with a case I'm working."

He cocked his head, and his eyes roamed from top to bottom. He was sizing me up. "I might be able to help you. What case are you working?"

"The disappearance of Donna Bernard. I've spoken to her family, friends, and neighbors. They say you knew Donna and that the two of you were an item."

His eyes widened and narrowed again. I'd guess Diego didn't want me to know he was surprised.

Diego shrugged. "Yeah, we went out for a while. It wasn't a big deal."

"How long were you together?"

"I don't know if I'd say we were together. We fooled around for a month or two—you know what I mean."

"I'm not sure I follow. What do you mean?"

"I mean, she was hot, but I had no intentions of marrying her. She was way more into me than I was into her. She was needy and clingy. I wasn't havin' it."

"What things did she say or do that you considered to be needy or clingy? I'm just trying to figure out what she was like."

"Like, one time she saw me talking to another girl. We were just talking, and she went crazy on me. She said I was a cheater and all that bull. She's one of those girls who wants a man to worship her like she's some kinda princess. I mean, she was hot, but not that hot. Diego doesn't bow down to no one, especially not some bitch. I dropped her after that."

"Do you remember when that was? The date?"

"I didn't write it in my journal or nothing, but it was before she graduated, so I'd say it was early June."

A month before Donna disappeared. Maybe he had been stalking her and then made his move. "Did you know she disappeared the next month?"

"Yeah, I heard that when I got back from Mexico, but I didn't think much of it."

"Did you have anything to do with her disappearance?"

He shook his head. "No, I had nothing to do with that girl after I dumped her."

Interesting choice of words. "Where were you the night of July fifteenth of that year?"

He smirked. "Probably getting busy with a girl, like most nights."

A real charmer. "So, you don't have an alibi?"

"That summer I was nowhere near Stone Island. I was in Mexico visiting family."

Damn it. If he really had been in Mexico, it was a solid alibi and that meant we had no leads. "Did you fly or drive?"

"I flew in an airplane."

"Which airline?"

"Man, I don't remember. One of the big ones. United or American, I think."

They should have records, even from back then. Or at least, I hoped they did. "What were the dates you were in Mexico?"

"I'd have to check the calendar but, it was the end of June to the beginning of August. Like I said, I was nowhere near Donna when she disappeared."

Assuming all this guy's information could be verified, we were at square one. "Any idea who may have had anything to do with her disappearance? Or wanted to cause her harm? Anybody who maybe was bugging her, or maybe someone she was dating?"

"Man, she had a lot of guys, but there was this one." He paused and eyed me again. "If I help you, what will you do to help me?"

This guy didn't have an altruistic bone in his body. "What do you want?"

"I could use some funding in my commissary. Maybe a change to a better locale."

Unless he had video of a crime, accompanied with physical evidence that could be used to convict, this creep wasn't going anywhere. But, sure, if he had something useful, the department could give him a few bucks to buy himself a cup o' noodles. "Look, I'm authorized up to a certain amount for your commissary, but a transfer is trickier unless you have something really good like the case wrapped up with a pretty little bow."

I remained stoic and stared into his dark-brown eyes, trying to imagine what he'd looked like back when Donna disappeared. He would have been in his early twenties back then. He was probably fresh-faced with far fewer tattoos.

Diego leaned back in his chair, crossing his arms. "Okay, here's what I'll tell you in exchange for the commissary money, and if the information I give you leads to an arrest, I get a transfer."

"If what you tell me leads to an arrest and conviction, I promise you we'll get you transferred."

Diego shifted in his seat, as if agitated. "You know they say I tried to kill that girl, I didn't. I don't belong here. I didn't do what they said."

According to his conviction, he had drugged a young woman, raped her, and then shared her with a couple of his friends before leaving her unresponsive at an abandoned house —where she would've died if a guy walking his dog hadn't found her. Diego deserved to remain locked up. I didn't care where. "Deal."

"Okay, so here's what I know. When Donna and I were hooking up, I saw her talking to an older guy. Standing real close, you know. At first I got mad, thinking she was banging him—I don't like sloppy seconds—but when I approached them, he rushed off. She told me I had it all wrong and that he wasn't a boyfriend. She said it was business."

"Business? What kind of business?"

"Man, I don't know. Shady, for sure. She said he gave her a grand a month to meet and talk."

What on earth had Donna gotten herself into? It didn't make any sense.

"Did she tell you what they talked about?"

"Nah. Which was really sketchy, if you asked me. She wouldn't tell me, but she swore she wasn't turning tricks or nothing."

"Did you believe her?"

He shrugged. "At first, no. I mean, what dude pays that much just to talk?"

A lonely man. A man who desired a "girlfriend experience" instead of just sex. I shifted in my chair. "What did you do? Is that when you broke up with her?"

"Nah. I got her to talk."

"And?"

"And, you get me money in my commissary and I'll tell you more."

I was not a fan of this guy and had to restrain myself from telling this punk off. "Not so fast. You'll get your money, but I at least need to know what the man you saw her with looked like."

"Dark hair, brown skin, and about my height. I didn't get a good look at his face since he ran off."

He could be the man on the levee that Kennedy saw with Donna. "I spoke with Donna's best friend, Martina, and she didn't know about any of this. Martina said she thought the money was coming from her parents."

He shook his head. "Martina, talk about a piece of work, I forgot about that chick."

I raised my eyebrows. "Not a fan of Martina?"

"Damn, she thought she was better than everyone. Said she was going to be some big Army person and all that. She said she didn't want me around her best friend. Like she was so great—she wasn't. What she up to? My guess, she's still in that trailer park with a tin full of kids living off the government."

"Not quite. She's very accomplished, actually," I said with a knowing smile. "Why would Donna tell you about her secret business and not her best friend?"

"I have to confess. In my younger years I wasn't as gentle a soul as I am now. I may have been overly upset when I was asking her about this guy. She didn't want to tell me, but eventually she did."

So, he had threatened her. Diego definitely belonged behind bars, and for good. "Is there anything else you can tell me that might help the case? Any other strange things happening around Donna?"

"That's it."

"Thank you, Diego. Like I said, you'll get the money in your commissary if your alibi checks out, and then I'll be back for the rest."

"Stop by anytime, Detective."

I shoved out of my seat and stepped outside the door, thanking the guard before hurrying out of the prison gates. I needed to verify the information Diego Tarantino had provided, and fast. If Donna had secret business dealings with an older man with dark hair and brown skin, that older man was likely the person who was last seen with Donna.

22

MARTINA

I took a picture of the page in the yearbook with Charlotte's photo and information. I collected my things and the yearbooks and headed back to the counter, wearing a wide grin. I said to the woman behind the counter, "Thank you so much."

She looked up from her computer monitor. "You find what you're looking for?"

"Sure did."

The woman pushed herself out of her chair and headed back toward the counter. "Well, what did you find?"

I opened the page to Charlotte's photo and pointed.

JJ's eyes widened. "Charlotte Henley? You're looking for Charlotte Henley?"

"Did you know her?" Based on my estimation, the woman appeared old enough to have attended high school with Charlotte.

"I was a few years older, but yes. It was such a tragedy for the Henleys."

"What do you mean? What tragedy?"

"I assumed you knew since you're looking for Charlotte."

"Please, if you could share with me what you know, I'd appreciate it."

The woman rested her elbow on the counter and propped herself up. "Well, Charlotte was the darling of the Henley family. She was beautiful, smart, and really going places, so we all thought. And then one night she was out with her brother, Frank—he's a state senator now, like his father. Well, anyhow, out of nowhere a drunk driver rammed right into the side of the car. Charlotte was killed instantly. Oh, how the family mourned her passing. I don't think the Henleys were ever the same after that."

JJ thought Charlotte died in Pennsylvania? And her brother and father were state senators? Not only had Charlotte been running from something or someone, but I had a hunch that somebody was also trying to keep her buried. "Was Charlotte married?"

JJ craned her neck back. "Heavens, no. She was college-bound until the accident ended it all."

Charlotte had lied about being married before Theodore. Why would she do that? "What else can you tell me about the Henley family, if you don't mind?"

"They practically own half this town. They have housing developments, shopping malls, and even a restaurant or two. Frank is the oldest, you know about Charlotte and then Amy, she's the youngest. A late in life surprise! Amy is a sweetheart. She's tried to stay out of the spotlight, but with her brother being a senator, it can be tough. I think he's got his eyes on the oval office."

"I went to Henley's Bistro for lunch. I presume it's owned by *the* Henleys?"

"Yes. It's great, isn't it? I just love their desserts. Amy runs it. She's such a darling girl. She's married and has kids of her own now."

"What about the parents?"

"Eloise is retired and mostly works on the boards of her favorite charities and that kind of thing. Big Frank died a few years ago."

"Did you know somebody named Alonso Davidson, who was friends with Charlotte and her brother?"

"Alonso Davidson, no I can't say that I did."

Maybe Alonso Davidson was an alias or not really connected to the Henleys at all? "Is there anything else you know about them? Are you in touch with the family now?"

"Just what I read in the newspapers or when I dine at the bistro and chat with Amy."

This was a lot to process. My hunch was correct. Charlotte's story about her life before she moved to California was completely fabricated. "You've been so helpful. Thank you, again." I exited the school with adrenaline pulsing through my body. I hadn't even remembered to zip my coat, but when the hail hit the side of my face, I was quickly reminded. I zipped up my coat and hurried over to my car. Quickly, I opened the door, and jumped in.

Thinking about what I had just learned about the Henleys, I lined up the information in my mind. Had her family faked her death? Charlotte had pretended that her entire family had died in a fire. The Henleys were a rich and powerful political family. If they had something they needed to keep hidden, surely they had the means to do so. But what? What had Charlotte known?

———

BACK AT THE HOTEL, I DROPPED MY BAG DOWN NEXT TO THE desk and paced the room like I often did when trying to figure out my next move. Obviously, I needed to go back to Henley's Bistro and question Amy Henley to find out more about the family. I checked my wrist for the time. My flight was scheduled to leave tomorrow morning. I had to act fast and determine how I'd maximize my few remaining hours in Doylestown.

Divide and conquer would fast-track the background checks on the Henleys. I picked up the phone and called the office. "Drakos Security & Investigations. How may I help you?"

"Hi, Mrs. Pearson, it's Martina. Can I speak with Angela, please?"

"Sure thing, Martina. I'll patch you right through."

I continued to pace the length of the hotel room and planned out all the things I would ask Angela to help me with while I was working on my plan. The more information we had, the better. I'd also put in a call to Hirsch and let him know what I'd found and see if he could help out too. "Hi, Martina."

"Hi, Angela. I need a big favor as soon as possible. We just got a big break in the case." I described to Angela everything I had found and what I needed her to research while I prepared to interview one of the Henleys. Assuming Amy was still at the bistro.

"You got it, Martina."

"Awesome, thank you." I was amped. I needed to go for a run to get some of the energy out, think clearly, and perfect my line of questioning for Amy Henley.

I changed into a set of workout clothes, grabbed my phone, and took the stairs down to the gym. Phone to my ear, I waited for Hirsch to answer as I climbed up onto the treadmill. I set the pace to 3.0 mph and warmed up. "Hey, Martina. What's up?"

"I found Charlotte's actual identity, and it's interesting." I filled him in on all the details.

"Okay, I'll run the family name through our databases and see what comes up."

"Great. Did you interview Diego yet?"

"Yep. He had some interesting things to say, but I don't think it was him with Donna that night."

My mouth dropped open as he told me what Diego had said. Donna had lied to me. Why? "None of that makes sense."

"It's strange, I'll give you that," Hirsch commented.

"Well, let me know if you find anything. I'm working on my strategy for interviewing Amy Henley and how much to share with her."

"Good luck."

"Thanks." I hung up and set the phone on the treadmill console before increasing the speed.

Sweat trickled down my temples, and my heart pumped as I pounded away on the treadmill and thought about Amy Henley and how I'd thought she had looked familiar when I was at the bistro. I must have been more jet-lagged than I thought to have not made the connection. She looked quite similar to both Charlotte and Kennedy. When I spoke to Amy, I needed to tread lightly before disclosing anything. If she was part of the coverup, I wouldn't want to disclose what I knew.

Thirty minutes later, I shut off the treadmill, wiped down the machine with a paper towel, and then plucked a fresh one to mop up the sweat on my face. After strutting out of the hotel gym, I jogged up the stairs and then exited the stairwell. When I reached my hotel room, I stopped dead in my tracks. Through the curtains, light was emitting from inside the room. I was sure I'd turned off all the lights before leaving. I steadied myself, slid the hotel key card in the slot, and slowly turned the handle and pushed. I inched forward, glancing from left to right. The two queen beds were untouched, as were the desk and dresser. Silence filled the room. Fists in fighting position, I crept toward the bathroom. I reached it and eyed right and then left. There was nobody in the room but me. Had I left the light on and forgotten?

I turned back around. I was the only person in my small hotel room. Had housekeeping entered, turned on the light, and left as part of a turndown service? Maybe that was it. I went back over to the door and engaged the safety lock at the top, and then peeled off my sweaty clothes and hopped into the shower.

Hot steam helped relax my muscles, but I was still on edge. I couldn't shake the feeling that someone had been in my hotel room. My mind had been preoccupied, and I was still on West Coast time when I'd left for the gym. I had to be overreacting.

I shut off the shower and dried off, redressing before heading back over to the desk to see if Angela had sent anything to my email. It had been less than an hour since we spoke, but Angela was fast and efficient at doing research. I slid my hand down to pull out my laptop and caught air. I glanced down and flipped open the lid to my messenger bag. My laptop was gone. This wasn't jet lag. Somebody had been in my room and taken it. But who? A thieving housekeeper or somebody related to the Henleys? Whoever had broken in only had a short window of time. My stomach flip-flopped. Was I being watched?

I dialed the office again. "Mrs. Pearson, this is Martina again. Somebody has broken into my hotel room and stolen my laptop. I wanted to report it right away. It was about thirty minutes ago. I need all the information wiped."

"I'll let IT know right away. Martina, are you okay? Do you need me to change your flight to get you home today?"

"Not necessary. I'll fly home tomorrow morning as planned."

Clearly, I was getting too close for comfort for the Henley family. Maybe I was jumping to conclusions that the Henleys were behind this, but my instincts were telling me I was on the right track, and no little break-in would stop me from uncovering the truth about what Charlotte had left behind.

Daylight was fading, and temperatures were dropping. I couldn't wait to go home to the sunshine and light breezes of the Bay Area. I exited my rental car and jogged up to Henley's Bistro. I pulled open the door and stepped inside. Scanning the restaurant, there were only a few tables occupied. It was a young crowd, nobody I would suspect to be tailing me. There was no sign of Amy Henley. I had little time and hoped luck was on my side and that she was in the back office. I approached the counter that had the same teenager from lunch standing behind the register. "I'd like a table, please."

"Go ahead and pick anywhere you want."

"Thanks." I chose a table closest to the back room and the kitchen. Soon after, a young woman with dark hair and braces approached my table with a smile. "May I take your order?"

"Yes, I'll have the tomato soup and the turkey avocado sandwich." It was a pleasant lunch, and I thought it would make a good early dinner too.

"Can I get you anything to drink?"

"A water and a latte would be great. Thank you."

"Coming right up."

I watched the bistro staff as they went to and from the dining area, to the register and beyond. Soon, the server returned with my latte and set it on the table in front of me. "Here you go."

"Thank you. Do you know if Amy is working?"

"She is. Do you want me to get her for you?"

"Yes, thank you."

Thank goodness. It was important for Amy to be there for my plan to work. If somebody was watching me and they were hired by the Henleys, they'd soon know I was talking to Amy, and it would draw them out of the shadows.

A few minutes later, the woman in the suit, whom I'd met earlier, walked out and approached my table with a customer-service-style smile. "I heard you requested me. Is everything okay?"

"Yes, everything is fine. My name is Martina Monroe, and I was wondering if I could ask you a few questions."

Amy stepped back. "Are you a reporter?"

"No, I'm not a reporter. I'm a private investigator from California."

Hand on her hip, Amy's apprehensive look had turned into a look of annoyance. "Look, I want nothing to do with my brother's political campaign. You can put that in your report."

I raised my hand to protest. "Please don't leave. I'm not here because of your brother. I was hired to investigate your sister, Charlotte."

Amy's mouth dropped open with apparent surprise in her eyes. "You want to know about Charlotte?"

"Yes."

She shook her head back and forth. "I don't understand. Charlotte died shortly after I was born. What are you looking for exactly?"

"Would you like to have a seat?"

I wasn't sure if I should tell her everything. The information would be a lot for anyone to take in. If Amy thought her sister had died when she was a baby, but in reality had been living a full life until about two weeks ago, it would be a real shocker.

Amy didn't move.

I met her gaze. "I have some news. You may want to sit down."

Amy glanced around the restaurant before pulling out a chair. Good. "What do you know about Charlotte?" I asked.

"I was told that she died a few weeks after I was born."

"And you are close with your brother, Frank?"

"We see each other at family functions and occasionally at a benefit, if he needs me to go for a campaign. Other than that, I try to keep to myself and my family. I prefer to remain out of the limelight."

"And you're married now. I heard you have children too?"

Amy cocked her head. "How do you know that?"

"I was at the high school and was asking about Charlotte's family. JJ told me about you."

"I still don't understand. Who hired you to look into Charlotte?"

"Before I tell you what I'm about to tell you, can you please look at a photo and confirm it is, in fact, your sister, Charlotte?"

"I only remember her from photographs, but okay."

I fished out the picture of Charlotte with the baby and handed it to Amy.

Amy studied the photo and placed her hand over her heart. In a whisper, she said, "That's Charlotte and me." She flipped over the photo and cocked her head. "It says Amelia?"

"Is Amy short for Amelia?"

"No, my name is Amy, that's what it says on my birth certificate."

She wasn't Amelia? Or perhaps it was a nickname that Charlotte had called her baby sister? The hairline, the nose, and the chin. Whether or not she knew it, I was fairly certain that Amy was baby Amelia.

"You're sure it's you and your sister."

"Yes. I've seen the picture before—or one very similar."

I braced myself. Amy was about to be given news that could rock her entire world. It wasn't a task to be taken lightly. "Charlotte's daughter, Kennedy, hired me to find out the identity of the baby in the photo. Charlotte died a few weeks ago."

Tears fell from Amy's eyes as she shook her head. "It can't be. Charlotte died when I was a baby, and now you're saying

Charlotte died two weeks ago, it doesn't make sense." Amy stared out the window above me. She returned her focus to me. "Unless they lied to me."

"They?"

Her face was long. "My father. My brother and mother."

"Kennedy hoped to find Charlotte's family. She said her mother, Charlotte, never wanted to discuss her past. Kennedy doesn't have a lot of family left and was hoping I'd help find her relatives."

Amy pushed back the chair and stood up. Her hands were trembling. "What did you say your name was?"

"My name is Martina Monroe, private investigator."

"You say Charlotte has a daughter named Kennedy?"

"Yes."

Amy raised her hand and placed it on her cheek. "I don't know what to say. Is she here?"

"No, she's not. She's in California."

Amy stammered. "I'm trying to process this information. I need to call my husband. Do you have a business card?"

"Yes, I leave tomorrow, to go back home to the Bay Area." I pulled the business card from my bag and handed it to her.

She stared at it with her head bowed before she went to the back of the restaurant. She didn't return.

I finished my meal, paid, and grabbed a business card. I'd follow up when I was back home—to check on her and see if she wanted more information about Kennedy.

I felt bad for Amy and soon, Kennedy, when I would tell her that her mother had lied about her past. It was a lot to deal with.

I bundled up and peered outside the restaurant. It was pitch black except for a few street lamps. I grabbed my phone and turned on the light. Considering I was convinced I was being watched, I needed as much visibility as I could get. I pushed open the door and hurried toward my car.

I reached my rental car and pulled out the key from my coat pocket. Suddenly, the wind was blocked, and I felt warmth close by. From the corner of my eye, I saw the blur of a swinging arm. I elbowed back and executed a powerful back kick. The person grunted but was able to grab my arm and twist it behind me. A sharp jolt of pain shot through me as a knee hit my kidneys. I screamed and a bulky arm stretched across my chest and covered my mouth with its gloved hand. In a deep, husky voice, he spoke into my ear. "Go back to California and don't return, ever. Leave the Henleys alone, or you'll end up six feet under and nobody will ever find you."

Another jab to my ribs and I crumpled to the ground. A few seconds later, I shot up off the ground, adrenaline fueling me and warding off the pain. I turned around, but all I saw was darkness. I crawled into my car and dialed 9-1-1. It was going to be a long night.

23

ALONSO

HE HOBBLED BACK TO HIS CAR, WINCING IN PAIN. THAT damn woman had gotten him pretty good—right in the groin. But he got her even better, and hopefully she received the message loud and clear because he wasn't messing around. It was one thing for her to poke her nose in things when she was back home in California. It was quite another to fly across the country and start snooping around and questioning one of the Henleys.

He didn't know how much more it would take to get this lady off the case, but he knew the boss would not be pleased when he got his next report. Safely back on the highway, he dialed the boss. "Hey, boss."

"This isn't a good time."

"Got it. I'll make it quick. I gave her the message after she had a cozy dinner at the bistro."

Silence from the boss. The message he'd delivered was cryptic, but surely the boss understood what it meant.

"Call me back in five minutes," the boss said, before the line went dead.

He continued down the highway, turned off at his exit, and

continued until he reached his driveway. Safe inside the garage, he entered his house and kicked off his shoes. He removed his jacket and gloves before dialing the boss again. "Hey, boss."

"Tell me everything that happened."

"I followed her back to the bistro. I could see from outside that she spoke with Amy again. I don't know what they said, but Amy looked pretty upset afterward. I caught up with the PI in the parking lot and let her know it would be in her best interest to go back home."

"I don't like this. Not one bit. I have a feeling this PI won't stop until she ruins everything. I want this over and done with."

"You got it, boss."

"Let her get back home and then have her taken out. I don't care how you do it. You can handle it yourself or contract out. I trust you to handle it."

He never enjoyed taking a life, but he didn't mind another trip to the West Coast either. Plus, after what that woman had done to his groin, he felt he owed it to Martina Monroe to be there when she took her last breath.

24

DETECTIVE HIRSCH

I waved to Vincent as he approached. Vincent was a young guy with a thick head of dark-blond hair and rosy cheeks. He worked in the records department, and I'd only had a few encounters with him, but he seemed competent and friendly. "What do you have for me?" I asked.

"I've got the records that you requested from the airlines. Looks like your pal, Diego, was in fact in Mexico when Donna disappeared."

If Diego hadn't lied about his trip to Mexico, maybe he'd been truthful about the older man that he'd seen with Donna, too. If true, that meant Donna had been working for the man on a secret project that paid more than a legitimate gig. Either that, or Diego still was fuming over the end of their relationship and had one of his buddies take care of Donna for him. It was a possibility I'd considered. Despite his nonchalant attitude about his relationship with Donna, based on what Martina had said, Donna was the one who had ended the relationship, and it hadn't been pretty. "Thanks, man. Any luck on bank records for Donna too?"

"I was able to get ahold of the records for the account her parents had opened for her. They were cosigners on the account. There weren't any regular deposits, like you'd expect if she was getting a regular allowance, a couple of lump sums of a few hundred dollars once or twice a year."

Likely birthday and Christmas money, but I'd have to ask the parents to be sure. "Nothing else?"

"It's possible she had another account that we just don't know about. Searching all the databases for any bank accounts registered to Donna Bernard from that long ago would be like trying to find a needle in a haystack. We can do it. It'll just take a little longer."

I was thinking it was time to revisit the Bernard home and start going through Donna's things. If she had another bank account, maybe she'd have bank records or an ATM card or something to that effect that could lead us in the right direction. It would be helpful to know when her business dealings with the older man had started and ended. Although, I wasn't sure we'd get that lucky. A thousand dollars a month was a lot, but if it were an illegal operation, they were likely all cash transactions.

I glanced up at Vincent. "Thanks, this is great."

"Sorry I don't have any better news, but I have one more thing," he said with a devilish grin before he held up a manilla folder and tapped it with his fingers.

"What's that?"

"I got a hit on a break-in at a veterinary office in Concord. Want to guess what was stolen?"

I straightened in my seat. "Ketamine?"

"You got it. Here's the police report." He handed me the folder.

"I also sent it to your email."

I took the folder, opened the cover, and began reading the report. What was this? Not only had ketamine been stolen but insulin too. I'd have to check with the medical examiner to see if they could match up the insulin and ketamine stolen from the veterinarian's office to what was used on Theodore Gilmore. We may have just found the origins of the murder weapon. I stared up at Vincent with a grin. "I think I owe you a beer."

"I'll hold you to that. I'm still compiling the background on the Henleys. So far, nothing unusual, but we'll keep digging. Anything else I can get you?"

"That's all for now."

It would've been nice to know if the Henleys had been involved in any suspicious activity sooner rather than later, but I'd just have to be patient. I thanked Vincent, and he left, presumably to continue his research. I returned my attention to the manilla folder. We had something to chase in the Gilmore murder. I picked up my desk phone receiver and dialed the medical examiner's number.

"Dr. Scribner speaking."

"Hi, Dr. Scribner. It's Detective Hirsch, I have a few questions for you about the Theodore Gilmore toxicology results."

"The official report should be available pretty soon, but I can see what the draft report contains. What do you need?"

"Is there a way to distinguish between veterinary-use insulin and human-use insulin?"

"The only thing that may differ is dosage. Hmm."

"What is it?"

"Actually, now that you mention it, give me a second. Let me pull up the draft report."

I waited for the doctor to return. Could this be the smoking gun, or in this case the smoking injection? I needed to work on my comedy routine.

Dr. Scribner returned to the line. "Okay, just as I thought. Yeah, based on the number of injections and the level of insulin found in Mr. Gilmore's body, it would align with a veterinary-grade insulin dosage."

"If I knew the dosage of the insulin, would you be able to match up the results based on the number of injections?"

"I sure could."

My adrenaline was pumping. "All right, we got a break-in at a nearby veterinary office just over the hill. Both insulin and ketamine, and a few other assorted drugs were stolen. I'll send you the report. It'll include the type of insulin and ketamine stolen."

"All right, I should be able to take a look later today."

"Awesome. Thanks, doctor. I'll send it right over."

"Anytime."

I hung up and forwarded the police report for the break-in at the veterinary office to the medical examiner. I looked down at the report on my desk and studied the responding officer's notes on the case. *Hot damn.* I made a quick call to a buddy over at the Concord Police Department before grabbing my keys from atop my desk. I pushed the chair back, slid on my coat, and hurried out of the building.

WEBB SMACKED ME ON THE BACK OF MY SHOULDER. "How the hell are you, Hirsch?"

Detective Webb and I went way back. He had been a coworker and friend, even introduced me to my soon-to-be ex-wife. He thought we would be a perfect match. I guess I did too. That was before the job turned me into what I what I had become. A somewhat-jaded workaholic who didn't do well around most people. "I'm all right. How are you, Kelly, and Nate?"

"I can't complain. Nate started first grade this year. It's amazing how time flies. Kelly is still at John Muir Hospital working in the NICU. Overall, not too bad. We'll have to have you over for dinner so we can catch up."

"Sounds good." I doubted the invitation would actually be extended, considering Kelly was close friends with my ex.

"I know this isn't a social call, so we'll get down to it. Let me take you back to my desk. I'll show you what we've got. We haven't gotten everything back yet, but we're hoping for forensics to come back with some good news."

We reached his cubicle. Webb sat in his chair and tapped on his keyboard before focusing on the monitor. I perched on the chair next to his desk.

"As you read in the file, we have video surveillance footage from outside of the vet's office. It's decent quality, but it doesn't help too much considering our perp wore a hat, scarf, jacket, and gloves."

"Sounds like he was definitely trying to conceal his identity." As did most of the smarter criminals.

Webb nodded. "He was careful. Here." He swiveled his monitor. "Have a look."

I leaned forward to get a closer look. Webb pressed the key for the video to start. I watched as a man, maybe five foot ten inches with a medium build, using a tension tool and lock pick, tried to unlock the back door to the vet's office. He wore a black baseball cap, black jacket, gloves, and a scarf. The only visible skin was from the nose down to his chin. He was either Caucasian or Latino with brown to olive skin tone. He didn't appear fresh-faced. More mature, maybe fifty or sixty. Successful in unlocking the door, he slid the lock-picking kit into his jacket pocket before creeping inside the building. Lights above the door flashed and a siren sounded. Less than a minute later, the perp rushed back out. "Hey, freeze that."

Webb reached forward and hit pause. The perp's jacket was bulkier in the front. Likely, he shoved the drugs down the front of his jacket and zipped it up before hightailing it out of there. I studied his lower face. There appeared to be a dark shadow on the left side.

I pointed to the screen. "Do you see that?"

Webb grinned. "You bet. Want to guess what it is?"

I stared into Webb's shining blue-gray eyes. Webb seemed to know exactly what it was, and I had a feeling as well. "Do tell."

"Dun. Dun. Dun." He mimicked dramatic music for effect. "Our pal broke the glass door on the drug storage cabinet. There aren't cameras in there, but we suspect it rained down on him and cut his cheek. Our forensic team has samples of the glass that had traces of human blood on them."

I had rushed down to Concord PD for the surveillance footage, but this was so much better. "Are you telling me you have the guy's DNA?"

"That's the rub. We have the sample, but the lab's backed up. We don't have priority, because it's not linked to a violent crime. But if it was..." He raised his brows at me.

"I think I could help you with that."

Webb smiled. "I'm all ears. Tell me what you have."

"Well, for starters, call the lab because it's connected to a homicide investigation." I described the details of the medical examiner's report for Theodore Gilmore, and how I suspected that this break-in was the origin of the drugs that were used to kill Mr. Gilmore.

Webb leaned back, hands behind his head. "Well, I'll be damned. I'll call the lab. All I need is a case number."

We exchanged the information needed to get the DNA

processed faster. A DNA match in CODIS (the Combined DNA Index System, which included state and national databases) meant we'd have the identity of the suspect for the veterinary break-in and the Gilmore homicide investigation. A two for one special.

25

MARTINA

I CAREFULLY STEPPED OUT OF MY CAR, ONE FOOT AT A time. My ribs and back were on fire. The ibuprofen had long worn off. I was tired. I was in pain. And I was pissed off. But at last, I was home. If it wasn't for the few hours of sleep on the airplane, I don't think I would've made it. At this moment, nothing sounded better than seeing Zoey's little face and sleeping in my own bed.

I braced myself on the car door and then stepped back and shut it. I glanced at the trunk where my suitcase lay and kept on walking toward the front of the house. My luggage could wait. I pulled out my keys from my jacket and unlocked the door.

Within moments, I heard the pattering of feet running down the hall. I shoved the door open and stepped inside. Zoey ran toward me. When she reached me, she flung her arms in a V and wrapped them around me. "Mommy, I'm so glad you're home."

I gently hugged her back, wincing. I didn't have the heart to tell her she was causing me agonizing pain. I sucked it up before untangling her dainty arms from around my waist. "How was your trip? I'm so glad you're home."

"Me too." I grimaced.

Zoey's face turned serious. "What's wrong, Mommy? Are you hurt?"

"I have a few bumps and bruises, that's all."

Zoey's eyes widened. "What happened?"

"It's a long story, honey. I'll tell you later." I glanced up and saw Claire standing in the hall. I let out a breath. "Hi, Claire, how's it going?"

She was solemn and not her normal, bubbly self. "All is normal around here."

"Good to hear." I hadn't told Claire or Zoey about my attack. As it was, ever since my accident the year before, Zoey had developed a little separation anxiety when it came to me leaving the house or going on trips.

Claire eyed Zoey. "Why don't we let your mom settle in. Maybe she needs something to drink or eat or to just rest. She went on a long trip."

Claire turned her focus to me. "Are you hungry, Martina? Can I get you anything?"

"Starved."

Zoey patted my arm. I gazed down at her. "Claire made some really fantastic enchiladas. Do you want some?"

"I would love some." *Have I thanked God for Claire today?*

"I'll get it for you, Mommy." And she ran off toward the kitchen.

I walked slowly toward Claire. She hurried to be closer to me. "What happened?"

"I was attacked last night in Pennsylvania. I haven't told Zoey yet. It's related to the case I'm working."

"How bad is it? Did you see a doctor?"

"Yeah, I called the police after the attack. They insisted I go to the hospital. I'm fine. A couple of bruised ribs, and some banged-up kidneys."

Claire frowned. "That sounds awful. Can I get you anything for the pain? How about some ibuprofen and an ice pack?"

My savior. "Both would be great. Thank you."

I knew I would have to tell her what happened in the parking lot outside of Henley's Bistro. It wasn't like I could hide it from Claire. She was studying to be a nurse and would be certified in a few short months.

She said, "Why don't you go in the kitchen, and I'll bring them to you. I also need to tell you about something else."

An uneasiness filled me. That didn't sound like a good something. "Okay."

I made my way to the kitchen and sat down at the dining table.

I watched as Zoey stood on the step stool that I'd purchased when she'd insisted she was ready to get her own plates and cups, if only she were taller. Miss almost-eight-going-on-eighteen. Zoey opened the door to the microwave and then lifted the plate with three enchiladas on it and placed it inside the microwave. She shut the door and then turned around to look at me. "A minute?"

I smiled. It was good to be home. "I think a minute will be perfect."

Claire arrived at the table with a glass of water and four ibuprofen tablets. She set the cup of water on the table and handed me the pills. I picked up the glass, popped the pills into my mouth, and washed them down with the water. Claire had the ice pack in her hand and kept it by her side. I wondered if she was gauging whether I wanted Zoey to see that I was injured. I nodded, took the ice pack, and sandwiched it between my back and the chair.

The microwave beeped. Zoey opened the door, grabbed the plate, and set it down on the counter before climbing down from the stool. She picked up the plate and brought it over to the table, then set in front of me. "Enchiladas for the best mommy in the world," she said with flair.

"It smells delicious. Thank you so much." I glanced up at Claire. "Thank you."

I took a bite of the chicken and cheese enchilada, shut my eyes, and softly moaned. It was amazing. Claire, at twenty-two years old, was an amazing cook, the best damn nanny I'd ever seen, and a nursing student. Some people, like Claire, were truly gifted. I continued to eat, feeling grateful for the home-cooked meal.

Zoey took the seat across from me. "How was your trip, Mommy?"

I swallowed my bite and set my fork down. "It was productive. I got a lot of excellent information."

"So, you can help your client?"

"Yes, I think it will."

"Was your client really happy?"

I wasn't sure how joyful the news would be to Kennedy. "I haven't told her yet. We have a meeting tomorrow to go over all the information."

"I bet she'll be so happy. Is this the one where you were trying to find a baby?"

Zoey had quite the memory. I probably needed to be more careful about what I told her. "Yes, I think we found the baby in the picture."

"Wow. I bet you're the best private investigator in the whole world."

I didn't know if that was true, but I was able to identify the baby in the photo, and hopefully, the additional information about the Henleys would be of some comfort to Kennedy—to know she had more family out there. Although, I had an inkling that most of that family would be people she may not want to know. If my suspicions were correct, there were a lot of rotten apples on that family tree.

"Guess what?" Zoey asked.

"What?"

"Grandma Betty called."

My chest tightened. Why was my mother calling? And why was I surprised? She had probably heard that I'd been on the island investigating a case. Hopefully, her call didn't mean she wanted to reconnect. That was one train wreck I'd like to avoid. "What did Grandma Betty have to say?"

"Well, she said that she heard you were on Stone Island and she wants to see us. She wants to come for a visit."

Over my dead body. "She did, did she?"

Zoey nodded emphatically. "She says she misses us. I remember I made her a Christmas card last year, but I can't picture her face. What does she look like?"

I'd been careful to not bring Zoey around my mother. The last time Zoey saw my mother, she was only two years old. When we had arrived for the visit, Betty had already been three sheets to the wind. Ironically, I didn't want my daughter around an alcoholic. At the time, I hadn't realized that I was living in a glass house. "Well, maybe I can find a picture to show you."

"How come we don't see her, like we see Grandma Mimi and Grandpa Jay?" Jared's mother and father. They lived out of state, but they always visited a few times a year, ever since Zoey was born. They had come out a few times after Jared's death to see if I needed help, but of course I'd sworn I didn't, but I'd been wrong. Luckily, Jared's parents hadn't witnessed the worst of my worst.

After my accident I feared that my entire world would be blown away. If they had deemed me unfit, they could have taken Zoey away, and I could've lost my job. I'd fought every day since then to stay sober and be there for Zoey and my clients. I needed to be that person for Zoey and for Jared. I could only imagine what he'd have done if he'd known how I'd spiraled out of control. "Well, I think Grandma Betty's pretty busy."

"I think it would be really cool to see her. Does she bake cookies?"

"Not that I can remember."

Claire leaned up against the refrigerator and crossed her arms. She said, "Your mother left a phone number for you to call her back. I spoke with her briefly as well. It may be a good idea to call her back."

Zoey chimed in, "I think so too. You know what she told me?" Claire gave me a knowing look. *Uh, oh.*

"She said that she's in AA now too! Like mother, like daughter." Zoey said with a silly smirk and a shrug.

Horrifying. So, Betty was going to AA. I didn't know if this was her first attempt or how long she'd been in. Maybe she had called to make amends, if she was at that step in the program. As an alcoholic myself, I supposed I should be more empathetic, but sometimes it was hard to let go of so many years of pain. If I'd learned anything in AA, it was to not only forgive myself but others as well. You never really knew what somebody else was going through, or what demons they had hidden and were fighting on a daily basis.

I took a deep breath. I hadn't talked to Rocco in two days. I'd been proud that I'd gone that long without needing to call my sponsor, but that streak would end shortly. He was a great sounding board, although I had a feeling I knew exactly what he was going to tell me. She was my mother. She was an alcoholic, and she deserved forgiveness, if not for her sake, then for my own.

"That is something, isn't it?" I looked back over at Claire. "Any other messages?"

"Just one," she said with a worried look on her face. Claire eyed Zoey. "Hey, Zoey. Why don't you show your mom the picture that you made at school today? I think she'll love it."

Zoey smiled and nodded before she hopped out of her chair and ran back to her room. When she was out of earshot, I asked Claire. "What's the other message?"

"They didn't identify themselves, but the voice was low and deep, like a man's. He said to tell Martina to drop it or she and her daughter would be sorry. And then he hung up. That was it."

Fury filled my being. "When did they call?"

"About an hour ago."

The Gilmore case wasn't the first time I'd been threatened to drop a case, and it wasn't likely to be the last. However, it was the first time someone had called my private home phone number and threatened my daughter. God help the man who did that, because I was good at defense but even better at offense. I would find him, and he would rue the day he messed with me and my family.

26

MARTINA

Stavros sat behind his desk and shook his head at me. What he was saying was outrageous. How could he expect me to walk away? I attempted to plead my case one more time. "Stavros, I'm fine. In Pennsylvania I couldn't carry my firearm, but here I can. I'm locked and loaded. I'm ready for whatever these people come at me with. I'm so close to uncovering what this family has been hiding."

"Yes, the family may have covered up and faked Charlotte's death. Yes, Charlotte may have lied and said that her family had died in a fire. That doesn't mean it's connected to Theodore Gilmore's murder. You were hired to identify the baby in the photo and to learn more about where Charlotte came from. You have fulfilled your obligation to the client. Martina, it's not worth yours or Zoey's life. Now you need to walk away. That's an order."

"You don't know that it's not related to the Gilmore death. Kennedy has lost both of her parents, and I've actually met the woman who was the baby in the photo."

"Have you found a connection yet?"

"No, but that family is hiding something, something serious. Why else attack me and tell me to leave the Henleys alone?"

Stavros stared me down, practically giving me the chills. "That's not your problem, Martina. This is your first real case back. You were almost killed, and now they're threatening you and your daughter. Why can't you let this one go? You've gone above and beyond the expectations in this case. Your instincts were correct, and you needed to go to Pennsylvania to find out Charlotte's true identity and where she grew up. You found the baby in the photo. I would say a lesser investigator would've taken a month, if not a year, to uncover what you did. You found her in less than two weeks. Consider it a job well done. Now meet with the client, share the information, and wish her luck in her future endeavors."

Stavros and I hadn't butted heads too much over the years, and yes, the last nine months had been strained, but this was the first time he'd ever ordered me off of a case. I didn't agree that it was over, or that I had fulfilled my duty to my client. Kennedy might be in danger if the Henleys wanted to wipe out anybody related to Charlotte. We didn't know how they operated. I felt like Stavros was treating me like a child, and I didn't like it. I disliked not having control over my work or being able to help my clients—to help Kennedy. Why was Stavros doing this? We risked our lives in our jobs. It was who we were as people. We protected. Was that what he thought he was doing—protecting me? I didn't need his protection.

"Well, then, I suppose there's nothing more to it then."

"No, there isn't."

I pushed myself off the chair and stormed out of Stavros's office. My heart was racing, and my adrenaline was through the roof. There was no way I was walking away from this. I reached my desk, but I didn't sit down. I was too amped up. I couldn't sit at my desk. I couldn't read emails. And I couldn't lie down and take orders like this.

Yes, I had been a soldier and yes, I'd always done what I thought was right. Leaving Kennedy at this point wasn't right. Stavros made a bad call, and we weren't in the Army anymore. I didn't have to follow his orders. My duty was to Kennedy.

I glanced at my watch. I was meeting Hirsch and Kennedy in two hours, downtown. I think I had enough time to go on a power walk, shower, and be ready to debrief Kennedy.

The stupid summary report could wait. I had everything I needed to tell Kennedy tucked away in my mind, and Hirsch and I needed to confer to determine if we thought any of the Henleys could be connected to Theodore's murder. I was not going to let anybody stop me from finishing my job. I bent over, ignoring my rib pain, and grabbed my gym bag from underneath my desk. I slung it over my shoulder and hurried out of the office.

27

DETECTIVE HIRSCH

I watched as she jogged across the parking lot. Even with battered ribs and kidneys, she was fast. Despite the attack, she looked good. She usually did. She was tall and lean but a little on the muscular side, with striking features—dark hair and amber-colored eyes. She was beautiful and tough. "How are you able to run with your injuries?" I said with a bewildered grin.

She shrugged. "Sometimes you just gotta get the wiggles out, even if physical pain is involved."

"Tough day?"

She shook her head. "My boss wants me to drop the case. He says I've fulfilled my duties since I've identified the baby in the photo and discovered where Charlotte grew up and the existence of more family members."

"Seriously?"

She huffed. "Yep. Stavros said it was an order."

"Someone attacked you in a parking lot. It's a rich and powerful family who is clearly hiding something major enough to threaten you and your daughter. How can he have you just back down now?"

"I don't know. Ever since I got back, he's had me on a short leash and I can't stand it."

"You were out?"

She seemed to deflate. "I'd rather not talk about it right now."

I could tell there was something she kept hidden away. She didn't want to share it with me, and that was fine. We'd only worked together for a little over a week, but we made a good team. It was easy between the two of us, since she seemed over the urge to want to punch me in the face.

"Thanks for meeting me before our talk with Kennedy. I thought you and I could go over some strategy and a few of the things that I found out."

"Sounds great. There's a little café right here that has great french fries."

She smirked playfully. "It's been a while since I've a had french fry."

"Well, if you don't eat fries, they've got some other healthy options as well. Come on, it's just up here."

I opened the door, and Martina gave me a look like she was a strong woman who didn't need a man to open a door for her. Either way, she walked in ahead of me. I hurried in and stood in line behind her. I listened as she ordered a garden salad with chicken breast.

No wonder she was so fit. She avoided the fries and cheese-burgers, unlike me. Not that I was out of shape. I hit the gym daily and didn't drink too much. Not that I ever really went out. Maybe my soon-to-be ex-wife was right, and I needed to get a life. A life outside of murder investigations.

Somewhat inspired by Martina, I ordered a chicken sand-wich and a side of fries. After finishing up at the cashier, Martina and I chose a small table at the back of the restaurant.

Sitting across from her, I could see she was more tense than she normally was.

"Are you sure you're all right?"

"Well, I just did a quick workout at the gym to blow off some steam, and well, the pain is coming back something fierce."

"Do you need anything? I might have some ibuprofen in the car?"

"No worries. I took some a few minutes ago. Thank you."

"Sure." I then filled her in on my interview with Diego.

She shook her head. "I'm not surprised. I remember him being a scumbag. It doesn't exactly shock me he's in jail for assault and attempted murder. Did you find anything in Donna's financials?"

"Nothing yet. Once Diego's story is verified, or not, I want to go back and find out what else he has to say. He may be a key witness."

Martina raked her fingers through her cropped hair. "It's strange, all of these memories and emotions coming back. Donna, my mother, and now Stavros is coming down on me hard. Life never really takes it easy on you, does it?"

Wasn't that the truth? "Definitely. When I got the transfer to the sheriff's department, it was shortly after—two days to be exact—that my wife filed for divorce. When it rains it pours."

Her eyes appeared a little surprised, even sympathetic, that I had been going through a crap time. Martina seemed like somebody who'd had her fair share of adversity. She gave me a reassuring smile. "Well, my husband died almost two years ago, so I know from experience it's weird starting over without the person you thought you'd be spending the rest of your life with. It's as if life never gets easier. You just get tougher."

"I'm so sorry. I didn't realize you had lost your husband."

She gazed down at her ring finger. "It's never occurred to me to take off my wedding ring, but I have wondered if I should.

I'd rather not have to keep explaining how I'd once had something so great and then lost it in an instant. It's hard to talk about," she mumbled.

Our food arrived, and a member of the waitstaff took away the number that sat on the table before telling us to enjoy our meals.

I'm not sure I'd ever seen Martina so vulnerable. This goes to show that we all have our own stuff we're dealing with. Maybe she and I had similar personalities that drew us to the work we did. Investigations were a great distraction from the rest of our lives.

"How much are you going to tell Kennedy?"

Martina set down her fork. "I think just the facts. I don't want to give her any of my theories. I don't want to spook her. I'm not going to tell her I was attacked, either. I figure since you have twenty-four-hour surveillance on her, there's no reason to alarm her even more. But, I will tell her she has family in Pennsylvania, and that she has an aunt named Amy that I suspect is, in fact, the baby in the photo."

I nodded as I chewed on the crunchy french fries. I swallowed. "Have you heard from Amy since you've been back?"

"No, she was pretty shook by the information I gave her. Afterward, she got up from the table and walked into the back of the restaurant, didn't return. She looked like it was more information than she could handle. I figure I'll give her some time before reaching out again, especially in the event Kennedy wants to get in touch."

"Now that you're not allowed to work on the case, is there something I can do? I will continue searching the background of the Henleys, and we can keep in touch if you'd like. And I'm assuming you still want to work the Bernard case, as well?"

Martina nodded as she chewed on her salad. She swallowed her bite and said, "I'd appreciate it. Regardless of what my boss says, I don't want to leave Kennedy not knowing if her family is dangerous. What if the Henleys see her as a threat and decide to take her out too?"

"My thoughts exactly." I illuminated my phone and saw that we still had twenty minutes until we had to meet Kennedy. "So, what made you decide to become a private investigator?"

Martina wiped her mouth with the paper napkin and set it down on the table. "I kind of fell into it, really. Stavros and my late husband were in the Army together—both special forces. They were pretty tight, and when I left the Army, he offered me a job, so I thought I'd give it a shot. It wasn't necessarily a concerted decision, just an opportunity, and I ran with it." She tipped her chin toward me. "Why did you decide to go into law enforcement?"

I should've known that was coming. I asked her about why she'd become a private investigator, so it made sense she'd turn it around and ask me why I entered law enforcement. "Someone murdered my older brother when I was fifteen. The police never caught his killer. The cops thought it was a random mugging that turned violent when my brother fought back. I think it was during the last update from the detective, when he told us that the case had gone cold, that I decided I would become a homicide detective. I wouldn't be one of these guys who just let cases go cold. I'd solve them and bring closure to the families." I watched hints of skepticism roll across Martina's face. I continued, "What I learned, once I made detective, was that the priority of bringing closure to families was important to me but not to the brass, at least not in my department at the SFPD. They were more concerned with stats and closing cases, even if they weren't right."

"Like the DeSoto case. Was it your choice to close the case? Or was it your LT?"

She was perceptive. "Off the record, I don't think it was a

robbery gone wrong. There wasn't anything taken from the house."

She shook her head in disgust. "So, the case was closed in order to bring up the department closure rates, while Julie DeSoto's husband, a murderer, is out there living his life."

"Yep."

"Is that why you chose to work cold cases, like Donna's disappearance?"

I nodded. "For the loved ones left behind, not knowing is the worst part. Not knowing who to direct your anger at, who to blame, and, worst yet, not having anyone being held accountable for taking away your loved one; it's just not right."

Martina nodded in agreement. This was more conversation I'd had with anybody in I didn't know how long. I wondered if Martina and I would become friends or continue to work together, if her boss allowed it. Martina pushed back her chair. "I'm going to use the restroom before we head out to meet Kennedy. I'll be right back."

I grabbed the last fry before I slid out of my seat. I exited the café and waited outside for Martina. I had little to give Kennedy in her father's case, but I could tell her that there was a promising new lead and then I'd keep my fingers crossed it panned out.

Losing Martina's help on the case would be a huge detriment. I wondered if there was any way I could talk sense into her boss. This case needed her insight. Not that I didn't believe in my own abilities, but she could do things I wasn't allowed to, like hopping on a plane to Pennsylvania and digging through yearbooks. By the time I got approved for that, it could be weeks, if ever. If Martina wasn't allowed to help with the investigations, maybe I could convince the department to hire another private consultant, but probably not. *Damn it.* I needed to make sure Martina stayed on the case.

28

MARTINA

Detective Hirsch and I sat across from Kennedy as she fiddled with a tissue. "How's it going, Kennedy?"

She shrugged. "It's fine, I guess. All the arrangements for my father's memorial are set for Saturday. You're both welcome to attend. I know last time, Martina, you wanted to attend my mother's to be able to question people."

"I'd like to attend." I turned to look at Hirsch.

"We'll be there. We will catch the person who killed your father," Hirsch declared.

She nodded as if she believed him. "So, you said you have a new lead in the case?"

Hirsch said, "Yes." He described what he'd discovered about the veterinarian's office break-in, the possible connection to her father's murder, and how they were waiting for DNA on the suspect.

She appeared surprised and hopeful. Hope was the best thing you could have when you had nothing else. It must be terrible not to have a single lead. That's how Donna's case had been, and it sounded like it was the same for Hirsch's brother's case as well.

I think I was completely wrong about Hirsch. In working together over the last week, I could see he was dedicated, hardworking, and probably a workaholic like myself. He was reserved but seemed to talk freely with me. Maybe he was happy to have someone to talk to, especially someone who understood the job. And someone who understood what it was like when life went downhill.

Kennedy dabbed her eyes. "It's so strange—all of it."

From the corner of my eye, I saw something dart across the room. My heart palpitated, and then I shook my head at my silliness. It was a cat. Zoey had begged me for a pet ever since she could talk. She wanted a snake or rat or kitten or dog, and once, even a lemur. I don't think I even knew what a lemur was when I was seven years old. Kids these days. Oh, jeez, I was starting to sound like my mother. I shook off the thoughts of my mother. I needed to focus.

"Like I promised, we have news on the baby in the photo and about your mother's past."

Kennedy's eyes brightened. She scrunched up the tissue in her fist. "Is it good news? I could really use some good news."

What a loaded question. Maybe it was, maybe it wasn't. Only time would tell. I didn't know how I would continue investigating, with Stavros standing on my shoulders. What would I do if I lost my job at Drakos Security & Investigations? Go out on my own? I could probably afford it with the life insurance, Jarod's pension, and my savings. The idea of not having to take orders certainly sounded great. At heart I was a soldier, but only if it meant I was doing the right thing, and turning my back on the Henleys did not seem right. "The name of the baby in the photoe is Amy Henley. She's your mother's younger sister."

Her mouth dropped open. "I have an aunt? My mother had a sister?"

"Yes." I then continued to explain what else I'd found out

about the Henleys, and the lie that Charlotte had died in a car accident.

Kennedy looked up and out the window, as if trying to comprehend what I was telling her. "Why did my mother tell me they were dead? Why would she do that? Did you find her ex-husband?"

"Your mother has never been married before. Or at least there's no record of it and the people I spoke to, who knew her, they didn't think she'd ever been married either."

Kennedy stared at the floor, and her eyebrows knitted together. "I don't understand. Everything she ever told me was a lie?"

The short of it was, yes. Her mother had lied to Kennedy her entire life. "I'm not sure why your mother told you the stories that she did, but I'm sure she had a good reason. I just don't know what that reason was. We may never know."

"Can you find out? I can pay."

I glanced over at Hirsch and then returned my focus to Kennedy. "It may be difficult to do that."

"You found this other information, and so fast. Rose was right, you're the best. Please find out why. Whatever it takes. I have savings and now all this money from my parents. Please, whatever it costs. I'm begging you." Tears streamed down Kennedy's face.

If Stavros saw Kennedy, would he tell me to walk away? That it wasn't my responsibility to find out why this woman's mother had lied to Kennedy her entire life, and why she kept the Henley family hidden from her? I stared into her eyes. "I'll do my best."

She leaped off the couch and came over to me, arms extended, and we embraced. "Thank you so much, Martina. You've given me so much. Thank you." She let go and looked over at Detective Hirsch. "You too, Detective. It sounds like you're getting close. Hopefully, the DNA will come back with a suspect." Kennedy's eyes welled with tears once again. "It's so much to take in."

I placed my hand on her shoulder. "Kennedy, do you have anyone to talk to? Do you have a therapist or a close friend? This is a lot to process. Losing your parents and finding out about your mother's family."

She shook her head. "I have friends. I don't have a therapist, but I guess it's not a bad idea."

"I can give you a recommendation for a good counselor, who has experience with grief and loss, that I think would really help you."

"I'd like that. Thank you." A meow came from below. I glanced down at Kennedy's orange tabby cat, who was meowing at her feet, wanting her attention.

"It's time for her lunch," she said with a weak smile.

"She's a cat that knows what she wants," I said, trying to lift the mood.

"That she is."

We said our goodbyes and exited Kennedy's apartment. Hirsch turned to me outside on the steps. "You're going to keep investigating the Henleys?"

"How could I say no?"

"I don't know. I wouldn't have been able to say no either." We continued down the steps and headed to my car. Now I had the choice to go behind Stavros's back or confront him, and tell him I was continuing on with the case. Either way, he could fire me if he wanted. It was a risk I was willing to take.

29

MARTINA

I STARED DOWN AT THE PIECE OF PAPER WITH MY MOTHER'S phone number scribbled on it. I'd been right about Rocco's advice. He'd told me I should call her, make amends, and forgive her. I just didn't know if I had the energy. My daughter's life and mine were being threatened, and Stavros was threatening my job. Did I really have to deal with my mother too?

As it was, we had nothing officially on the Henleys or on Alonso Davidson. We didn't even know if that was his actual name or if he was even connected to the Henleys.

What I really needed was to return to Pennsylvania and continue the investigation. If I went out there, I could get the answers that Kennedy needed and potentially stop whoever had been threatening me. These people needed to know that Martina Monroe didn't just lie back and let things happen to her. I was a woman of action, and that was exactly what they were going to get.

My phone buzzed on the kitchen table. I walked over to it and picked it up. "Hirsch, how's it going?"

"I received some bad news about Donna's case."

"What happened? They're not shutting it down, are they?"

"No, but they found a key witness dead in his cell this morning. Diego is dead."

"Suicide?"

"No, he was most certainly killed."

"How did he die?"

"Stabbed. The warden thinks it was gang-related."

Damn it. He was our best lead. "Well, I took the day off work and would like to head out to Stone Island and see if the Bernards will let me go through Donna's things. I'm sure they still have them."

"What do you think you'll find?"

"I'm not sure, but I have to find something." It still surprised me that Donna had kept secrets from me. We had been so close for so long.

"I'm not sure I'll be able to go out there today, but call me if you find anything, okay?"

"Will do. Did you get anything back on the Henleys yet?"

"Not yet. So far they're looking squeaky clean, which is pretty strange for a political family."

"Tell me about it. You know anybody in Pennsylvania law enforcement?"

"I have a friend in the FBI. I could ask him for a favor."

"That would be great."

"I'll check into it. Let me know if you find anything at the Bernards' place. I'll be at the station."

"Okay. I'll talk to you later." I hung up the phone and looked at the time on the screen. I had five hours before Zoey would get out of school. That should give me enough time to make it out to Stone Island, search Donna's room, and get back in time. Zoey had been ecstatic when I told her I'd take the day off and would pick her up at school, and we could have dinner together. Now, I had better make good on that promise.

I pulled into the driveway of the Bernards' house, and an

eerie feeling washed over me. I didn't know if I'd ever shake this feeling of being transported back in time to my wild teenage days, hanging out during the long summer nights with my best friend. I shook it off and continued up the steps toward the front door of the Bernard residence.

I glanced to the left at the Gilmore house. It was dark, with no signs of life. I wondered what Kennedy would do with it when all was said and done. Would she move back to her home-town or sell it or keep it as a vacation rental? I'm not sure I'd be able to sleep in a house where my loved one had been murdered. I had a feeling Kennedy wouldn't either. I knocked on the door. The door creaked open, and Sandy greeted me with a smile. "Always good to see you, dear."

"You too, Sandy."

"Please come in."

I stepped inside and felt that there were ghosts everywhere. I stared at the framed photograph of Donna that hung on the wall. Her bright smile, blond hair, and blue eyes. She was young, beautiful, spirited, and strong but also had secrets. Secrets she didn't share with her best friend. I'd be lying if I said it didn't hurt that she had chosen not to confide in me that she had a side thing going on.

I had thought we'd shared every dream and every whim that crossed our minds. I wondered if this was how Kennedy felt knowing that her mother had lied to her all those years. She'd said they were close and didn't hide things from one another.

It was like I hadn't known her at all. I would have liked to have known her, all of her, even her secrets, even if she was doing something that wasn't right.

"What are you looking for today?"

"Do you remember Diego Tarantino?"

Sandy rolled her eyes. "Don't remind me."

"He was found murdered in his jail cell today, but before he died, Detective Hirsch had gone out and talked to him. He said that Donna had been working for someone, somebody he saw her talking to. He told us they were working on something together and promised he would tell us more after his first payment, but by the time Detective Hirsch followed up, he'd been killed."

Sandy's face went pale. "You think the person who took Donna, killed Diego?"

It had crossed my mind but the thought slipped out shortly after what Hirsch later explained to me. "The warden thinks that whoever killed Diego is from a rival gang or that he'd angered another prisoner. Diego wasn't a pleasant person and could have made the wrong person mad."

Sandy nodded. "Donna's room is exactly how she left it. I didn't change anything, in case she ever came back."

I placed my hand on her shoulder. "I hope she comes back too."

Sandy didn't have to show me where Donna's room was. I was quite familiar. I walked down the hall and stepped into Donna's room for the first time since she'd gone missing. My chest tightened, and I had to fight to not shed any tears. I was there to find out what happened to her, not to mourn. I could do that later. I had a job to do.

I walked over to her closet and thumbed through her clothes. Each one flashed me back to a memory of when she wore it last. I glanced up, looking for any memory or keepsake boxes. Then it hit me. I swiveled around and rushed over to her bookshelf and knelt down. I scanned past the Nancy Drew novels before staring it straight in its black plastic eyes—a pink and purple teddy bear Donna had since she was a baby.

It brought me back to a memory of the two of us sitting on the floor. Giggling, she'd said, "I got something."

"What did you get?"

"Let me show you." And then she pulled down the teddy bear and turned it over, splitting the seam and pulling out a baggie of marijuana. Her eyes had lit up like stars in the sky. "Tonight, we get high," she'd said in a singsong voice. We'd both chuckled, grabbed the pot, and ran out of the house to meet our boyfriends.

I grabbed the teddy bear and turned it upside down, digging into the torn seam. I pulled out a few hundred-dollar bills and a slip of paper with a message in blue ink.

Beth's Pond.
Every fourth Saturday.
Midnight.

Beth's Pond? I wanted to search the rest of the room for additional clues, but I had an immediate need to be at Beth's Pond. I rushed out of her room. Sandy was in the kitchen mixing something in a pot on the stove. "Is there something wrong?"

"No, I found something. I'll be back." I rushed out of the house, ran down the steps, lightly gripping the rail as I descended. I didn't need to tumble down a flight of stairs.

I hopped into my car, drove two blocks down, and pulled to the side of the road, parking near the path to Beth's Pond. I hurried out to the entrance of the path. It was lined with tall grasses and weeds. I surveyed the area and didn't see a soul. I returned to my vehicle, pulled my weapon from the glove box, and secured it in its holster, then grabbed a flashlight and stuck it in my jacket pocket.

I stepped out of the car, shut the door behind me, and looked around. Donna and I hadn't gone to Beth's Pond since we were kids. There was no reason. There weren't any boys or booze.

I continued down the path, swatting away the foliage for several minutes until I reached the clearing. The term pond was being generous. It was more like a large puddle. I walked around the pond and saw nothing unusual. I pushed back grasses, looking for clues—anything that would tell me what had happened to Donna.

After thirty minutes of scouring the surrounding area, I was deflated. I was frustrated and angry. I wanted to scream. It wasn't fair that Donna was gone. It wasn't fair that I had to stop working on the Henley case. It wasn't fair that Kennedy lost her parents. It wasn't fair that Jared was gone. Why couldn't this world be more fair? Why did I have the alcoholic gene? Why had my parents decided to reproduce and give that to me? Why?

I took a deep breath, and glanced up at the sky. It was dark and gray, with menacing clouds. I felt the first drops of mist, then the drizzle and then raindrops. Of course. Now I was going to be soaked. I shook my head. There I stood at Beth's Pond, alone and wet. Tired. Angry. Sad. I hadn't found Donna, but that didn't mean that I'd ever stop searching.

Head down, I continued around the pond and back to the path that would lead me back to where I'd parked my car. My body went rigid, as if a force was holding me in place. My attention was drawn to a sparkle on the ground. My heart sped up, and I knelt down to the ground and stared at the shiny object. I brushed off the remaining mud the rain hadn't washed off. I lifted it up, and my mouth dropped open. The sparkling diamond and pear-shaped emerald earring sent chills down my spine. It was Donna's earring.

30

DETECTIVE HIRSCH

I thanked Webb and hung up the phone. The DNA testing on the blood sample from the veterinary office break-in still wasn't back yet. I knew I didn't have to call. Most likely, Webb would let me know right away once the test results came in, but I'd thought maybe he was out of the office. He wasn't.

I switched gears and reviewed the names of family and friends of Theodore Gilmore that were expected at the memorial the next day. The memorial would bring out everyone who had cared for him—and potentially his killer too. My cell phone buzzed. "Hi, Martina, what's up?"

She said, "I found something," and then explained what she'd found.

"How do you know it's Donna's earring?" I asked.

"Her parents gave her the earrings for a high school graduation gift. I've got a feeling, Hirsch. I feel like she's here."

"Did you find anything else other than the earring?"

"No, but it's raining, and it's getting muddy. I don't have any tools to dig, and I'm guessing you don't want me to mess up any forensic evidence, right?"

"You're right. Let me see what I can put together. I can't

guarantee I can get CSI out there today, but let me talk to my sergeant to see if we can get a team together and maybe some cadaver dogs. It might have to wait until next week."

"Next week? If the killer comes back, he could try to move her body."

"You seem awfully sure that her body's there."

"It fits. The paper said that she met here every fourth Saturday at midnight. I'm telling you, Hirsch, she has to be here."

"Let me see what I can do."

I lifted myself off the desk and walked back to my sergeant's office. If I kept this up, soon I'd be known as the guy who was always going to the sergeant's office, asking for favors. "Sarge."

"Hey, Hirsch, what's up?"

I explained to him what Martina had found at Beth's Pond and what she was requesting.

Sarge leaned back and scratched his head. "All the evidence we have is a slip of paper and an earring?"

"It's the first piece of physical evidence since her disappearance."

He let out a loud breath and shook his head back and forth. "I hope they find her because if they don't—you'll have a lot of answering to do." He eyed me. "Put in the request and let's get a team out there today."

"Thank you." I didn't wait to get back to my desk before calling Martina and letting her know. "Are you still at the site?"

"I am, but I have to pick up my daughter at three. I don't have a lot of time to wait."

"I'll head out now. Can you wait until I get there, so I'll know exactly where to direct the team?"

"Will do. Thanks, Hirsch."

I hung up the phone and grabbed my keys before rushing out of the station.

Several hours later, I stood under the tent while the rain pattered, sounding like someone was shooting pellets at us. The forensic team had been working diligently to search for clues. It was a slow, agonizing process. We didn't have a lot to go on, but I hadn't seen Martina be wrong yet. If she thought it was worth digging, it was worth digging.

Brown, the forensic lead, stood up and waved his hand. I hurried over to the adjacent tent with my boots getting sucked into the mud, slowing me down. As I approached, Brown pointed down at the ground. My heart nearly beat out of my chest.

It was a bone.

I glanced at Brown. "Is it human?"

"We won't know for sure until we excavate the entire area or test it, but it looks like a phalange to me."

"Nice work."

Brown's team continued to work. As I stood there discussing the case with Brown, I asked, "How long will it take to dig up?"

"Assuming the complete skeleton is here, it could be a while. We don't want to destroy any evidence or damage the bones. Maybe we'll get lucky and it will be intact. If so, it may be just a few more hours. If you have to go, it's okay. We've got this."

"No, I'm not going anywhere. I was just curious."

I stood back in silence as Brown went back to work, kneeling down in the mud, carefully scratching back the dirt and brushing it off the bone. Within minutes he exposed an entire skeleton of a human hand. *Holy crap*, Martina had been right.

We'd have to check dental records, but considering she found Donna's earring there, what was the likelihood it wasn't Donna?

I rushed over to the other tent and pulled out my phone. It was late, but I didn't think Martina would mind. "Hey, Martina. Sorry, it's late."

"No, it's fine, I'm up. What did you find?"

Adrenaline pumping, I said, "I think we found her."

"What exactly did you find?"

I explained, and then there was silence on the other end.

"Are you all right, Martina?"

"Yes, I will be. I knew this was the most likely outcome, but I guess part of me still hoped that she would come back, you know? Any idea how long before you can confirm identity?"

"I'm guessing she had dental records?"

"She had braces when we were teenagers, so yes."

"Well then, it may only be a day or two."

"Thank you for calling, Hirsch. Have you notified the family?"

"I plan to call over there now, and then head over to their house, since I'm already here." I paused. "Or would you prefer I wait until tomorrow when you and I can go there together, before Theodore Gilmore's memorial?"

"I don't want to be the reason they have to wait another minute," she said with a shaking voice.

"All right, Martina. See tomorrow."

"Thank you, Hirsch."

I shook my head. I'ds been excited to let Martina know what we found, but in my rush, I'd lost sight of the fact that it was Martina's best friend and that she was a loved one. I probably should have handled that more carefully.

I glanced up at Brown. "I'm going to notify the family that we found something. They only live a couple blocks down the road. I'll be back."

I knocked on the door. Mr. Bernard stood with a long face. His wife Sandy stood beside him, holding his hand. It was as if they were bracing for the worst. "Mr. and Mrs. Bernard."

Mrs. Bernard waved me in. "Please, come in, Detective Hirsch. It's a mess out there."

They didn't let go of one another. It was a terrible thing that they were waiting for, but I could tell in their eyes they knew what was coming. "Earlier today, Martina found a note in your daughter's bedroom with the location, Beth's Pond. I'm not sure if you're familiar with the place?"

"Beth's Pond? Is that the place they would go when they were little?" Sandy asked her husband.

"Yes, I think they named it after that little girl that moved away, remember?"

"Oh, yeah. I remember now."

"We found something." I lifted the evidence bag that contained the earring Martina had found and handed it to Mrs. Bernard.

Mr. Bernard lowered his head, and Mrs. Bernard had tears streaming down her face. "It was Donna's. We gave them to her for her graduation," she said through tears.

"It's not all we found." Their eyes were both on me. "We'll need to confirm identity, but we've unearthed a skeleton. They should be able to finish the excavation in a few hours. We would like to compare the remains against dental records for Donna. If you could give me the name of her dentist, we can speed up the process." Neither of the Bernards moved a muscle. It was as if they were frozen in time.

Mr. Bernard said, "So it may not be her?"

"We won't know for sure until we compare the records." Without a word, Mrs. Bernard rushed to the kitchen, opened a drawer and pulled something out before hurrying back over to me. She handed me a refrigerator magnet with the dentist's information on it. "That was her dentist. He's retired, but the office is still there. They should have her records, right?"

"Most likely, yes."

I continued to answer their questions, and it was clear all their fears seemed to be coming true. It brought me back to the day that the police officer notified my mom, dad, and me that someone had killed my brother. It was a feeling that I wouldn't wish upon anyone, not even my worst enemy.

I waved and headed back to Beth's Pond. I hurried toward Brown. "Anything new?"

He turned up to look at me. "It's female, you can tell by the pelvis. Late teens, early twenties."

If it wasn't Donna, I'd have another case to solve.

31

MARTINA

I HUGGED ZOEY AND SAID GOODBYE TO CLAIRE BEFORE walking out to the driveway. What a week. I was practically on pins and needles, waiting for the call that confirmed that the remains at Beth's Pond belonged to Donna. I had few doubts, but was aware that being "nearly sure" and being told "it is" was a different thing all together. After finding her earring, I realized I had kept a sliver of hope we'd find her alive. That sliver had become a speck of dust.

At least I hadn't received any additional threats on my life or Zoey's in a few days. Hopefully, the threats were only intended to scare me, and then that would be the end of it. But my instincts had me on high alert.

It would be interesting to see who showed up at Theodore Gilmore's memorial. Would the so-called family friend, Alonso, return? Or was the killer somebody entirely different? An old acquaintance? A former coworker? A secret lover's spouse out for revenge? My money was on the Henley connection, but even so, it still didn't make sense. What was the motive? Theodore didn't tell us anything salacious, or anything that seemed like it was worth killing over. The only true thing he could disclose to us about Charlotte's past was the name of her hometown in Pennsylvania. Surely that wasn't enough to kill someone over, was it?

I opened the car door, slipped off my blazer, and laid it on the back seat before sliding into the driver's seat. I didn't like to expose the weapon on my hip, or the one on my ankle, but it was going to be a long drive, and I didn't want to wrinkle my coat.

I buckled up and backed out of my driveway. Turning out of my neighborhood and toward the highway to start the journey to Stone Island for Theodore Gilmore's memorial, I soon found my thoughts drifting back to Donna. I could kick myself for not having looked for her earlier. I'd been so hell-bent on turning my back on Stone Island and the life I had before I joined the Army, that although Donna had stayed in my heart all of these years, I couldn't bring myself to return and find out what really happened to her. I guess we all have a bit of coward in us.

I still hadn't returned my mother's phone call. What would I say? "Hi, Mom, want to be AA buddies?" I shook my head. Ridiculous. Not only did I have Donna and my mother on my mind, but I also had to consider my job with Stavros. I had been their top investigator, but was being treated like a child. I didn't like it. I needed to confront Stavros. He couldn't use the excuse that a situation was too dangerous for me to be involved in. I could take care of myself. I'd proven that time and time again. Did he treat the male investigators with kid gloves? It was sexist, and it was wrong.

I made a right at the light and continued on toward the highway. I glanced at my dashboard to see how much fuel I had in the tank. I supposed I could stop and get gas. It was still quite a drive out to Stone Island, and the last thing I needed was to run out of gas.

I checked my mirrors and continued down the road. I was about to make a left, re-checking my mirrors, when I spotted the same silver Ford Escort three cars back. I made the left-hand turn and then another left. My heart raced as the silver Ford remained on my tail. If it was the person who was threatening Zoey and me, I knew one way to stop them.

My stalker was about to learn that he couldn't bully me or make me step aside. I wasn't easy to get rid of. I took another left —sure enough, it followed me. I pulled into a gas station, stopping at the first pump. The car didn't follow me into the gas station; instead, it whizzed past. In a blur, I saw that the driver wore a black baseball cap, sunglasses, and black gloves that gripped the steering wheel. It sped down the busy road until it was out of my sight.

The sun was out, but there was still a chill in the air. The outfit wasn't completely out of character for the season, but something told me this person was following me for a reason, not to just keep eyes on me. I grabbed my blazer from the back seat and stepped out of my vehicle, putting it on quickly in order to conceal my weapon. People got nervous when they saw someone with a gun strapped to their hip.

I grabbed my wallet and pulled out my credit card. I was there, I might as well fill up. I shut my door and walked over to the pump. After I slipped my credit card into the card reader, I heard the light patter of footsteps rushing toward me.

Before I could turn around, a powerful object struck me, knocking me to the ground. Heavy boots connected with my sore ribs, and I yelled out in pain. Before he could get in another kick, I grabbed his foot and twisted, knocking him on his butt. Adrenaline flowing, I rolled over and used the gas pump as a crutch to get to my feet. I stood and our eyes locked.

A moment later, I kneed him in the groin before delivering a roundhouse to his chest. He fell to the ground, clutching his privates. I kicked him in the ribs before retrieving my gun from the holster. While he was still on the ground, I launched on top of him, straddling him. I aimed the gun at his face and glared at him. "Don't move."

The man who had once introduced himself as Alonso Davidson, stopped squirming. It was a common response when one had a gun in their face. "Who are you?"

He smirked. "I want a lawyer."

"I'm not a cop. You don't get a phone call. And a lawyer will not help you right now." I raised my voice, as my heartbeat thumped in my ears. "I asked who are you?"

He arched his head forward. "Lady, I think there has been a misunderstanding."

I steadied my grip on my weapon. "I will shoot you."

"Will you, little lady?"

I really didn't like this guy. But I also didn't want to splatter his brains out there in public view or anywhere, really. I preferred for the bad guys to rot in prison—a far worse sentence than an instantaneous death.

Despite what you saw in movies, it was a little difficult to pull out your cell phone and call the police while you're straddling a bad guy with a gun pointed at his face. I needed both hands for that, and I needed my concentration. Best I could do was hope that someone would call the police, and fast. After all, there was a lady holding a gun on a man at a gas station in broad daylight.

"I'll ask you again. Who are you and why are you following me? Why are you trying to kill me?"

"My name is Alonso Davidson We've met before. There's no need for this. We can sort this out. Why don't you put the gun away, and we can talk about it."

He was bold. I'd give him that. Attacking me on a busy street in the middle of the day and maintaining his innocence? "Do you really think that whoever sent you is going to help you after they throw you in jail?" I stared into his deep-brown eyes. I thought I saw a bit of hesitation. I'd struck a nerve. "I assume it's the Henleys who have sent you. Do you really think they're going to muddy their hands with you?"

"Lady, you don't know what you're talking about."

"You will go to jail."

"I'm superb at keeping quiet."

"That should serve you well while you're spending the rest of your life in prison."

"We'll see about that." He started to squirm, and I pressed the gun to his forehead. "I wouldn't do that if I were you. I'd be a good little boy and wait for the police to get here so that you don't find yourself with your brains all over the concrete."

I heard sirens, and a trickle of relief ran down me. My arms were cramping, and I did not like sitting out in public with a gun pressed to a man's face. I wanted him to talk and tell me why he'd chased me across the country to take me out. "Why didn't you try to take me out while I was in Pennsylvania?"

Alonso continued practicing his skill of being quiet. I, on the other hand, had no plans to do that. "I know you're working for the Henleys, and the cops will know it too. You won't get away with any of it." I stayed steadfast, with the muzzle of the gun pressed to his forehead, despite the sound of uniformed officers running toward me. "Put the weapon down," they yelled.

I tossed the weapon across the pavement and slowly stood up with my hands in the air. I knew better than to get shot over this guy. They rushed toward me and handcuffed my hands behind my back. I looked at the officer in the eyes. "He attacked me. They should have it on surveillance video."

"That may be so, ma'am, but I need you to come with me." They hauled me off to the back of the police car and sat me down. "Ma'am, what's your name?"

"Martina Monroe."

"Do you have any other weapons on you?"

"Ankle."

Two officers stood with fists on hips as the one in charge lifted my pant leg and removed the weapon from my ankle. He stood back up. "You're awfully armed for a civilian?"

"Sir, I'm a private investigator. My life and my family have been threatened. I have a license to carry. You can look it up. That man who attacked me is a potential suspect in a previous attack. He had been following me, so I pulled over. He attacked me from behind and I fought back."

"How did he attack you?"

"He hit me with something on the back of my head." Seated and out of imminent danger, my skull was throbbing and nausea was starting to hit me. I leaned back in the cruiser and took some calming breaths. *Darn it, that jerk probably gave me a concussion.*

Before responding, the officer in charge called out to another officer. "Call an ambulance. He hit her in the head, and the other guy may need attention as well."

He refocused his eyes on me. "Any idea why he attacked you?"

I nodded slowly. "Yes, I'm working a case, and I'm pretty sure he's the same guy who attacked me before." I explained the connection to Theodore Gilmore's murder investigation, the Henleys, and my attack in Pennsylvania. He nodded at the officers and said, "Let me go see if I can get a hold of Detective Hirsch and verify your information. Sit tight." I watched as he hurried off. *Darn it. Because of this stupid guy, I was going to miss the memorial.*

A few minutes later, the officer in charge returned. Without a word, he placed his phone up to my ear. "Martina, are you all right?"

Relief flooded me. "Hirsch, it's good to hear your voice." And it was. It was surprising how much so.

"McKenna says you had a blow to the head and you may be concussed. I'll meet you at the hospital."

"You'll miss the memorial. I think you should go to the memorial and question the attendees. There is a possibility Alonso, or whatever his name is, may not be the killer." Hirsch was quiet. "You can meet me after. Kennedy will need you," I insisted.

"Okay, I'll come by the hospital after I finish questioning the guests and am sure Kennedy is safe."

"See you then."

McKenna, I presumed, took his phone back. "How are you feeling?"

With heavy eyelids I said, "I've been better."

"Try to stay awake. The ambulance just got here. We'll get you taken care of. Turn around so I can remove the cuffs."

I nodded and then let sleep take me.

32

DETECTIVE HIRSCH

I stepped into Martina's hospital room and paused. She was in the far bed, next to the window, and had two visitors. A young female with big blue eyes and a sparkly shirt stood next to a younger woman with blond hair and a worried look on her face. My guess, being a detective and all, was that it was Martina's daughter, Zoey, and her nanny, Claire. I inhaled the disinfectant-filled air in the hospital room and continued forward slowly to make myself known. I lifted a hand to say hello. "I hope I'm not intruding. I can come back."

All eyes were fixed on me. The younger women clearly didn't know who I was.

The blond woman said, "No, it's fine, we were just about to go down to the cafeteria to get a snack."

"But before you go, this is Detective Hirsch. Detective Hirsch, this is my daughter, Zoey, and her nanny, Claire."

Zoey hurried over to me, extending a tiny hand to shake. I shook her hand and said, "It's very nice to meet you, Zoey."

"Nice to meet you, too, Detective Hirsch. Are you a detective like in the movies?"

"Yes, kind of."

"That's so cool," she said with a gleam in her eyes. Claire opted for a wave, and a brief, "hello, how are you," before she ushered Zoey out of the room and left.

Once we were alone, I approached Martina's bedside. Her head was bandaged in gauze, but her face was mostly untouched. "How are you feeling?"

Martina shrugged. "I have a wicked headache. I'm pretty tired and feeling banged up. The jerk kicked me in the ribs— same place he got me before."

"What does the doctor say?"

"It's just your run-of-the-mill concussion. I'll be fine."

"When will they let you out of here?"

"They want to keep me overnight, but I'm trying to nego- tiate an earlier release."

"Maybe you should stay, just in case."

"Well, the doctor should be back in an hour. We'll see what she says."

There was an awkward pause between the two of us. I could tell by the look in her eyes that she was happy to see me. Maybe we were becoming friends. Before I could say anything, she started up again. "How was the memorial? Did you find out anything that would indicate somebody other than this Alonso character murdered Theodore Gilmore?"

I adjusted my stance, preparing to give her the full report. "I couldn't find anything out of the ordinary. From what I could tell, he'd never had any extramarital affairs. There were no dirty business deals gone wrong, and the records show a healthy financial status. No obvious reasons that anybody would want to kill him, other than his wife's murky past. I still don't know what the motive could be."

"Have you found anything about who this Alonso person really is?"

"I talked to the arresting officer. Apparently, his first name is

Alonso, but he goes by Lonnie, last name, Ricci. He hasn't been in the system for quite some time, but he did some petty stuff in his late teens and early twenties. After that, he seemed to clean up his act."

"Is his DNA in the system?"

"Not yet. There's a warrant for it now. He'll have to give us a swab."

"Good. I had a gun to his head, and he still wouldn't give anything up about the Henleys." She adjusted her bed to prop herself up. "Any updates on the remains found at Beth's Pond?"

"Not yet, but it's the weekend. I'm hoping to get dental records on Monday, then the ME can do a comparison."

Martina deflated into her hospital bed.

"I'm sorry, this isn't looking like it will have a happy ending."

"I knew this was the most probable outcome. But..." Martina didn't finish her thought.

I finished it for her. "But there was always a little hope that we would find her alive."

"Exactly," Martina said before she asked, "Anything new on the Henleys?"

"No, but I called my buddy at the FBI, who is working in Pennsylvania. He hasn't gotten back to me yet, which isn't really like him. He's usually pretty responsive. I'll follow up."

I leaned back against the window sill and contemplated Martina's situation. Her life was full.

"Is your life always like this?"

Martina cracked a smile. "Not all the time. You?"

"It's not usually so complicated."

"I'd say after all this is over, I'll owe you a beer."

Martina's smile faded. "Not a beer. Maybe a coffee?"

"Not a drinker?"

She stiffened. "Actually, I'm an alcoholic. A recovering alcoholic. I'm nine months sober. Nine months ago I got into a car accident after drinking too much, and I almost died and almost lost my daughter and my job."

The puzzle pieces were falling into place. Now it made sense why her boss was on her case about every little thing. "You have a sponsor?"

"Yep, Rocco. I don't know what I would do without him."

"It's pretty brave. From what I've heard, it's not easy to get sober."

She shrugged. "It's difficult, but I have a lot to fight for."

I looked straight ahead at an unknown visitor approaching. There was something familiar about her, but I didn't think we'd ever met. She was tall and husky, with a lot of lines on her face. "Can I help you?"

"I'm just here to see my daughter." I glanced over at Martina, who seemed surprised by the visit.

"Mom, what are you doing here?"

"I called the house, and Zoey told me you were in the hospital. I wanted to see you, Martina."

Martina eyed me, and something told me she wasn't happy to see her mother. My phone buzzed inside my blazer, and I pulled it out. I glanced back up at Martina. "I gotta take this." She waved me on, and I hurried out of the hospital room. "Hirsch."

"Hey, man, sorry it's taken me so long to get back to you. It's been crazy with crime around here."

"No worries. What did you find?"

"Well, it's interesting that you called. I'm curious, why are you looking into the Henleys?"

"Did you find something?"

"I ran it up the chain and have been told I can't discuss any potential investigations over the phone. Tell me, what's the case you're working, and how does it connect to Frank Henley?"

I glanced around the hall. And mouthed a *yes*. He had to have something. "It's a doozy." I explained to Callahan the web of connections between Alonso and the Henleys and Theodore Gilmore.

"If you can make it here to Pennsylvania, we could meet, and a friend of mine might be able to help you with some background. I'll give you his number. Just give me a couple hours to let him know you'll be calling."

Callahan was too evasive to have come up empty-handed. "Thanks, man, I totally owe you one."

"I'll hold you to that."

I stepped back toward Martina's hospital room. She seemed to be having a somewhat-heated conversation with her mother. I figured I'd give them a moment or two.

My stomach growled, and I gave them some space by heading to the caféteria. I made my way down the hall toward the elevator. After it dinged and the doors opened, I stepped into the elevator with a couple of nurses wearing blue scrubs and a doctor wearing a white coat. I nodded and pressed the floor to the caféteria.

Arriving on the first floor, I spotted Zoey and Claire right away. Zoey was munching on french fries. I wondered how Martina would feel about that. Zoey spotted me, and ran toward me. "Hi, Detective. Can I ask you some questions?"

"Sure, I was just going to grab a bite to eat."

"I highly recommend the fries. They're great," she said emphatically.

I'd been working with Martina for nearly two weeks. When she had spoken of Zoey, I had pictured a miniature version of Martina, but what stood before me was a ball of sunshine wrapped in glitter. Not exactly Martina's clone. For that, the girl would need to be dressed in head-to-toe black and wearing sensible shoes. "What questions do you have?"

"Well, first of all, I'd like to know more about the case. Mommy hasn't told me a whole bunch, but I know that it's something big."

I glanced over at Claire, who shrugged, as if to explain—this is Zoey. "Well, your mom's been helping me to investigate some crimes that a bad person did."

"Are you helping find the baby in the picture?"

"Sort of. That is mostly your mom's investigation."

"Do you have any kids?"

"I don't."

"Any pets? Like a snake or a rat."

"Nope." *Never.*

"Not even a goldfish?"

"Not even a goldfish."

Zoey frowned. "You must be really lonely."

They say children are brutally honest. Zoey Monroe was no different. "I work a lot."

"Oh, one of those."

Zoey was something else. Claire tried to wave the girl over. "Zoey, why don't you let the detective get something to eat, and you come over here and finish your snack."

"Okay. See you later, Detective," she said with a smile, before running back over to the table to join her nanny.

I couldn't imagine coming home from a day like I'd had and a day like Martina had had, to all the energy of a seven-year-old girl. I didn't know how Martina did it.

33

MARTINA

"WHAT ARE YOU DOING HERE?" I HADN'T MEANT FOR IT TO come out as harsh as it sounded, but it was what it was. My mother walked around to the other side of my bed where Hirsch had been standing. She folded her arms across her chest. "Look, I know I wasn't an excellent mother, Martina. I was a lousy drunk, and so was your dad. I don't blame you for being gone all these years. I don't. But I'm clean now. I've been sober, one year. I just got my chip." She fished the disc out of her pocket and held it up with a proud smile.

It was becoming increasingly more difficult to be righteous when Betty had been sober longer than I had. I supposed, though, she'd done a lot more damage than I had, or was I just trying to make myself feel better?

I swallowed my pride. "Congratulations. I know that's not an easy thing to do," I said as I tried on my newfound humility. It fit okay. There were worse things.

Her amber eyes twinkled. "Thank you. My sponsor finally convinced me to reach out to you. I was scared, ashamed, and frankly, I was weak. I know I did you wrong, for so long. I see that now. It's all clear and fuzzy at the same time. It's like I know it was bad, but I can't always recall the details."

The haziness was likely due to the booze; I would know. "I get it."

"I'm not sure if you can forgive me, and I guess I wouldn't blame you if you didn't." She looked down at the tile floor, took a breath, and then refocused her watery gaze on me. "I came here because I was afraid it might be my last chance to say what I need to say. You seem to have a dangerous job, and from what I've heard, trouble seems to find you."

I smirked. "Or you came here because you knew I couldn't run away."

She shrugged. "I suppose that might be true too." She unfolded her arms and stepped closer to my bed. "Martina, I came here to apologize and make amends. I should've been a better mother. I should've protected you and taken care of you and your brothers. I have a job now, and I volunteer at the homeless shelter. I'm doing my best to make my life right, after it had been wrong for so long." Tears rolled down her cheeks.

It was strange to see my mother breaking down. She was never one to be anything but angry or passed out. There was something different about her. She seemed to be stronger and maybe even stood taller, too. I didn't need to be a jerk and wreck that. "I forgive you."

Betty choked out a, "Thank you, Martina." She buried her face into her hands and sobbed briefly before she glanced down at her purse, seemingly searching for something inside. She pulled out of a small package of tissues and appeared to calm herself, and then wiped her tears.

"I appreciate that, Martina. It's been a hard year, but I feel good."

Darn it. This is the part where Rocco and God would advise me to have a little grace. "I understand. I'm actually in AA myself."

Betty's face softened. "I thought Zoey had said that. Something like—like mother, like daughter. I wasn't sure if it meant you were in the program too. I guess I'm happy to hear you're sober, yet sad to hear that you got the gene. How long have you been sober?"

"Nine—going on ten months," I said, with as much pride as I could muster—which wasn't much.

"Good for you. I know how hard it can be. What was your bottom?"

"Car accident, I was drunk, and I almost lost everything."

"That's usually how it works." Betty relaxed. "How do you like your sponsor?"

I nodded. "He's perfect, and I feel like I owe him everything. He's tough when I need it, but also compassionate when I need that too."

"That's great," Betty continued. "Now that I hit my one year, I decided I was ready to be a sponsor."

"That's amazing. I'm proud of you." I never thought my mother and I would have anything in common other than our eye color. This life was turning out to be pretty strange.

"It's been a few years since we've seen each other. Zoey must be what, eight now?"

"She'll be eight next month."

Betty nodded. "I've missed so much."

"She's talked about you practically non-stop since you called. She's actually down in the cafeteria right now." As I finished the last syllable, I heard small footsteps running toward the room, followed by heavier footsteps. "Mommy, Mommy, guess what? I talked to Detective Hirsch, and I told him he should try the french fries, and he took my advice and got the french fries. I like him." She nodded and smiled. But before I could say a word, Zoey froze in her tracks as she studied my mother. She then glanced over at me with questioning eyes.

I supposed it was as good a time as any to reintroduce her to her grandmother. "Zoey, honey, this is Grandma Betty. Do you remember her?"

Zoey tilted her head. "Your face looks familiar, but maybe it's because I saw a picture recently."

My mother covered her mouth with her hand and then moved toward Zoey. "Zoey, it's so good to see you. Aren't you a vision? I sure do like your shirt. I love sparkles too."

Zoey bit her lower lip and glanced up at me. It wasn't like her to be shy. Was she looking for my approval? "Zoey, isn't that something? You and Grandma Betty both love sparkles. You should tell her about your collection."

Zoey's eyes lit up, and she returned her focus to my mother. "I have more than twenty tubes of glitter! All different colors! Claire and I, that's my nanny. We do art projects almost every day. Maybe you can do a project with us? What's your favorite color of glitter?"

Betty smiled wide. "I like pink."

Zoey's eyes got huge. "Me too! I'm glad you're here, Grandma Betty. Mom, are you glad that Grandma Betty is here?"

I gazed over at my mother, whom I hadn't seen in almost six years. The woman I never wanted to be like. Yet there she was, clean and sober, making amends. Maybe my brain wasn't the only thing that needed healing. "Yes, I'm glad Grandma Betty is here too."

Claire stepped forward and waved to my mother. "Hi, I'm Claire, the nanny."

"Nice to meet you, Claire."

"Martina, I hate to do this, but I have a major study session tonight, with a lab on Monday. I need to go soon. Do you know if you'll be discharged tonight?"

"The doctor will be back soon to let me know if I can go home tonight."

My mother jumped in, "With a concussion? I don't think they'll let you go home tonight."

I watched Claire's desperation. She'd sacrificed so much for me and my family. I couldn't let her miss out on studying for her exams. She was so close to becoming a nurse and fulfilling her dream. "Don't worry, Claire, we'll figure something out. I don't want you to miss your study session. Don't worry about it."

"Are you sure? I could try to study back at your house with Zoey... If you need me to?"

My mother shook her head back and forth. "Nonsense. Martina, I can watch Zoey, if you're okay with that."

Did I trust my mother? Did I trust a woman I hadn't seen in six years with the love of my life—my daughter?

I looked at Zoey, her eyes wide and hopeful. I knew she wanted to know her grandmother. "I suppose if I can't get out of here tonight, that would be okay. If it's not an imposition."

"Nonsense."

I looked over at Claire. "When do you need to go?"

Claire gritted her teeth. "Fifteen minutes."

My mother stepped toward Claire. "Why don't you go. I can take care of Zoey and Martina."

My heart raced, and I wondered if I was making the right decision. I needed to make sure the doctor let me out tonight. "Claire, it's fine. Please go. We've got it covered."

Zoey turned to my mother and explained, "Claire is going to become a nurse. She's really close to graduating and becoming the best nurse ever."

Claire smiled. "If you guys are really okay with it, I'm going to go. I'm studying with some classmates, but if there's an emergency, please call me, Martina."

"Thank you, Claire."

My phone vibrated on the table.

Zoey ran over to the table. "I'll get it for you." She grabbed it and handed it over with a grin on her face.

"Thank you." I looked at the screen. I didn't recognize the number, but I recognized that the area code was from Pennsylvania.

"Hello, is this Martina Monroe?"

"Yes."

"This is Amy Driscoll, maiden name Amy Henley. Do you have some time to talk?"

"Give me just one second." I put the phone down. I waved Zoey over and whispered, "I need to take this call. It's about the case with the baby in the photo."

Zoey gave an exaggerated thumbs up and went over to my mother, grabbing her hand and talking softly before leading her out of the room. I never thought I'd see such a thing. I put the phone back up to my ear. "Amy, it's good to hear from you. What is it I can help you with?" I asked with bated breath.

34

DETECTIVE HIRSCH

I stepped into the room and caught a whiff of the all-too-familiar combination of dust and body odor in the visiting room of the county jail. I eyed the suspect in front of me. I had a feeling he wouldn't be easy to crack, but I'd give it my best shot. I owed it to Martina and Theodore Gilmore.

Without a word, I pulled back the plastic chair and sat down, overemphasizing each move. I placed my hands in my lap, opting for a friendly, prim-and-proper approach. I stared ahead as Alonso Ricci sized me up. By the grimace on his face, I could tell he wasn't impressed with me, and probably not law enforcement, either. I smiled. "Alonso, my name is Detective Hirsch. How are you today?"

He remained stoic. "I've been better."

I nodded, as if I, too, had been in his position. "I would think so. I'm here because I'd like to hear more about what happened with the woman you attacked at the gas station."

"I have nothing to say."

"Nothing at all? You must have known that the gas station had surveillance cameras."

He shrugged and leaned back in his chair. He was cocky

and overly confident despite all the evidence we had against him. He either wasn't very bright, or he had something up his sleeve. "You know, it takes a real set of balls to attack a woman in broad daylight."

He smirked. "I don't know what you're talking about."

Did this man live in a fantasy world? Did Alonso really think pretending like it wasn't him would make anyone believe it wasn't him? There was surveillance footage of the attack, and there were statements from people who witnessed part of it. There were several police officers who saw Martina pressing a gun to his forehead. Being so brazen, I would almost think he wanted to get caught. That, or he'd thought he could get away with it before hightailing it back to Pennsylvania. "I have to ask, why? Why attack a woman in broad daylight? You clearly didn't know her very well, considering she clearly got the upper hand and knocked you right on your butt, before sticking a gun in your face."

Alonso shifted in his chair. His dark hair was thinning at the temples. His face was ruddy, with dark-brown eyes. His arrest record said he was five foot ten, one hundred ninety pounds. From what I could tell, he was well built. He was fit for a sixty-year-old. Despite his best efforts, he must not have realized what kind of self-defense skills Martina had. Or that she carried a weapon. Or that she was waiting for him. "You know, I've known Martina for a little while now, and honestly, I don't think I would want to go toe-to-toe with her. Did you know she used to teach Krav Maga, and that she's one of the best shooters in the state?"

Alonso seemed mildly amused and maybe even a little impressed.

"You didn't know that, did you?"

"I didn't know she had a gun. If she hadn't, I would've been able to take her."

At least he was finally ready to talk. The crap about not understanding what I was talking about was getting old, pretty fast. I tapped my finger on the table. "What I still can't figure out is why you attacked Martina."

Alonso's eyebrows arched up, but just for a moment. He didn't seem to know we were working together. "That's right. Martina and I are teamed up on a couple of cases right now. One of them she's consulting on is a break-in at a local veterinary office. Did you know that?"

His eyes went dark. "I know little about Martina or what she's working on," he said with steely calm.

"No? I assumed you must've known a little about her and what she's been working on. She swears that you're the person who attacked her in Pennsylvania."

"I know nothing about that."

I leaned over, unzipped my briefcase, and pulled out the file from the veterinarian's office break-in. I set it down softly in front of me, slowly flipping open the front cover, exposing a printout of the man who had broken into the vet's office. I slid it slowly over to Alonso and leaned back in my chair. "You know what I find interesting?" I asked, before glancing across the table at Alonso, who sat stiff as a board. He could sit there silently for all I cared. The evidence was piling up, and I didn't think he'd be going anywhere anytime soon. "I think that the guy on the surveillance video, breaking into the veterinarian's office, looks a lot like you. I also think it's interesting that some of the items stolen from the vet's office were used to kill Theodore Gilmore. So how I see it." I paused and scratched the side of my head. "You came to California to take out Theodore Gilmore because Martina was looking into the Henleys. I think you got the drugs needed to kill Mr. Gilmore from the veterinarian's office. The office that you can see there in the photo. If you look close, you can see that it's you breaking into it." I gave him a smug smile.

Alonso pushed the paper away from him and folded his arms and looked to the side. "I'd like my lawyer now."

"That's fine. We'll get you your phone call and your lawyer, but just so you know, this isn't all we have on you. If you talk to us, maybe we can help you; otherwise, I hope you like it here because I don't think you're ever going anywhere else. California is beautiful, don't you think?"

Alonso remained stoic, but the scowl on his face told me he was angry because he knew I had him. Unfortunately, it was mostly circumstantial evidence. I needed a little luck that the lab would come back with a DNA match to Alonso, so I could make sure this guy spent his retirement years behind bars. If they did, I could wrap up this case and focus my energy on finding out who killed a young woman and buried her remains at Beth's Pond.

35

ALONSO

H<small>E</small> <small>TURNED HIS BACK TO THE OTHERS IN THE HALLWAY</small>, lowered his eyes, and whispered into the receiver. "Hey, boss."

"How are you? What's happened?"

"I've got a problem. I need a lawyer—a really, fantastic lawyer."

"What do they have you on?"

"A few things. They seem to think that I broke into a veterinarian's office to steal some drugs to kill some guy named Theodore Gilmore, and that I attacked some lady private investigator named Martina Monroe, who apparently has been liaising with the police department on both cases."

He braced himself for what the boss may say. "You've got to be kidding me. Let me think this through. I'll see what I can do."

"Thanks, boss." He gave him details on where he was being held, before he hung up the receiver and swaggered back toward his cell with his head held high. He knew the boss would come through for him. He'd always come through for him, which was why he would remain loyal and would never tell his secrets. Soon this nightmare would be a distant memory. He used to be quite fond of the Golden State, but it quickly began to cramp his style.

36

MARTINA

I secured my weapon in its holster and threw my jacket on. If I didn't hurry, I was going to be late again. I ran into the living room, where I saw Betty and Zoey sitting on the sofa, looking at pictures that Zoey had made with glitter and markers. Should I be suspicious that Betty had offered to stay just Saturday night, yet it had been Monday and she was still there? She'd told me she called her job at the restaurant to let them know she needed a couple of days off to help her daughter. But were they lies? Had my mother really become a new person?

I shook my head. I had zero time to think about this. My mother looked up. "You off now?"

"Yes. I gave you my cell phone number, Detective Hirsch's cell phone number, and my office number. If you can't reach me at one of those, you probably won't be able to, because I'm likely out of the cell phone service area."

"Don't worry, Martina, we'll be fine," my mother said, fairly convincingly.

Zoey glanced over at me. "It's fine. Grandma Betty and I are planning to make an art project where we use every color glitter. Cool, huh?"

Well, I guess it was settled then. Zoey sure seemed to enjoy my mother's company. It was sweet and a little spooky at the same time. I had to have faith. If God could heal me, he could heal Betty and turn her into a new woman too. "All right, you two have fun." I ran up to Zoey and gave her a quick peck on the cheek. "Love you, Zoey."

"Love you, too, Mommy."

I hurried out of the house and out to my car. My phone buzzed. "Hey, Hirsch."

"Hi, Martina. Are you on your way?"

"I'm just getting in my car now. I'm still at home. Is everything okay?"

"I just got confirmation that the remains they found at Beth's Pond belonged to Donna."

It felt like someone had thrown a brick at my chest, and I braced myself using the hood of my car. I had known that the remains at Beth's Pond were likely Donna's. Why did it still hit me like this? "How did they match it?"

"Dental records. It's definitely her. The ME still wants us to come down and discuss a few things."

"Okay. I'll see you when I get there." I entered my car, shut the door and pounded my fists on the steering wheel while screaming silently at the Universe.

THE FOG HAD BURNED OFF, BUT THE AIR STILL HAD A CHILL in it. I zipped up my jacket as I approached Hirsch, who stood outside the entrance of the medical examiner's office. "Hey."

"Have you heard from Amy Henley?"

I shook my head. "Not yet."

"Any thoughts as to why she wants a DNA test to determine if her and Charlotte really are sisters?"

"I have a few theories."

"Me too. You want to share?"

I squinted. "Not yet." I didn't want to sway Detective Hirsch's opinion if and when more evidence became available. I'd rather have his initial, unbiased thoughts.

"Okay then. Shall we go see the ME?"

"We shall." I followed Hirsch into the building and stepped into the autopsy suite after him. The smell hit me hard and fast. I instinctively held my breath and glanced around. Despite the scent of decay, the only remains visible were a set of bones arranged anatomically on a metal table. The heaviness returned to my chest, and I hoped I could keep it together long enough to get through the meeting with the medical examiner.

A woman wearing green scrubs and a lab coat eyed Hirsch and gave him a wide smile. "Hirsch, it's good to see you. I tell you, you are the winner for bringing me the most interesting cases."

"Oh yeah, how so?"

"First things, first, Hirsch." She stepped toward me and extended her hand. "You must be Martina Monroe."

I accepted her gesture and answered, "Yes. Dr. Scribner, it's nice to meet you."

"Likewise. You're building quite a reputation around here too."

It wasn't the first time I had heard such a statement. I supposed my life could be lower profile, but I had yet to figure out how. Dr. Scribner continued, "Come on over. I'll show you the remains."

Hirsch and I quietly stepped over to the table where Donna's bones were displayed. I studied her from her skull down to her feet bones. A lump formed in my throat, and I couldn't speak. I placed my hand on my chest.

Hirsch bent over and asked quietly, "Are you okay?"

I eyed him and nodded. I focused on Dr. Scribner. "I'm sorry. I don't know if Hirsch told you, but Donna was my best friend in high school. I was with her the night she disappeared. This is tougher than I thought."

Dr. Scribner nodded. "He told me. Please take your time. This is hard. It's never how we want to see our loved ones."

I shook my head. "No, it's certainly not." I took a few more moments to myself to process what I was seeing. I shut my eyes and pictured Donna's beautiful face before silently promising her I would find out who did this to her, and I would, even if was the last thing I did. Donna deserved so much better than being buried in the ground, when she should have been living her best life. She could have been a mother, a professor, or whatever she wanted to be. I took a deep breath and glanced back up at Hirsch and Dr. Scribner. "Okay, I'm ready. What can you tell us?"

She stepped toward Donna's skull and pointed at the back of her head. "You see the cracks and breakage? That's not from time or any other natural process. It indicates a heavy blow to the back of her head. It's most likely the cause of death."

"Any idea what could have done this type of damage?" Hirsch asked.

"It could have been any number of things, from a big rock to a bat, depending on how strong her attacker was."

I winced at the description of what had happened to my best friend. I shoved the emotions down into the deep dark place inside myself where I hid those kinds of things. It was how I got through most tough situations. It was how I'd get through this conversation and how I'd stay calm enough to figure out who did this to her. "Did she die quickly?"

"My guess is she bled out in a matter of minutes."

"Any trace evidence? Anything to help us find out who did this to her?" Hirsch asked.

"Not yet, but the forensic team took soil samples around her body, which you might get some evidence from. You should check in with Brown."

"Thank you, Dr. Scribner."

"I'll let you know if I find anything else. This is just a preliminary review."

We said our goodbyes and exited the suite. Out in the hallway, I asked, "Have you notified her parents yet?"

Hirsch shook his head. "Not yet. I'd found out just before I called you. I want to notify them in person."

"I'll go with you." It wasn't a request.

"Are you sure you want to do this? It's going to be a tough one."

"I'd like to be there for the Bernards."

"I can drive."

I was thankful that Hirsch offered to drive. I was keeping it together, but I was distracted, too. Now that I was a mother myself, I couldn't imagine what Donna's parents would be going through when they saw her skeleton lying on the exam table. Their baby girl. And to learn that all these years, she'd been buried less than a mile from their house.

"There's going to be a press conference about Donna's case."

"When?"

"Tomorrow. My sergeant wants me to announce that we've found her remains. I'd like to be able to publicly thank you for your role in finding her and explain to the media that it was a team effort. Are you okay with that?"

It had been a long time since I'd felt like I was part of a team. But Hirsch and I had definitely become one over these last few weeks. "It's okay with me."

My phone buzzed. I pulled it out. I hoped it wasn't Zoey in

trouble. It wasn't, thank goodness. I gave Hirsch a knowing look. "Hi, Amy, how are you?"

"Not great," she said, voice cracking. My mother, Eloise, died by suicide."

"I'm so sorry. My deepest condolences."

Amy sniffled on the other side of the call. "I'm calling because in addition to her suicide note she left a letter. It's pretty private, and I can't let it get into the wrong hands. Is there any way you could come back to Pennsylvania? I think it will provide some answers for Kennedy."

I stared at Hirsch. "Of course, I can make a trip to Pennsylvania. Let me check my calendar, and I'll get back to you."

37

DETECTIVE HIRSCH

I TURNED TOWARD MARTINA. "WHAT WAS THAT ALL about? You're going back to Pennsylvania?"

Martina's face was long and solemn. "Amy just told me that her mother took her own life, and that she left a letter. It sounds like it may contain some very sensitive information, and she doesn't want it to get into the wrong hands. She says she'll only show it to me in person. I told her I would check my calendar and get on a flight to Doylestown."

Her eyes were fierce with determination. She'd suffered a concussion just two days before, yet there she sat, without hesitation, willing to hop on a plane and go across the country to continue investigating a case. Not to mention, she was told by her boss that she could not continue investigating the Henleys.

I was sensing that Martina Monroe basically did whatever she wanted, regardless of what her orders were. Perhaps that was why she was more suited to be a private investigator than a police officer.

"When do you plan to go?"

She shook her head. "I don't know. I need to find someone to watch Zoey and figure out how to go and not get fired. I need to think about it, but there's no way I'm not going back there to finish what I started."

I still hadn't told her about the phone call from my friend at the FBI, and that I, too, needed to go to Pennsylvania. I hadn't mentioned it based on Martina's current health status, and it wasn't like I actually had any information, other than a hunch there was an active FBI investigation into one or more of the Henleys. She didn't need any more stress—she had a head wound, and I didn't want to overwhelm her, but she was tough. I should've told her. It was clear she could handle it. I had a feeling she wouldn't be pleased that I had withheld the information for two days. "Well, I got a call from a friend at the Philadelphia's FBI Field Office. He says he can't tell me if he found anything on the Henleys, but he has a buddy I could talk to if I fly out to Pennsylvania for a meeting."

Martina's mouth dropped open. "He wouldn't have told you that if they didn't have something on the Henleys."

"I agree."

"So, the Henleys are under investigation by the FBI?"

"That's what I think."

She glanced down and then back up at me. "Why didn't you tell me this? This is huge."

"You had just been attacked, and you were in the hospital. You seemed to have enough on your plate, and I was still figuring out how to convince my department that I needed to go. For that type of travel, I need pretty compelling information. Now based on the call from Amy, I think it'll be enough."

She let out a breath. "All right. I'm going to talk to Stavros so that he and I can come to an understanding, and then I can book my trip. After you talk to your boss, let's coordinate our travel. Two minds are better than one. What do you say?"

I knew there was no romantic connotation to Martina's invitation, but it was confirmation she enjoyed working with me, and she thought we made a good team. "Deal." I started the car and pulled out of the parking lot. Now for the hardest and most rewarding part of the job—to notify the family their loved one had been located.

———

WE MARCHED UP THE WOODEN STEPS TO THE BERNARDS' home. Before we reached the front door, Martina and I both stopped and glanced over at the Gilmore house. It still didn't sit right with me. The coincidence that there were two murder victims who lived next door to one another. I didn't like coincidences and didn't think they existed.

I turned to Martina, who was looking down at the ground, and then turned the other way to stare out at the water. It must be difficult for her to be there and to give a death notification to her best friend's parents.

I could only imagine what she was going through. I hoped that mixed in with her grief, she also felt proud that she was about to give closure to a family who had been waiting and hoping for so long.

I turned around and stared out at the dark, choppy water. I hugged my jacket tighter to my chest. It was colder out on the island than on the other side of the bridge.

Martina pivoted toward me. "You ready?"

I nodded and took the steps toward the front door. I knocked once before the door eased open. An unfamiliar face resembling Donna Bernard greeted me. Before I could say anything, Martina stepped forward. "Dave, I'm glad you're here." I glanced at her, and she eyed me back. "Detective Hirsch, this is Dave Bernard, one of Donna's brothers."

"It's nice to meet you."

"Please come in." He was somber, as if he knew what we were there to tell them.

I entered their home and stood near the recliner while Martina approached Mr. and Mrs. Bernard, who sat huddled together on the sofa. Mr. Bernard had his arm around his wife as if bracing for the worst, which was exactly what they were about to receive.

I flashed back to my family's worst moment. I had stood next to my father when the detective told us that my brother, Sam, had been killed. My heart ached for Sam and for the Bernards. I rarely froze up in these moments. Not that I was great at delivering notifications, but usually I was at least able to remain more emotionally distant.

I steadied my nerves. "Mr. And Mrs. Bernard. Dave. We received confirmation that the remains found at Beth's Pond belong to Donna."

Mr. Bernard's head bowed as he tried to conceal his grief. Mrs. Bernard shook her head and tears flowed down her cheeks. "You found our Donna? You're sure it's her?"

"Yes, and actually, Martina found her."

I watched as Martina approached Dave and embraced him and then stepped back. "I'm so sorry. I'm sorry it took me so long to find her. I should have looked sooner."

"No, you brought her back to us. Thank you."

"It wasn't just me. Detective Hirsch and his forensic team helped as well. He's the one who reopened the case and had the backing of the department." She turned to face the parents. "Sandy and Mr. Bernard, I'm so sorry." She leaned over, wrapping an arm around each of the Bernards, embracing in a three-way hug. When Martina eased back, Dave passed her a box of tissues. She plucked a few from the box before handing it off to Mrs. Bernard.

While they consoled one another, Dave approached me. "Do you know who did this to my sister?"

"No, not yet. The forensic team is still evaluating the evidence found at the scene."

He shook his head. "I can't believe it. You know, we always hoped she'd come back, that maybe she'd run off with a new guy or something. I never wanted to believe she was gone. My brother, Tim, is out of the country right now. It will crush him when he hears. I need to call him."

"I understand. We will find out who did this to her." And I believed in my gut, Martina and I would do just that.

38

MARTINA

I CLIMBED UP THE FRONT STEPS TO THE HOUSE. MY LEGS felt like jelly. My head was pounding. Oh, what I wouldn't give for a hot bath and to go straight to bed and be able to sleep for a week. Before I could even put my key in the door, I heard the pattering of footsteps on the other side. The door flung open, and Zoey stood there, holding up a picture that she'd likely created with Betty. "Welcome home, Mommy. We made this for you."

I looked past Zoey. My mother, Betty, stood in the background wearing a cheerful smile. I received the picture from Zoey. It was heavy and constructed almost entirely of colorful glitter. A rainbow sky with people and trees. Betty must have drawn the outlines for the glitter. Zoey was pretty good with art projects, but she'd never drawn such intricate shapes. I hadn't known my mother had artistic talent. Maybe there were a lot of things I didn't know about her. "Mom, did you help draw this?"

Before she spoke, Zoey answered for her. "She did. She's so good at drawing. Mom, you have to see what else she drew. She's an amazing artist. Like, the best in the world!"

"I'd love to see it."

Betty turned to Zoey. "Why don't we let your mom come in. She's had a long day."

Zoey nodded before running back toward the kitchen. I shut the door behind me and made my way down the hall into the living room that was connected to our kitchen. My mother turned around. "Long day, huh?"

"Do I look that bad?"

"I've seen you look healthier. I'm guessing you could use some dinner and then maybe an early bedtime."

"That sounds heavenly."

"I was hoping maybe once you're settled in, we can have a talk about Zoey."

My heart rate sped up. "What about Zoey? Is she okay?"

"Yes, she's fine. What I meant to say is that we can talk about Zoey's care. I spoke to Claire, and she said that she's graduating from school soon, and you still haven't chosen a new nanny."

Right, I still have to choose a new nanny. If I don't decide soon, I'll have no help with Zoey or the house. My mother's eyes were shining.

"Yeah, that's just one more thing on my list of to-dos. Let's discuss it later," I said before walking into the living room and plopping down on the sofa. Zoey soon joined me, as did my mother. Zoey nestled her head in the crook of my mother's shoulder and grinned up at her. Part of me was surprised, and part of me was offended that Zoey wasn't cuddling with me. I was her mom. Before I could feel too sorry for myself, Zoey scooted over and wrapped her little arms around me. Before sitting up, she glanced at her grandmother and then back at me. "So, Grandma and I were talking..."

I studied their gleeful faces. They had conspired together. It had only been two days, and I was already the odd man out. "What were you talking about?"

Before Zoey could catapult into one of her long-winded explanations, my mother put her hand on Zoey's shoulder and said, "Let me talk, okay?"

Zoey nodded and used her fingers to mimic zipping her lips closed. She listened to my mother, which was good, I supposed. Not that Zoey was ever particularly defiant—at least not yet. I focused on my mother, the person whom I had been estranged from until forty-eight hours ago. "So?"

"Like I mentioned earlier, Claire and I spoke about how you still hadn't picked an au pair or live-in nanny so that you would always have someone here for the times that your job has you being whisked away at the last minute."

It was true. I was currently in a whisking situation, seeing as how I needed to be in Pennsylvania. I guess I couldn't deny that either would be a good option. "True."

"Now, I know I'm just now back in your life, but maybe I could take the job."

Zoey nodded enthusiastically. My mother had clearly made quite an impression on her. Perhaps it was the fact our family had dwindled down to the two of us, that she was hoping for a familial connection. Or maybe it was that she was worried about the fact her nanny was going to be gone soon. I sat up straight. "To be honest, I'm not sure I'm comfortable with this."

"I can understand your hesitation. It's been a long time since you and I have been in each other's lives. Despite that fact, I love you, Martina, and I love Zoey. How about I help with the house and Zoey on a trial basis while Claire is still here? That way, if it doesn't work out, Claire can fill in, and you can continue looking for a different nanny."

"Claire is okay with this?" *Would I have to pay for two different nannies?*

"Claire says she has so much studying to do that she could

really use the extra time. I think she's being spread thin between studying for her finals and taking care of Zoey."

We had an extra room or two. I didn't use my home office, since when I worked from home, it was usually late at night in my bedroom.

Part of me was suspicious that my mother had returned and was already offering to move in with me and had charmed the pants off Zoey. I was desperate, and maybe she knew that and figured it was her perfect opportunity to... I wasn't sure what the potential motive was. Did she need money? A place to live?

I needed help, but I needed it from someone I could trust. I just wasn't sure Betty was that someone. I supposed if it didn't go well, Claire was still around, and I wouldn't be any worse off than before.

I could do that, or stick to a strict nine-to-five schedule and pass on the tougher cases. Zoey could go to after-school care, and we'd both be miserable. I already knew from my time off, after the accident, that being a full-time PTA mom wasn't in my nature. I had gone nearly crazy with boredom and lack of adult conversation. Plus, I loved my job. I loved figuring out the puzzle and helping people, whether it was bringing closure to a family or finding their missing loved one. It was what I was meant to do.

I hoped I wouldn't regret this. "Okay, we can do it on a trial basis."

Both of their faces lit up like it was Christmas. Zoey cheered, and I gave her the best smile I could, despite the day I'd experienced.

"What's wrong, Mommy? You're not happy about this."

I shook my head. "No, that's not it. I've had a long day, and I'm sad."

"How come?"

I didn't have to explain death to Zoey, we had already had

the talk after her father had passed away. "Do you remember when I told you about my best friend, Donna?"

Zoey nodded.

"We found her today."

"Then why are you sad?"

"Because we found her body, and now we know she's been in heaven all this time."

Zoey's face went long, and her eyes stared at the rug. "She's dead, like Daddy."

"Yep." In that moment, I lost all my composure. Everything I had been holding inside. The stress. The anger. The sadness. I let the tears flow down my cheeks as my little girl hugged me. My mother joined soon after.

Zoey whispered, "I'm sorry, Mommy."

I sniffled and wiped my tears with the back of my hand. "Thank you, baby."

My mother's eyes welled up. "I'm so sorry, Martina. I know how much Donna meant to you."

I had run out of words, so I simply nodded. Zoey leaned back and looked me in the eyes. "Did somebody kill her?"

"Yes."

"Are you going to find the person who killed her?"

My mind cleared. "Yes, I am."

"And is Detective Hirsch going to lock them up and throw away the key?"

I hoped so. "He will."

"Good," Zoey declared.

After Zoey went to bed, I reentered the living room and spotted my mother sitting on the couch, reading a novel. She set her glasses down. "How are you feeling?"

"Just another day in my life. I'll be all right."

"It's terrible about Donna."

"Yes, it is. There was something I wanted to talk to you

about. Since you so graciously offered to come and help with Zoey, are you up for your first challenge?"

"Oh?"

"The case I've been working on has had a break, but I need to travel to Pennsylvania." I quickly recapped my last trip to Pennsylvania and that I needed to follow up.

"Wow. Zoey has been telling me you're the best private investigator in the whole world. It sounds like she was right."

I didn't know about that. Sometimes I felt like the worst.

Betty continued. "Of course, I'll be here for Zoey. How long do you think you will be gone?"

"Two to three days, tops."

"Is it safe?"

"This time, I'll be with an armed police officer. Hirsch is going too."

"Well, that's good to hear. So, are you and the detective friends?"

I saw the implication in her eyes. It wasn't like that. "We've just started working together recently and we make a good team. I suppose we're kind of friends. We've come a long way, actually." I chuckled as I recapped the last time, before the Gilmore case, I'd encountered Detective Hirsch. After he told me he was closing the DeSoto case, I had wanted to strangle him and it took all I had not to. "He's definitely grown on me since then. He's a good detective, and it's nice to have someone to bounce ideas off of."

"It sounds like your job can be a lonely one."

It hadn't been, before Jared died. He'd been my sounding board. He was the one I had bounced ideas off of. Not only did I miss my husband, I missed my best friend. Jared had been my partner in everything.

"It can be." I let out a breath. "Now to tell my boss that I'm going. He sort of ordered me to stopping working the case."

My mother cracked a smile. "I don't recall you ever taking orders from anybody. I remember thinking it was so strange when you'd decided to join the Army where they give nothing but orders."

"The Army had been a challenge at first. I suppose we all have the capability for change."

Betty's demeanor turned serious. "You know, I've always admired your determination and your smarts. I knew you wouldn't stick around the trailer park for long. I want you to know, I'm really proud of you, Martina. You're a wonderful, caring mother and an excellent private investigator who helps people."

I hadn't realized I needed those words from my mother. When had I gotten so broken? I was an alcoholic. I was lonely. I carried guilt and grief. When had I needed my mother's love and approval? Maybe I'd always been broken, and I had somehow put myself together with duct tape without even realizing it. Could it be that there was some honest-to-goodness healing going on? "Thank you, Mom."

Now I had to tell Stavros I was continuing to work on the Henley case. I hoped he was half as gracious as my mother had been about my lack of desire to follow orders.

39

DETECTIVE HIRSCH

I drummed on my desk while I waited for Martina to answer the phone. Voicemail again. My gut stirred. It wasn't like her to not answer her phone. I hoped she wasn't lying somewhere in a parking lot or on the pavement at a gas station or any other place she had been attacked at since we'd started working together.

She would want to be in attendance when I stuck it to Alonso, I was sure of it. As a last effort, I pulled up the number to Drakos Security & Investigations and dialed. The receptionist picked it up after two rings. "Drakos Security & Investigations, how may I help you?"

"Yes, I'd like to speak to Martina Monroe, please."

"May I ask who is calling?"

"This is Detective Hirsch."

"Hold one moment, please."

Relief trickled through me. She was at the office and not lying in a ditch somewhere. Although, I wondered if the only thing capable of taking her out was an entire army.

"I'm sorry. Martina is in a meeting right now. Would you like me to have her call you back?"

Damn it. I needed to talk to her, but at least she was alive. I wondered if she was meeting with her boss, Stavros, and finally telling him she was still working on the Henley case. "I'll try again later. Please let her know I called."

"Will do. Have a nice day."

I hung up and contemplated if I should wait until Martina was available. I'd try her cell phone one more time before giving up and heading to the county jail.

I sat across from Alonso Ricci, who seemed less than enthusiastic to see me again. I smiled. "Mr. Ricci. Good to see you again. Do you mind if I call you Lonnie? I hear that's what your friends call you."

He remained stoic, refusing to even budge or acknowledge my presence. "You know, Lonnie, I hear you're still not talking." My grin faded, and I shifted forward in my seat. "Not even to your lawyer." I leaned back and folded my arms. "Actually, I've heard your lawyer hasn't come to visit you yet. That's got to be disconcerting. If you'd like, I can order you up a public defender. I can call right now." I held up my phone for effect.

Alonso stared toward the ceiling as if I were boring him. But I knew he must be squirming on the inside. Why hadn't his lawyer shown up yet? He'd been locked up for three days. Whoever he was working for hadn't come through for him yet. It wasn't a good sign for Alonso, and he was likely all alone in his defense.

I folded my hands in my lap and focused on Alonso. "I rarely like one-sided conversations, but I wanted to share some information with you that may be of some interest to you. You can choose to just listen if you prefer, but you are welcome to comment at any time. We just got DNA results back from the break-in at the veterinarian's office and guess what?"

He turned his gaze to me. And I smiled, a genuine I've-got-you-you-bastard smile. "That's right, Lonnie. It's your DNA. Now if you add it all up, we have you on video breaking into the vet's office, and we've got your blood matched to the scene of crime. Not only that, but we've been able to link the stolen drugs from the veterinarian's office to the drugs that killed Theodore Gilmore. If you're keeping score, those are charges for breaking and entering, felony theft, and first-degree murder. But that's not all, is it? We also have you attacking Martina Monroe in broad daylight on video and with eyewitnesses." I waited for a reaction.

He turned to the side and evaded my stare.

I ignored his lack of speech and continued. "Now if I were you, which I'm not. I'd be talking and trying to cut a deal because whoever you're working for has let you stew all alone for three days in a county jail cell on murder charges, attempted murder charges, and felony theft. My goodness, those three alone will get you life in prison. Here in California, we call that three strikes and you're out. Three felonies and you go away for life. If you insist on keeping quiet, well, I'd recommend you get real cozy because you're not going anywhere—ever again." I sat back in my chair and watched him fidget. Finally, a reaction.

His eyes locked with mine. "My lawyer will be here any moment now. So, if you have nothing else, Detective, I'd hate to take up any more of your day."

He acted like he was confident, but it had to be a show. The best lawyer in the world couldn't get him off the hook from these charges. The only way he would ever even have a chance to be a free man again is if he attempted to plea, but maybe not even then. "Okay, but as soon as this goes to trial, I'm afraid I won't be able to help you."

Alonso stared straight ahead. My guess was that it was his best attempt at appearing unfazed by all of this information. I pushed back from the table and stood up. "If you change your mind and you want to talk, you know where to find me." I shrugged. "I certainly know where to find you—you'll be in your jail cell."

Alonso didn't look at me. So be it. I practically waltzed out of the county jail, knowing we had this guy. There was no way he was going to walk on any of these charges, and soon the case would be closed.

I loved closing cases. The sense of accomplishment and knowing the bad guys were locked up was a feeling akin to a first kiss or watching the sun rise. Not to mention, it would bring some closure to Kennedy Gilmore. She'd been through enough already. It was too unfair for her to not know who was responsible for her father's death. *Damn.* I still didn't have the why. Alonso hadn't cooperated, so I couldn't explain why he had killed Theodore Gilmore. It certainly wasn't random. My feelings of elation faded. I wasn't done with Alonso yet.

I reached the parking lot and slid into the driver's side of my car when the inside of my jacket vibrated. I pulled out the phone. Finally. "Martina, how are you?"

"Oh, you know, things could be better."

"What's wrong?"

"Nothing really. I just finished a rather difficult conversation with Stavros. He was pretty against me continuing on the Henley case. After a long, drawn-out debate, I had to threaten to quit for him to allow me to continue. It wasn't pretty."

"But he's on board now?"

"Yep."

That must have been rough. Going toe-to-toe with a superior was not for the faint of heart. "Well, if you want some good news. I have some."

"Yes, please," she said with a ring in her voice.

"The DNA came back from the break-in at the vet's office. Guess who it's a match to?"

"Alonso?"

"Yep, I'm just leaving the county jail now."

"How did he take the news?"

"He tried to make it appear he didn't care. He's still not talking, but I could tell he's rattled. His lawyer hasn't shown up yet."

"Interesting. Whoever he's working for doesn't want to step up."

"I think that's what Alonso is figuring out."

"Good news for the case."

"Yep, I offered him a public defender, but he declined."

Martina chuckled. "You don't say? All right, we should meet to discuss our approach for the Pennsylvania mission."

She was definitely ex-military. All missions and commands. "I have a meeting with my sergeant later today. He's endorsed the trip, but we're going over specifics before the official approval. If you have time, we can meet and discuss it around four?"

"Sounds good."

I hung up the phone. We had a plan. Martina and I would go to Pennsylvania and figure out how the Henleys were tied into this whole mess. I was sure they were at the heart of it all, despite the lack of confirmation from our closed-lipped friend, Alonso Ricci.

40

ALONSO

Alonso shook his head, bewildered. Why hadn't the boss been taking his calls? The boss had always cautioned him to never call his offices, but he had to know Alonso was getting desperate as he sat in jail. Now that they had DNA connecting him to the murder, he needed a damn good lawyer and fast, or he was going away for life. That stupid detective was right. He knew he should've taken the time at the vet's office to clean up the broken glass, but he hadn't realized he'd been cut until it was too late. Not to mention the blaring alarm that had been piercing his eardrums.

Everything he'd done was for the family and for him, the boss. Now it was Alonso's time of need, and he'd been certain the boss would be there for him. The three days in county jail, without a peep from a lawyer or the boss, were saying the contrary.

Against his better judgment, he dialed the office number. "East Coast Securities. How may I help you?"

"I need to talk to Frank Henley, please."

"May I ask who is calling?"

"This is Mr. Ricci."

"One moment, please."

Heart racing, Alonso hoped the boss would take his call. He needed to talk to him. The situation had gone from bad to worse, and he needed his help. Alonso had some money stashed away to pay for a decent lawyer, but it would likely clean him out.

Considering Alonso was facing the loss of his freedom, which was no small thing, Frank Henley had a heck of a lot more to lose than that. It was in his best interest to help him, so why hadn't he?

"I'm sorry, Mr. Ricci. Mr. Henley is not available right now. If you'd like to leave a message, I can have him get back to you."

Anger seared through Alonso. "I want to talk to Frank. I want to talk to him now. Tell him to get on the phone or it's all over."

"Sir."

"Look lady, just give Frank the message."

"One moment."

His hands were vibrating on the telephone receiver.

"Frank Henley here?"

"Frank, it's Lonnie. I need your help."

"I'm sorry, but I don't know anybody named Lonnie. What's your last name?"

Alonso's mouth dropped open, and he stared at the phone. He was acting like he didn't know him. His temperature rose, and he curled his hand into a fist. "Frank, don't mess around with me. I need a lawyer, yesterday."

"I'm so sorry, sir, but I think you might have me mixed up with somebody else. Who is that you are trying to get a hold of?"

Anger bubbled out of him as he spat at Frank, "You will be sorry," before he slammed the receiver down. If that was how Frank wanted to play it, that was how he'd play it.

41

DETECTIVE HIRSCH

I STOOD OUTSIDE AND LET THE RAINDROPS FALL DOWN ON me. The pattering on my skin and the chill reminded me I wasn't dreaming. I had just received the call. The call that we were about to break this case wide open. The cherry on the hot fudge sundae of the case. I grabbed my phone from my pocket and called Martina. "Do you have time for a field trip?"

"Where to?"

"County jail. I got a call from our friend Alonso Ricci, and he wants to talk."

"Did he say about what?"

I didn't think Martina understood the gravity of the situation. I thought Alonso was about to tell us who he had been working for and why he'd ordered the hits—the last pieces of the puzzle. "I think he'll give us his boss and maybe motive."

She hesitated. "All right. Where are you now?"

"I'm at Concord PD, talking to a buddy of mine, the guy who worked the veterinarian's office break-in."

"Is he coming too?"

"No, it'll be just you and me. We'll finally get answers, Martina. I can feel it."

"I hope so. I'll be there in thirty minutes," she said.

"I'll be here waiting for you." I hung up and headed back inside the station.

My hair was wet and rain trickled down the sides of my face, but I didn't care. I headed back toward Webb's desk. "Hey, man."

"Hirsch, you did it."

"We did it. I'm about to head down to the county jail with Martina Monroe and try to get his full confession."

"Case closed."

"Fingers crossed." I hoped by the end of the day we could finally dot the i's and cross the t's and erase the case from the board.

Webb leaned against his desk. "So, I was talking to my wife. Are you available Saturday night? She's trying a new chili recipe. You like chili?"

"Love it."

"So, you're in?"

It wasn't like I had anything else to do. As it was, I hadn't brought myself to open up the envelope that sat on my dining table. I knew what was inside—divorce papers. All I needed to do was sign them, and it would be official. I'd be divorced. Like so many other detectives before me who couldn't hold on to a relationship. It was a difficult thing to do, when most of the time, all you could think about was the job. "I'll be there."

"Great. It'll be good to catch up."

"Thanks, Webb."

———

Martina and I entered the county jail. She still seemed a little down from the tough conversation with her boss.

Hopefully, whatever Alonso told us would cheer her up and remind her of why she fought so hard to stay on the case.

We were escorted back to the interview room. It was the same dank little box where I had visited Alonso twice before. I had asked Martina if it would be strange to confront her attacker, but she'd shrugged it off like it was no big deal. That woman was tough as nails.

We entered the room, but it was empty, except for the guard. "Where is he?"

"He'll be down in a minute. Can I get you anything?"

"Another chair."

"No problem."

A few minutes later, he returned with a plastic chair. I sat down. Martina did the same. "Here goes."

The sounds of footsteps and chains jingling were audible and growing louder. I watched as Martina's eyes followed Alonso's every move. The guard closed the door, and all eyes were on the prisoner. "I heard you wanted to talk."

"I've had a change of heart."

"Glad to hear it. This is my associate, Martina Monroe, but I think you two have met."

"Martina Monroe," he said, squinting his eyes curiously.

"What did you want to talk to us about?"

"I have decided to do the right thing and tell you what you want to know."

I lifted my hands. "Great, we're all ears."

"Not so fast." He sat up a little straighter in his chair. "I want to do what's right, but I also want to do what's right for me. I'm willing to talk for a price, of course."

"What do you have in mind?"

"Well, I've got some information that I think that you'll want."

"What kind of information?"

"Well, I believe earlier you asked me some questions. Now, I'm not admitting anything mind you, but you had asked me why I wanted to kill Theodore Gilmore, why I had broken into the veterinarian's office, and why I had attacked Ms. Koltz here."

Was he losing his memory? Koltz was her maiden name—how did he know that? I exchanged glances with Martina before refocusing on Alonso. "I did ask those questions. Are you saying you may have answers to those questions?"

"Not only that, sir, ma'am, but I may have additional information that may be useful to you both."

"Okay, what do you want?"

"Immunity."

"What kind of immunity?"

"Full immunity. I'm not the guy you really want. I'm a gentle soul who may or may not have committed terrible acts only at the behest of my employer. If you give me immunity, I'll give you what you need to close your cases, and we can let bygones be bygones."

Was he delusional? He'd murdered a man. Did he really think he'd get full immunity with such vague statements? "You'll need to provide more details to determine whether the information you give would warrant such generous compensation."

"Is your DA around?"

"I could get the district attorney in here pretty fast. I've got him on speed dial." Not true, but I could get him quick enough.

"Good. Now, if I were to be able to tell you who may have asked me to attack and kill Ms. Koltz, murder Mr. Gilmore, and a few other things, would that be enough?"

Why was he continuing to refer to Martina as Ms. Koltz? "Why do you keep referring to Martina as Ms. Koltz, when I've told you her name is Martina Monroe?"

He glanced at Martina. "Oh, sorry, old habits die hard. Ms. Koltz is your maiden name, isn't it?"

I turned to look at Martina's expression. She seemed as curious as I was. I had the distinct feeling he was dropping bread crumbs, but to what, I didn't know.

"That's correct. How did you know that?" Martina asked.

"I did my homework on you." A Cheshire-cat grin spread up Alonso's face, before he returned his focus to me.

"Okay, let me make a call."

"I'll stay here," Alonso quipped.

I thought, *So, he's now chatty, funny Lonnie?* I gestured to Martina to follow me out to the hallway.

Out of earshot of the interview room, I faced Martina. "What do you think of this guy's story?"

"He seems pretty ticked off at whoever hired him. If we get him immunity, I think he'll spill all the beans. Beans we don't even know about."

"I agree. Let me call the DA and see what kind of terms we can get."

"Sounds like a good plan." Martina leaned up against the wall as I dialed my office to get the number of the district attorney's office and then spoke with a district attorney who had never heard of me but had heard of the case. *Thanks, pal, like I needed any more blows to my ego.*

I thanked him for the information and hung up the phone. I was authorized to provide full immunity if Alonso had what we needed for a full conviction of his employer.

I nodded at Martina, and we headed back into the interview room to share the good news with our pal, Lonnie. "The DA said that he will give you full immunity in exchange for the name of the person who hired you to attack Miss Monroe, break into the veterinarian's office, and kill Theodore Gilmore. Besides naming the person, you'll need to provide evidence that the transaction had taken place between you and that person. In other words—we need proof."

"What if I don't have all the proof now, but can get it?"

"That'll work as long as it's in a timely manner, which I would think is beneficial for both of us, considering this is your permanent address until you do."

"Understood. Let's do it."

Adrenaline was pumping through me like I was in the middle of a 10K race. "Okay, let's start with Theodore Gilmore. Why was he killed, and who asked you to kill him?"

"Senator Frank Henley asked me to kill Theodore Gilmore after his wife, Charlotte, died. I think you may know by now that Charlotte was Frank's sister. Frank was worried that Charlotte had told Theodore some sensitive information about the family, and he wanted to keep him quiet."

"Why now?"

He looked over at Martina and then back at me. "After Charlotte's Memorial, I bugged Mr. Gilmore's house so I could listen to his conversations and assess how much he knew. A few days after Charlotte's memorial, I listened as he told his daughter and Martina what he knew about Charlotte's past. Although it wasn't exactly accurate, Frank had a feeling he knew more, and that maybe he was just making up that story to placate his daughter. Frank thought it was too much of a risk to keep him alive and was convinced Charlotte had confided in him about the family."

"What about the family were they trying to hide?"

"Look, I don't know what he was looking for. I don't know what this big family secret is, but apparently Charlotte knew it, and Frank needed to ensure that she told no one and that it never became public."

"So, he asked you to kill Charlotte's husband after she died so that he wouldn't tell her family's secret, and you don't even know what the secret is?"

"He never told me and I never asked."

"A good soldier," Martina said.

"I was."

"Until he left you behind," I commented.

Alonso shrugged, attempting to look tough, but there was hurt in his eyes.

"Tell us about the break-in at the veterinarian's office."

"You saw the video. It was me. I broke in to steal the drugs—ketamine and insulin—to kill Theodore Gilmore."

"Why did you attack Martina?"

"It wasn't personal. She was getting too close to the Henleys, and Frank didn't like that she was talking to his little sister, Amy. He nearly flipped his lid when he found out. He didn't like it one bit."

"So, all of this was to keep some family secret? The Henley family secret. And you don't even know what it is?"

"That's correct."

"And you have evidence that Frank hired you to do all of this?"

"I have some, but I could get more and you'll likely need more. If you can get him on the phone with a tap, I'll get you all the evidence you need for a nice and tidy conviction against the senator."

Alonso was talking to save his own butt and frying Henley in the process. I didn't blame him. Frank Henley burned Alonso the second he needed help. I said, "This won't be good for the senator's reelection campaign."

"Or his run for president," Alonso added.

"All right, I'll see what I can do with the wiretap. If you put it in writing, and we can corroborate your story, you'll get full immunity. Until then, sit tight."

"And the immunity is for all crimes committed on behalf of Frank Henley?"

"Yes." *Sure, why not.*

"All right."

I picked up my recorder from the table and glanced over at Martina as she stood up. Alonso leaned back in his chair. "Oh, before you go, I just wanted to say, Martina, you've done well for yourself. I'm impressed, but then again, you always were a firecracker."

42

MARTINA

I swung my body around and stared Alonso straight in the eyes. "What exactly do you mean by that?"

"I meant nothing by it. It was a compliment. I recall you were always kind of the leader, you know."

My patience had officially left the building. "No, I don't know what you mean. I don't know you, so what are you implying—that you know me?"

"I remember watching you when you were young," he said with a smug smile.

The bastard was hiding something, and he was clearly egging me on by eluding my questions. "Whatever you're implying, just say it already," I demanded.

"Calm down. I only want to help you, Martina."

I glanced back at Hirsch. "Do you know what the hell he's talking about?"

"No."

I turned back to Alonso. "Why do you keep referring to me by my maiden name? Did we know each other when I was younger and lived on Stone Island?"

"We never met, but I felt like I knew you."

I leaned over the table, my hands planted on top. "Look, just spit it out. What are you trying to say?"

He shook his head back and forth. "I don't know, Hirsch. I'd like to tell her, but I'm afraid it needs to be covered under the immunity agreement."

I stepped back as a wave of nausea rolled through me. My mind churned like gears locking into place. I shut my eyes, and it was as if I could see it all on a slideshow.

"Is the new information in the same vein—as in it was ordered by Frank Henley?" Hirsch inquired.

"It sure is," he said with a gleam in his eye.

"Then it'll be covered."

Alonso returned his gaze to me. "You're looking a little pale. You may want to have a seat while I tell you my story."

I sat as the rage and disbelief shot through me. "Talk," I demanded.

"Like I said, Martina. I knew you, but you didn't know me. I used to watch you and Donna. The two of you were best friends, right?"

I blinked rapidly. It was all true.

He continued. "I'm surprised Donna never told you about our arrangement."

"Get on with it, Alonso," Hirsch commanded.

"Fine. Here's what happened. Frank Henley needed someone who could have eyes on the Gilmores at all times. That's where Donna came in. I swore her to secrecy and threatened to kill her if she ever told anyone. It was good money, and there was no reason for her to tell anyone. She must've agreed, since she hadn't even told her best friend. Anyhow, Frank had me hire her to watch Charlotte, Kennedy, and Theodore. We needed to know of any major events, like a move or a separation or major issues in the family. Donna would give general reports on how things appeared at her next-door neighbor's house.

Mostly, Donna told us they seemed happy and never fought. That kind of thing. I came back once a month to meet with Donna to get my report and she would get her payment."

"How long was she doing this?" I asked.

"A year. Until she told that stupid lowlife boyfriend of hers what she was doing."

"Diego?"

"Yeah, he was a real piece of work. I don't know what she ever saw in him. She was too good for him."

"So what—you killed her because she told Diego about the arrangement?" Why had she told Diego and not me?

"Pretty much—once I'd told Frank of the breach, he ordered the hit," he said with little emotion.

My mind was processing the fact I was sitting across from Donna's killer.

"How did it go down?" Hirsch asked.

"I told her I had another deal for her where she could make even more money. When we met that night, I told her we needed to go somewhere private, so she brought me over to Beth's Pond. When she was distracted, I struck her in the back of the head with a big rock. Thankfully, it didn't require another blow. She was out nearly instantly. It wasn't how I'd planned to do it, but when I saw the rock, I figured it would be faster than if I'd strangled her. I didn't want to do it, but it was a direct order from Frank so my hands were tied."

My head was throbbing. I squeezed my eyes shut to help control it. I gritted my teeth. "How did you know she told Diego?"

"She confessed. I thought she was smarter than that. I liked her, to be honest, and I'm sorry that it had to end that way. I'm glad you finally found her. Hopefully that brings some closure to the family."

My body shook, and I had to control myself because I

wanted to reach over the table and strangle him until that smug look on his face turned to shock and surprise as the life drained out of him. Instead, he'd get full immunity. It wasn't right, not even if he delivered Frank Henley. He'd killed two people and tried to murder me. Before I lost my control, I stormed out of the interrogation room and ran outside of the county jail. Out in the rain, I let the drops splatter down on me and was reminded of the moment I saw Donna's earring at our place—Beth's Pond.

My chest heaved, and I cried out to no one at all. We had found Donna, and we'd found her killer, but with Alonso looking at full immunity, we hadn't gotten Donna the justice she deserved. Alonso needed to be locked up tight, and the key destroyed. My body vibrated as the grief overtook me. I fell to my knees onto the pavement in the parking lot. I needed the water to wash away the pain and fury. Why was life so damn unfair? Alonso walking free wasn't fair to Donna and the Bernards, or to Theodore and the Gilmores. There had to be a way to make him pay for what he'd done.

43

DETECTIVE HIRSCH

I stepped outside the interrogation room and called Callahan at the FBI in Pennsylvania. After his voicemail greeting, I said, "Callahan, it's Hirsch. The person we were talking about has just been implicated in some serious crimes in California. Call me back." I hung up the phone, shoved it into my pocket, and headed off to find Martina. She had looked pretty upset when she left. She'd had a rough couple of days. I can't imagine what it would be like to be in her shoes. Having to listen to Alonso callously describe how he murdered my best friend would have sent me over the edge. Not to mention, thinking Alonso would get away with the murder and all the other horrible things he'd done.

What I needed to explain to Martina was that I didn't think Alonso could ever prove that Frank Henley had called the shots on all of these things. Unless he'd recorded their earlier conversations, which was highly unlikely, considering how long ago Donna had been murdered. In my mind, both Henley and Ricci would pay for what they did—one way or another.

In my experience, the district attorney had a clever way of writing loopholes into immunity agreements, especially when murder was involved. Ricci had given up his crimes far too quickly. He clearly wasn't as smart as he thought he was. The smart criminals knew to get it in writing before speaking a word. Even if Ricci had immunity in California, he'd been dumb enough to admit to the attack on Martina in Pennsylvania, which wasn't in our jurisdiction. One phone call to the Doylestown Police Department and an email of the recording of his confession was all it would take to ship him to Pennsylvania to do time for attempted murder. There was no way Alonso Ricci would be a free man—ever again.

I exited the building and saw a figure in the parking lot on her knees. I jogged toward Martina. I reached her, and she glanced up at me before she shook her head in defeat.

I extended my hand to help her up, and she accepted. I stared into her amber-colored eyes and said, "Let's talk."

She nodded silently as I led her to my car, and she climbed into the passenger side. Once we were both out of the rain, I turned to her. "He will not get away with this."

"How? What about the immunity deal?"

"At the bare minimum, he'll do time in Pennsylvania for attacking you, which we'll call attempted murder—he has no immunity agreement in Pennsylvania. Not to mention, he's probably done other things that we haven't uncovered yet. I'm telling you, this guy will never get to see the light of day again, except for his one hour of mandatory outdoor exercise. Trust me, Martina. We will make sure he is never a free man again."

She stared down at the floor of my car. "I don't know why she didn't tell me."

"You heard what Ricci said. He had threatened to kill her if she said anything about the arrangement. She probably only told Diego because he had threatened her. I spent enough time with Diego to know what kind of man he was."

I hoped Martina heard me as she shifted her gaze to the window.

"Should we tell Kennedy now, that we caught the person who killed her father, or do we wait?"

Martina was obviously still processing the last hour and didn't want to discuss Donna further. I said, "I think we should hold off until we hear from the FBI. I called my buddy, and if they have an active investigation, this could screw things up. We can hold Alonso until he can produce evidence against Henley. Are you booked for the trip to Pennsylvania?"

She returned her attention to me with confidence in her eyes. "I'm booked."

I stared into her eyes. "We'll make sure that Donna and Theodore Gilmore get the justice they deserve. We will ensure Frank Henley pays for what he did."

"Let's take him down," she commanded.

That was the plan.

44

DETECTIVE HIRSCH

I HURRIED FROM THE RENTAL CAR AS THE WIND AND SNOW whipped at my face. We were definitely not in the Bay Area anymore. I opened the door and held it for Martina before entering the FBI building in Philadelphia. I shut the door behind me and watched as Martina shook the snowflakes out of her hair. I grinned. "So, have you ever considered moving to the East Coast?"

She chuckled. "No, and I don't think I ever will. I prefer sunshine over freezing temperatures any day."

I was pleased to see her in better spirits. It had been two days since we'd discovered Alonso had murdered Donna. Martina had taken the news hard but appeared to be coping.

I stepped up to the front desk and explained to the clerk we had an appointment with Special Agent Deeley. The woman wearing a headset made a call and then assured me he'd be out shortly. While we waited, we provided identification, my badge, and signed the visitor log. I declared I had a weapon, but my buddy, Callahan, had arranged for me to keep it on me since I was law enforcement. Martina wasn't licensed to carry a gun in Pennsylvania, and based on her last visit, I didn't want her to be anywhere without me by her side. I hadn't told her that, since I guessed her response would be akin to a karate chop. Yes, I thought she could take care of herself, but bullets were fast and didn't need to know Krav Maga to kill. Henley could easily send another goon to come after her. I guessed Ricci wasn't his only henchman.

Martina and I stood in the lobby. "Any guess to what the FBI investigation is focused on?" Martina asked.

"I don't know. He's a politician and a businessman. It could be anything." And I meant it. It could be anything from money laundering to serial murder. Some people were damn good at hiding their true selves.

"Do you think whatever they're investigating is related to Charlotte and the secret that she kept?"

"Could be. The suicide by Eloise Henley is a bit too coincidental for my taste." So far, every coincidence on this case had turned out to be nothing of the sort.

"I think something has the Henleys under pressure, which is why I think the body count keeps rising," Martina said.

Footsteps on the tile drew my attention ahead. I smiled and waved. Callahan and a black man, with a bald head and thick mustache standing nearly six feet three inches tall, approached. I grinned and shook hands with Callahan before focusing on the other man. "You must be Special Agent Deeley?" I extended my hand. "I'm Detective Hirsch, and this is Martina Monroe, a private investigator my department is working with. She's been investigating the Henleys for several weeks."

"That's right. Callahan's told me a few stories from your college days. A class clown turned homicide detective," Deeley said, with a bright smile.

Martina eyed me quizzically and said, "I'd like to hear some of those stories." She winked at me before she shook hands with Deeley and said, "It's nice to meet you."

Deeley returned the sentiment. "Why don't you head back with me, and we can play a little show and tell. It'll be interesting to see what you've got and how it may tie into our case."

So, there was definitely an investigation into the Henleys. It did not surprise me. Callahan wouldn't have had me fly out if there wasn't.

They led us back to a hallway and into a conference room. Deeley shut the door behind us, and I focused my attention on one of the walls. My mouth dropped open. There was a wall of photographs and strings connecting to note cards.

"Tell us what we're looking at here."

Deeley explained, "This here is the Henley investigation. Currently, Frank Henley is under investigation for a whole slew of financial crimes. The first thing that got us interested in Henley was because of this guy here." He pointed to a photograph of a middle-aged man with dark hair. "A whistle blower at his investment firm. He said that Henley was taking secret kickbacks from different investment fund managers. Basically, he'd put his clients' money in their fund for a kickback. These kickbacks come in the form of fake consulting contracts. We soon found that the kickbacks were just the tip of the iceberg. This guy is so dirty, he makes a pig in slop look like a clean freak."

"This started as an SEC investigation?"

"Yep."

I watched as Martina eased up to the board of photographs. She pointed at one and turned back to me. "There's Alonso, right there."

"I'll be damned," I commented. Alonso wasn't lying that he had worked for Henley.

"I hear you have our pal, Ricci, in custody."

"Yep, he's confessed to two murders and an attempted murder on Martina. He alleges all his crimes were direct orders from Frank Henley."

"Who did he kill?"

"The first murder was thirteen years ago. Donna Bernard, who had been hired to monitor her next-door neighbors, the Gilmores, aka Charlotte Henley's family in California. The second was Theodore Gilmore, Charlotte's widower."

"And he attacked Martina, twice?"

"Yep. Once during her last trip to Pennsylvania and last weekend in California. She got the drop on him both times. That's why he's in custody now."

Deeley leaned up against the wall and crossed his muscled arms. He said, "Nice work" and gave Martina a slight smile. "Well, from what we have on wiretaps and based on our undercover agent's assessment, Alonso's probably telling the truth. Frank is one sick man whose only concern is power. Alonso is just one of his henchmen. Did Alonso tell you why Frank wanted the hits?"

Martina shrugged. "According to Alonso, there is some family secret that Charlotte had carried. He says he doesn't know what it is."

"Must be pretty big to hire a hit."

Martina nodded. "My thoughts exactly. Rumor has it, Henley wants to run for president, so the secret must be bad enough that it could jeopardize his campaign."

"Any leads?" Deeley asked.

"Amy Henley has a letter her mother left after she died."

"A letter? In addition to the suicide note?"

"Yes. She says she can only show it to me in person. She's also asked to have her DNA compared to Charlotte's. Did you guys look into Eloise's suicide? Are you sure she wasn't murdered?"

Deeley said, "It had all the hallmarks of a classic suicide. No obvious signs to raise suspicion. She took a bunch of pills, which she had a prescription for, no sign of a struggle, and she left a note. We questioned Amy, and she seemed pretty convinced it was suicide as well. I thought she was hiding something, now I know what."

Martina said, "I have a meeting with her this afternoon. Since telling her that Charlotte had been alive until a few weeks ago and that she has a niece, Kennedy Gilmore, she wants to get to know her newfound family. What's your take on Amy?"

"She is pretty far removed from Frank Henley and all his shady business deals. She works at the bistro, which is a clean operation. Most of the Henley businesses are. But then I think Frank got greedy. We have enough charges to arrest him on most of the SEC violations, but to ensure a lengthy prison sentence, we have an operation going down tomorrow morning, on the golf course, of all places, to get him on money laundering and racketeering too. Our boy, Frank, has been playing with the Philly mob." He eyed Martina. "As for Alonso, we have him on a wiretap discussing Theodore Gilmore's murder and taking down 'the PI' back in California. Frank gave Alonso the option to contract out, but I guess he wanted revenge, since you got him good in the first attack," he said, with a playful smirk.

"I got him pretty good the second time too. He's lucky I have self-control, otherwise his brains would have been all over the pavement."

"You would have done the world a favor. He's not a good guy, and you may have guessed by now, not the brightest bulb."

Unfortunately, that meant the wiretaps corroborated Alonso's story that he was following orders. I explained the immunity deal to Deeley. He shook his head. "I wouldn't worry. If you can't get him in California, we'll take good care of him here in Pennsylvania."

Martina seemed to relax. "Good. Donna Bernard was my best friend, and I want him put away for the rest of his life. I'll tell you this, I'm not sure my self-control would have existed had

I known he was responsible for her death when he'd attacked me at the gas station."

Deeley's hard features softened. "I'm so sorry, I hadn't realized that. My condolences. We will take him and Henley down, I promise you that. As a matter a fact, we'll put you on the call list once we have Henley in custody, in case you and Hirsch want to interview him."

"I'd appreciate it," Martina said.

"Absolutely," I confirmed.

We continued to exchange information between our two investigations. By the end, I was eager to get our front-row tickets to watch Frank Henley get exactly what he deserved.

45

MARTINA

WE PULLED UP IN FRONT OF THE TWO-STORY, COLONIAL-style house with gray trim and white siding. There were no cars in the driveway, and snow covered the front of the house, presumably where a perfectly green lawn would be in the spring. I turned to Detective Hirsch. "I think you should stay here. Her and I have a rapport."

"I'll be here if you need me."

"Thanks." I stepped out into the freezing cold and hurried up the front steps. I knocked on the door with a gloved fist. A moment later, the door creaked open and Amy stood before me. She looked pale and had red-rimmed eyes. My guess was that she had experienced a heck of a week. "Martina, please come in. It's freezing out there."

I walked inside and stopped into the hallway.

"Let me take your coat," Amy offered.

I pulled off my gloves and removed my coat. Amy hung it on a rack behind her. "Can I get you anything: coffee, tea, or water?"

"I'll have some herbal tea, if it isn't too much trouble."

"Mint, okay?"

"Perfect. Thank you."

My nerves were already going haywire with all the adrenaline and jet lag. I didn't think extra caffeine would be useful at this point. She led me past her formal living and dining rooms and back into the large modern kitchen, which had an island in the center, displaying a bouquet of colorful wildflowers. "You have a beautiful home, Amy."

"Thank you."

The home was quiet. I didn't hear children or anybody else in the house. "Are your kids at school?"

"They are."

"How old are they?"

"They're six and seven, a first grader and a second grader. They're a handful, so I figured it was best to have you come over while they were out." She poured the tea, set the cups on a tray, and carried them out of the kitchen.

I followed behind.

"Is it okay if we sit and talk in here?"

"Of course." I pulled out a cloth-covered dining chair in the formal dining room and sat down in front of the gold placemat, where she set down my tea. She sat across from me. Next to her placemat sat a purple folder. "Do you have any kids?" she asked.

I smiled warmly. "I have a daughter. She'll be eight next month."

"They're so active, aren't they?"

"Yes, they are. My daughter has so much energy and everything is sparkly."

Amy grinned. "My girls too. After a weekend of art projects, there's glitter covering nearly every inch of my house." She paused and turned somber. "I'm sorry. It's been a difficult few days."

"I'm so sorry for your loss."

"Thank you. I'm afraid it's worse than that."

I took a sip of the tea and set it back down. "How so?"

"I don't know if I can read it aloud. It's the letter my mother left—it's in this folder. I also received the DNA test results a few hours ago. I printed them out too."

She slid the folder over to me. "I don't even know what to say. It's... Well, you'll see."

"No worries, I'll take a look and then we can talk about it." I took the folder and opened it. The first page was a handwritten letter, presumably from Eloise. I read and my mouth dropped open, and I covered my heart with my hand.

My dear Amy,

I can no longer live with all the secrets and lies and the pain that we've caused. Your brother has his own demons, but I won't get into that, as it's his cross to bear. I feel I owe you the truth after all these years. I loved you from the day that you were born. Your father was a terrible man and I know that. I blame myself for what he did to you and to Charlotte. It wasn't right to send her away, but I didn't have the courage to stand up to your father. I should have demanded Charlotte stay with us and to let her raise you as a mother should have the right to raise her own child. She loved you and didn't want to leave you behind, but I'm afraid your father gave her no choice. She wanted to call you Amelia, but your father wouldn't have it. He'd agreed on the name Amy, and so you became Amy. I truly believe leaving you behind broke Charlotte's heart. I am ashamed and feel sick that I allowed this to happen to my own baby girl. Please forgive me and know that I will always love you.

Love,
Eloise "Mom" Henley

. . .

Eloise's letter was an admission and an apology. How could she have let her husband send away her daughter? And what had the Henley's father done to them? I had an awful guess. If I were right, how on God's green earth could a mother let a man, or any person, abuse their child? I flipped the next page over to the DNA report and scanned it. *Oh geez.* It was as I had suspected. I glanced up at Amy, who sat stiff as a board. "Did you read the DNA results?"

"Charlotte was my sister, but she was also my mother."

"I'm so sorry, Amy. Are you okay?" That was a stupid question. Of course, she wasn't okay. She had just found out she was a product of incest and wasn't even allowed to know her mother.

"I called my therapist. We have a session tomorrow. I'll be okay. I'm a survivor."

"Yes, you are." Her strength inspired me. She reminded me of Kennedy, and not just her physical appearance. "Did you suspect that Charlotte might be your mother? Is that why you asked for the DNA test?"

She nodded, and teardrops fell from her eyes. "My father, like my mother, Eloise, alluded to, was a vile man. He sexually abused me through my teen years. I left home after high school, graduated from college, and went into counseling. I've been in therapy for a long time, and now I have a healthy marriage and two beautiful children." She paused, drying her eyes before taking a sip of her tea. She set the teacup down on the saucer. "It's not something I've ever shared with anyone other than my husband and my therapist. When you told me that Charlotte had been alive up until a few weeks ago, I hadn't considered that maybe what my father had done to me, he had also done to Charlotte. After I found the letter, I confronted my brother, and he told me if I didn't keep it quiet, I would ruin his political career and destroy our family's reputation. He said he wouldn't stand for it and then threatened me and my family if I ever went public with the truth about Charlotte and me, and my father's abuse."

It must have been devastating to have her own brother prioritize his reputation over her mental health and her life. "I'm so sorry, Amy." I needed to stop saying that. I was beginning to even annoy myself. "I think you're really brave to come to me and share this with me. Your brother was wrong to tell you to keep it a secret if you don't want to. For some survivors, it can be very therapeutic to share their story."

I understood the secret that Charlotte had kept and why. She had been a victim of incest, and her daughter was also her sister. Based on what a devoted mother to Kennedy she had been, it must have broken her to leave Amy behind. Frank Henley must have known everything, which is why he'd done all he could to keep it a secret. I wished I could tell Amy that her brother was going to prison and very soon, but I couldn't jeopardize the operation.

"Maybe one day. I'm not quite there yet."

"I'd like to share this information with Kennedy—is that okay with you?"

Amy nodded. "I'd like to meet her. She's my sister." She looked out the window. "I have a sister." She returned her focus to me. "What is she like?"

My heart broke for Amy and for Kennedy. "She works in corporate communications and lives in San Francisco. There is a striking resemblance between the two of you. She has the same long, straight strawberry-blond hair and freckles. She's strong and smart and kind. I actually went to high school with her and knew her while growing up."

"Really?"

"Yes, she lived next door to my best friend."

"Isn't that something?"

"When I told her about you, Kennedy expressed interest in

reaching out to you, but at the time she didn't know that you were her sister."

"Is it possible for you to arrange a meeting between the two of us? After you've explained everything to her, I could come out to California. I discussed it with my husband, and he wants to come too and bring the girls."

"Absolutely." Amy had a rough life. An unfair beginning, but I felt lighter knowing that I could bring her and Kennedy together. Maybe it would provide some closure for both of them.

We said our goodbyes, and I returned to the car where Hirsch sat by himself. I opened the door and hopped in. I didn't speak, still thinking about Amy and Kennedy's situation.

He frowned. "Was it that bad?"

"It's not great." I explained the tragedy that spanned generations. Maybe Kennedy and Amy would unite and bring comfort to one another.

46

MARTINA

THE NEXT MORNING, I SAT ACROSS FROM HIRSCH AND sipped my latte, enjoying the warmth of the liquid running down into my belly. I'm not sure how people handled these freezing winters. I admitted it; I was a Bay-Area-weather wimp. I nodded as I agreed with Hirsch's assessment of the Henley investigation. "Any idea what time they will take him down today?" I asked.

"I think soon. All we can do now is wait to get the call from Deeley."

I took a bite of my veggie omelet and swallowed. I was pumped. I couldn't wait to stare into Frank Henley's eyes and watch him crumble. "So how do you know Callahan—that's your connection in the FBI, right?"

Hirsch wiped the corner of his mouth with his napkin and set it back down in his lap. "College buddies. We were roommates the last year, and we were in a lot of classes together. We both majored in criminal justice. I wanted to be a detective and went into police work. He went to Quantico. But we've kept in touch all these years. He's a good guy."

"What is this class clown business?" I teased.

"I may have made light of some of our more boring classes. My professors weren't terribly appreciative, but I passed."

"Where did you go to college?"

"UC San Diego."

"Were you also raised in California?"

"I was. I grew up in Marin County."

So, he came from money. It was an interesting choice to go into law enforcement, especially after obtaining a four-year degree. "Did you ever consider going into the FBI?"

"When Callahan decided to go that route, I had considered it, but at the time, I was under the impression the FBI typically focused on financial and white-collar crimes and that didn't appeal to me. From what I understood, it wasn't very glamorous. But now, seeing how they had the reach to take down someone like Henley, I wonder if I made the right choice."

"It's not too late to make a switch."

"True, but I'm finding I like the position at the sheriff's department. Any other questions?" he asked, with curiosity in his eyes.

"Actually, yes. What's your first name?"

Hirsch lowered his eyes like he was embarrassed. "August."

August Hirsch. It's not a name you heard every day. "Is your family German?"

"Yep, on both sides. We've been in the U.S. for a long time, but our ancestors were from Germany." It made sense. He was tall, with fair skin and baby-blue eyes.

He tilted his head toward me. "What made you decide to join the Army after high school? You don't seem like someone who enjoys following orders."

"Am I that obvious?"

"I am a detective."

A grin crept up my face. "Touchè. No, not really. I didn't take school too seriously when I was young. The Army seemed like a good way to see the world, and then I figured I'd go to college afterward."

"Where did you go to college?"

I shook my head. "I didn't. Shortly after I was married, I got a little surprise we now call Zoey. Everything changed after that. I started working with Stavros and really enjoyed the work. I don't regret joining the Army. I learned a lot about leadership and responsibility. I think it was the right path for me, but no, I'm not a fan of taking orders if I don't think they're the right orders."

"I get that. Zoey seems inquisitive, perhaps a mini-investigator in the making."

I chuckled. "That she is. She likes to hear about my cases. I usually leave out anything too dark or graphic, obviously. I mostly tell her about cases where I get to help people. The cheating spouses and fraudsters aren't usually something we discuss. Speaking of helping people, we're not far from closing Donna's case and the Bernard murder case. What's next for you?"

"I'll get whatever new murder pops up that needs investigating, and then I'll pick out my next cold case."

"How did you decide to look into Donna's case? How do you pick your cold cases?"

"After reviewing some of the files, Donna's case seemed to have the least amount of investigative work done on it. Based on the statements and the lack of follow-up, I figured Donna didn't get a chance to be found, and I thought she deserved that. I guess I was trying to right a wrong."

Hirsch was a good guy. There was no question about that. "Have you ever looked into your brother's case?"

"Probably too much. I have a copy of the case file but no luck so far. It's tricky when I don't have any forensic powers, and there are hardly any leads in the investigation."

Hirsch's phone vibrated on the table. We gave each other knowing looks before he answered. "Hirsch." He nodded. "All right, we'll be there in fifteen minutes."

He slammed the phone down. Hirsch was excited. "They got him. Henley's in custody and they're reading him his rights. Deeley says we can interview him once they get him settled in and booked."

"All right, time to take this jerk down."

"With pleasure," Hirsch said with satisfaction.

The past few weeks had been a whirlwind. Hopefully, all this would come to one nice and neat conclusion. I was looking forward to getting my piece of Frank Henley. I wanted to watch him squirm. I wanted to see the look on his face when we told him we had him on conspiracy to commit murder and that he'd never be a free man again. I wanted justice for Donna and for Theodore Gilmore and for myself. The jerk ordered my death and threatened my daughter. Nobody gets away with that.

HIRSCH AND I SAT DIRECTLY IN FRONT OF FRANK HENLEY, while Special Agent Deeley leaned up against the wall, arms crossed. The energy in the room was a mix of adrenaline-fueled excitement and panic. The panic was all Frank Henley's.

We all wanted to grill him until there was nothing left. I studied his face and his demeanor. He was partially bald, with strands of gray hair along the sides. His eyes were a dark green like dirty emeralds, and he was fit.

Hirsch agreed I could get first crack at Henley, since he had killed my best friend and then tried to kill me. I didn't mind playing that card. "Hello, Senator, or is it okay if I call you Frank?"

He ignored my question and my presence.

No worries. "My name is Martina Monroe, private investigator. You may know the name since you conspired to commit my murder? Does my name ring a bell now?"

He looked to the side, ignoring my gaze. "Or maybe you know me from my younger years? I was Donna Bernard's best friend. The same Donna Bernard you ordered Alonso Ricci to murder." He wouldn't meet my stare.

My heart was racing, and I wanted to pounce on top of him and strangle him. But I was in control. I wasn't the one facing a life sentence and didn't plan on it in the future.

He turned and glanced up at Special Agent Deeley. "I said I want my lawyer."

Deeley shrugged. "He's not here yet. As soon as he gets here, I will let you know right away. Don't you worry."

Frank Henley looked ahead at me. "I think you've mistaken me for somebody else and just so you know, I'm not saying a word until my lawyer gets here."

I nodded. "That's probably smart, but it won't help you. You see, your friend Alonso Ricci, sang like a little birdie. And before you deny knowing him, you should also know that the feds had wiretaps on your phones and have you and him on tape discussing my murder. Alonso took a deal. He told us about how you ordered him to murder Donna Bernard and to murder Theodore Gilmore and to have me killed. Between those charges and what the SEC and the FBI have on you, there isn't a lawyer in this country or this universe that will get you out of this. I won't get into what the FBI has on you, but they've got a lot, which is why you're sitting here. But, what we have on you back in California may be even worse." I glanced over at Hirsch.

It was Hirsch's turn. "Yes, I'm sorry I didn't introduce myself. My name is Detective Hirsch. I'm a homicide detective out in California. I'll be the one who will charge you with the murders of Donna Bernard and Theodore Gilmore, and the attempted murder of Martina Monroe."

The senator rolled his eyes as if all of this was preposterous. There was a mountain of evidence against Henley. According to Deeley, the FBI and the SEC had the evidence to put him away for a long time.

As I continued to watch the senator, he remained stoic and unaffected by the entire situation. He was a cold man. A cold man that had threatened his own sister, even though she had endured horrible abuse and separation from her biological mother.

Hirsch described to Henley the extradition they would pursue after the FBI was done with him. Hirsch turned to me. "Anything you'd like to add, Martina?"

"Just one more thing. Frank, I thought you might be interested to know that we know everything. And when I say everything, I mean everything. We know your family secret. I've been in contact with your sister, Amy."

Frank flinched.

"The FBI and Detective Hirsch are willing to keep that out of the press if you're willing to talk and avoid a trial. I personally spoke with Amy and Kennedy Gilmore, and they're both willing to go public with the truth. You will be destroyed in the public's eye."

The last bit was a fib. I hadn't talked to Kennedy yet. I felt that type of information was better served in person. She had already endured so much that this latest news about her family was going to be another shock to her world. I didn't want her to be alone when she learned the news. Frank glared at me with his green-brown eyes. "I don't know what you're talking about."

"No? We tested Amy's DNA against Charlotte's daughter's DNA," I said, without emotion.

Frank lowered his head, his face turning crimson. He looked back up at me. "Amy wouldn't ruin all of us. She's one of us."

"Kennedy is also one of you. And despite what you think, Amy is not to blame. This isn't her burden to carry. She wants to tell her story, but she has agreed that if we could avoid a trial and avoid destroying your family's reputation, she'd be willing to remain anonymous when she did."

It wasn't true. I didn't know if or when Amy would ever want to go public with her story, but it seemed to be just the thing to rattle Frank Henley. Finally, it appeared as if the senator was contemplating his predicament.

I sat quietly and glanced back over at Special Agent Deeley and Detective Hirsch. I'd said my peace. I was done with Frank Henley. The rest was up to law enforcement.

Deeley stepped forward. "We have enough evidence to put you away for twenty years, which means you'd finish your sentence when you're eighty years old, at which point we will extradite you to California to serve out your time there for the before-mentioned crimes. If you cooperate, your family name remains untarnished, other than, of course, the fact that you're going to go to prison. Your political career is over, however you look at it."

"I'm not talking until my lawyer gets here." He was more clever than his pal Alonso.

Hirsch set his hands down on the table. "All right then. I suppose we're done here. Martina, are you ready to go?"

"I sure am," I said with satisfaction as I strutted out of the FBI's interrogation room.

In the hallway, the three of us met up. "I think that went well."

Deeley nodded. "He's not going anywhere. He can be as tight-lipped as he wants, but there are so many charges against him it just doesn't matter. You could tell he was shaken that you knew his family secret."

"Oh, absolutely. The guy is a classic narcissist that doesn't care who gets hurt as long as he doesn't look bad. He can deny the charges and even go to prison, but he can't deny the DNA testing results of his baby sister."

"Exactly."

"What's next for the two of you? Are you heading back to California now?"

"That we are. I need to meet with Kennedy Gilmore to give her the updates on her father's murder, the investigation of her family, and the latest news about Amy Henley."

Deeley asked, "How's Amy holding up?"

"She's tough. I think she'll be okay. She wants to meet her sister. I spent some time with Kennedy and now with Amy. I'm hoping the two of them can do some healing together and be a source of comfort for one another. They are both survivors, but they're also both strong women who believe in family connection."

"Best of luck to you both. It was great meeting you. Next time you'd like to collaborate on a case, we'll welcome you both with open arms here at the FBI."

Hirsch said, "I appreciate that."

"And we might take you up on it," I said with a smile.

Deeley nodded, a twinkle in his eye. "I hope so."

We said our goodbyes and then strode out of the FBI building. I turned to Hirsch. "Do you think we should go see Amy and let her know what's happened? She'll have the news vans swarming any minute. She'll be ambushed."

"I agree. She deserves some warning."

Indeed. She'd been through enough. They all had. After a quick stop at Amy's house, we were headed to the airport. I was more than ready to go home and hug my little girl.

47

DETECTIVE HIRSCH

"ARE YOU READY?"

Her lips curled up. "I'm more than ready."

"Okay, then let's give him the good news." We stepped into the room where Alonso sat with a smug look on his face. He had no idea his world was about to be blown apart. "Alonso, how are you doing?"

"Pretty good. Looking forward to getting out of here."

Martina dramatically pulled her chair out and sat down, placing her hands in her lap. "Hi, Alonso."

Alonso hesitated, probably disturbed by the cheerfulness in Martina's voice.

I took a seat next to Martina and said, "Alonso, we talked to Frank Henley, and of course, he denies everything. And he decided not to talk to us. He told us things like, 'he didn't know anybody named Alonso,' yada yada yada. But the thing is, the FBI had a wiretap, and we have a recording of him talking to you and ordering you to kill Theodore Gilmore and Martina. So, we didn't believe him."

Alonso leaned back. "The FBI had wiretaps?"

"You didn't know?"

Alonso's face paled. "No. Why were they tapping Frank's phone?"

I wondered how many other crimes Alonso had committed that we didn't know about.

I enlightened Alonso on the FBI investigation and all the charges against Frank Henley. "They took him down yesterday," I said with a smile.

"Frank's in jail?"

I nodded slowly. "He was. I hate to be the one to inform you. This morning, Frank took his own life, and the feds could not corroborate that he ordered you to kill Donna Bernard." It was unfortunate to hear from Special Agent Deeley that Henley had taken his own life. It was a cowardly move but consistent with his life choices. My guess was that Frank Henley couldn't face the world once his true greedy, selfish, and criminal self was revealed. However, it would avoid a trial for Amy, so that was something. Yet, it didn't seem fair that Frank was able to make the decision to end his life—or not—when he had taken that decision away from Donna Bernard and Theodore Gilmore.

Alonso clenched his jaw.

"That's right, he's dead. Which means your deal with the district attorney is null and void regarding Donna Bernard, unless you have some other evidence you'd like to provide."

"You have that he asked me to murder Martina, right?"

"Yep, but not Donna Bernard."

He twisted his neck and stared up at the ceiling, clearly trying to figure out his next move. I supposed if I were in Alonso's position, I'd be trying to dig my way out too. He returned his focus to me and then Martina. "I have more on the senator I could give you."

I glanced at Martina, who shrugged. "He's dead and no longer our concern."

"The FBI and Doylestown PD may have some unsolved cases they might like to close," Alonso retorted.

"That'll be up to Pennsylvania law enforcement, but here in California we're charging you with the murder of Donna Bernard. And, if for some reason your sentence for her murder ends before your death, you'll be extradited to Pennsylvania for the attack on Martina and whatever else the FBI has implicated you in. So, like I told you the first time we met, you'll never be a free man ever again." I pushed my chair back and said, "I think we're done here."

Martina grinned at Alonso before sliding out of her chair and walking out of the room without saying a word.

Alonso called out, "I have names of people he had me kill in Pennsylvania. I'll talk if we can make a deal."

I turned around. "If you can help Pennsylvania law enforcement close out some cold cases, they may be able to pull a few strings in California regarding sentencing and prison conditions, but I don't want you to get the wrong idea. You are never getting out of jail."

Alonso deflated.

I said, "Take care" and exited the interview room, making a mental note to call Special Agent Deeley and let him know Alonso may have valuable information on other cases. Who knew, maybe it would get Alonso more comfortable accommodations or a few extra bucks in his commissary account.

We pulled up to the Gilmore residence on Stone Island. Kennedy had said that was where she wanted to be when she heard about the Henleys, since it had been her family home. It was convenient for Martina and me, since we needed to talk to the Bernards as well. There had been so much heartbreak and tragedy to cover up the abuse that was inflicted upon Charlotte. Talk about insult to injury. I turned to Martina before we got out of the car. "Now for the better part of our job. We can bring some closure to the Gilmores and the Bernards."

"It's all we can do," she said.

We exited the vehicle and climbed up the wooden steps to the Gilmores' door. I tapped lightly and waited a few seconds before the door opened. Kennedy looked better than she had the last time I saw her. She had color in her cheeks and dry eyes. She was dressed casually in a pair of jeans and a sweater and was even wearing lip gloss. "Hi. Please, come in."

Martina entered, and I followed behind. We sat at the dining table. I began to explain. "First off, we have news on the investigation into your father's murder. We have the man responsible in custody. He told us he had been hired to commit the act, which we know to be true, due to the FBI investigation of his employer..." I stopped myself and turned to look at Martina.

She nodded.

"This may be tough to hear, Kennedy, and I understand that, but I'm just going to be straight with you." I then explained Frank Henley's criminal activity, motives, and the end of his life and Eloise Henley's.

Kennedy didn't shed a tear. She sat stoically. "My uncle hired someone to kill my dad?"

"Yes."

She glanced over at Martina. "So, this is all related to my mother's past? Were you able to determine what the secret that they were hiding was, and why my mother had lied about her family history?"

That moment, I realized Charlotte's and the Henleys' lies had come true. Charlotte's entire family, except for Amy, was dead. And Charlotte was also dead.

Martina explained, "Yes. Like we discussed, Amy had requested a DNA sample so that they could test her DNA against your DNA to determine her relationship with Charlotte. What we discovered is that Amy is actually Charlotte's daughter."

"Not her sister?"

Martina raked her fingers through her hair. "Technically, Amy is Charlotte's daughter and her sister."

Kennedy covered her mouth and lowered her head. Tears escaped, and she looked up. "My mother was a victim of incest?"

"Yes, her father had abused her. What we can gather is that they sent Charlotte away after Amy was born to conceal the fact that she, one, had a baby out of wedlock and, two, that her father had been abusive. We think Frank knew about the whole thing, and he was trying to cover up that fact because he's a politician and didn't want to tarnish his family's name."

"My mother had escaped an abusive home but also had to leave behind her daughter. Amy's my sister?"

Martina nodded. "Yes, and she would very much like to meet you."

Kennedy placed her hand on her cheek. "It never occurred to me I might have a sister."

"Right now, there's a lot of press around Frank Henley's arrest and subsequent suicide, but she said she'd like to visit."

Kennedy shook her head. "So wait. Frank Henley, my uncle, died by suicide and my grandmother, Eloise, also died by suicide?"

"Yes, your grandmother was also aware of the abuse against your mother, and we think she couldn't live with it anymore. There was a letter that said as much."

"Wow. That's a lot."

"I'm so sorry, Kennedy. The only silver lining is that you

and Amy have found one another. She's a strong, pleasant woman with two adorable daughters and seems to have a very supportive and loving husband."

Kennedy stared down at the carpet. "Is there anything else?"

I looked over at Martina, who looked like she was having a difficult time delivering this news to Kennedy. "That's everything."

"Thank you."

"Well, actually, it's not everything. It's everything related to your mother and father, kind of." Martina shut her eyes and nodded slightly. "We also found Donna's killer. It's the same person who murdered your father."

"What? I don't understand the connection?"

I explained the motive and connection.

Kennedy wiped her eyes and let out a breath. "Thank you for coming by. I think I need some time to digest all of this."

"Understandable. Is there anything we can do for you?"

"Can you share Amy's information with me? When I'm ready, I'd like to call her."

"Yes, of course," Martina replied. We offered our condolences once again before heading next door to tell the Bernards that we had caught their daughter's killer.

48

MARTINA

TWO WEEKS LATER

THE SUN SHINED DOWN THROUGH THE TREES WHILE A light breeze brushed my face. I stared down at her gravestone and felt her beside me.

Donna Kay Bernard
Daughter. Sister. Friend.

She'd finally come home, and I hoped, no, I believed Donna was at peace. I squeezed Zoey's hand as she knelt down and set a pink Gerber Daisy next to the gravestone. Zoey had said that she had a feeling that Donna would've liked it. I thought that was probably true. Zoey stood up and said, "Mommy, we're the only ones left up here. Should we go down where the other people are?"

I glanced down at her and nodded. Donna's parents had been grateful that we had located her body and that Hirsch was able to get justice, and that the man who had taken her life was behind bars and would be for the rest of his days. They could finally say goodbye and bury their daughter. I, too, could say goodbye and begin to work through the grief and the guilt of leaving Donna that night.

I felt the wiggling of my hand that Zoey clutched with all her might. "Okay, let's go," I said.

We strolled down the hill where folks were gathering before the procession down to the reception hall. Hirsch wore a black suit with a white shirt and gray tie. I'd never seen him look so dressed up. August Hirsch cleaned up nicely. I'd be sure to give him a hard time about it.

Hirsch stood next to my mother, Betty, talking about God only knew what. In the three weeks she'd been back in our lives, I'd seen firsthand the change in her. It was the type of change that I think all of us were capable of, if we tried hard enough. She was different from how I remembered her from my childhood. She was strong and loving. Zoey adored her to the point where, at times, I felt a little replaced. I supposed they called that jealousy.

The timing was strange, in that, it was as if my mother had come back just when I needed her the most. And that was what really mattered, wasn't it? When people are there for you when you need them the most, that's what really counts.

Betty had officially moved in with us, taking over the spare bedroom. Zoey had been delighted. I was still adjusting to having another person in the house, but it was nice. My mother insisted on cooking dinner every night, except for Tuesdays, which was her bingo night. Zoey declared Tuesdays pizza night, and I couldn't deny her.

I glanced over to the left where Kennedy and Amy stood, talking amongst themselves. I'd spoken with Kennedy a few times. Once about her family and another time about Donna. She'd told me she'd felt somewhat responsible, since it had been her own family that had ordered her to be killed. I told her she was not responsible. I hoped she believed that.

I glanced down at Zoey. "Why don't you go over by Grandma Betty and Detective Hirsch. I need to say hello to some people, okay?"

"Okay, Mommy, but we don't want to be late."

"We won't. I promise."

I approached Amy and Kennedy, offering each a light embrace. "Thank you both for coming to Donna's memorial. Kennedy, how are you?"

"Doing well. Thank you. I'm so glad you found Donna. She was such a ray of light."

"She was."

"I remember one time, when we were about ten years old, we were out on the levee in front of our houses, and she told me we should make up a song and dance. I had asked her why and she replied, 'because we're alive and that's a reason to sing and dance, don't you think?'"

That sounded like Donna, the eternal optimist. "That's a great memory. Thank you for sharing."

"I'm sure you have a million stories like that."

"I do." I should share them with Zoey. I think she'd like to hear about Donna. My childhood wasn't all bad. I'd had a best friend and lived into adulthood, where I found love, had a beautiful baby girl, and a meaningful career. If Donna were there, I thought she'd be telling me I should be singing and dancing.

"Amy, how are you?"

"I'm doing well. We actually have some news."

"Oh?"

"My family and I have decided to relocate to the Bay Area. With all the media attention surrounding Frank and all my childhood memories, we decided a fresh start was exactly what we needed and, of course, to be closer to Kennedy. We've lost a lot of years." She wore a smile, showing that there truly was a silver lining amongst all the tragedies. Amy and Kennedy had found their family.

"That's wonderful news." I wished them well and continued back over to my mother, Zoey, and Hirsch. "All right, are we ready to go?"

"Yep."

"Hey, Martina, can I talk to you for a minute before we head out?" Hirsch asked.

"Sure. Zoey, Mom, I'll be right there. I need a few minutes." I stepped to the side and looked at Hirsch. "What is it? Don't tell me something happened and Alonso's out?"

He shook his head. "Oh, no, he's never getting out. No, I was talking to my boss, who apparently talked to yours. You see, the thing is, we have a whole storage room full of cold cases, and we could use some help to solve them. If you're willing, we have the budget, and Stavros Drakos has approved it."

I cocked my head, not sure what to make of what he was saying to me.

Hirsch chuckled. "The sheriff's department would like to contract you to help solve more cold cases. We would work side-by-side, similar to what we did here. I think you and I make a pretty excellent team. What do you think? Are you in?"

By finding out what had happened to Donna, we had brought closure to her family and friends so they could begin their journey of healing. By unraveling Charlotte's past, we were able to solve Theodore Gilmore's murder and bring closure to Kennedy, as well as connect her to her newfound relatives. If my focus would be doing the same for other families, I was definitely in. "Can I call you August?"

Hirsch grinned. "You can call me whatever you want—you could even call me your partner."

I extended my hand. "You've got a deal."

Three months. Three missing women. One PI determined to discover the truth.

Back from break, PI Martina Monroe clears the air with her boss at Drakos Security & Investigations and is ready to jump right into solving cold cases for the CoCo County Sheriff's Department.

Diving into the cold case files Martina stumbles upon a pattern of missing young women, all of whom were deemed runaways, and the files froze with minimal detective work from the original investigators. The more Martina digs into the women's last days the more shocking discoveries she makes.

Soon, Martina and Detective Hirsch not only uncover additional missing women but when their star witness turns up dead, they must rush to the next before it's too late.

Order your copy today!

THANK YOU!

Thank you for reading *What She Left*! I hope you enjoyed reading it as much as I loved writing it. If you did, I would greatly appreciate if you could post a short review.

Reviews are crucial for any author and can make a huge difference in visibility of current and future works. Reviews allow us to continue doing what we love, *writing stories*. Not to mention, I would be forever grateful!

Thank you!

JOIN H.K. CHRISTIE'S READER CLUB

Join my reader club to be the first to hear about upcoming novels, new releases, giveaways, promotions, as well as, a free e-copy of the prequel to the Martina Monroe series, *Crashing Down*.

It's completely free to sign up and you'll never be spammed by me, you can opt out easily at any time.

Sign up today at
www.authorhkchristie.com

ALSO BY H.K. CHRISTIE

The Martina Monroe Series is a nail-biting suspense series starring Private Investigator Martina Monroe and her unofficial partner Detective August Hirsch.

What She Left, Book 1

If She Ran, Book 2

All She Wanted, Book 3

The Selena Bailey Series is a suspenseful series featuring a young Selena Bailey and her turbulent path to becoming a top notch kickass private investigator as led by her mentor, Martina Monroe.

Not Like Her, Book 1

One In Five, Book 2

On The Rise, Book 3

Go With Grace, Book 4

Flawless, Book 5

A Permanent Mark: A heartless killer. Weeks without answers. Can she move on when a murderer walks free?

For a full list of books by H.K. Christie, visit her website at

www.authorhkchristie.com

ABOUT THE AUTHOR

H. K. Christie watched horror films far too early in life. Inspired by the likes of Stephen King, Dean Koontz, and a vivid imagination she now writes suspenseful thrillers featuring unbreakable women. *What She Left* is her tenth book.

When not working on her latest novel, she can be found eating & drinking with friends, walking around the lakes, or playing with her favorite furry pal.

She is a native and current resident of the San Francisco Bay Area.

ACKNOWLEDGMENTS

Many thanks to those who helped me shape and create this story. First, many thanks to my Advanced Reader Team. My ARC Team is invaluable in taking the first look at my stories and helping find typos and spreading awareness of my stories through their reviews and kind words.

To my editor, JTO, big thanks and I'm not sure what I would do without you.

To my cover designer, Odile, thank you for your guidance and talent.

Last but not least, I'd like to thank all of my readers. It's because of you I'm able to continue writing stories.

Made in the USA
Monee, IL
10 April 2022

94497701R00173